DISCARD

Virginia

Virginia

Susan Hughes

 KCP FICTION

For Anne Churchill-Smith, my dear friend

KCP Fiction is an imprint of Kids Can Press

Text © 2010 Susan Hughes

Kids Can Press acknowledges the financial support of the Government of Ontario, through the Ontario Media Development Corporation's Ontario Book Initiative; the Ontario Arts Council; the Canada Council for the Arts; and the Government of Canada, through the BPIDP, for our publishing activity.

Published in Canada by
Kids Can Press Ltd.
29 Birch Avenue
Toronto, ON M4V 1E2

Published in the U.S. by
Kids Can Press Ltd.
2250 Military Road
Tonawanda, NY 14150

www.kidscanpress.com

Edited by Tara Walker
Designed by Marie Bartholomew
Printed and bound in Canada
Jacket photo © Shutterstock Images

CM 10 0 9 8 7 6 5 4 3 2 1
CM PA 10 0 9 8 7 6 5 4 3 2 1

This book is printed on acid-free paper that is 100% ancient-forest friendly (100% post-consumer recycled).

Library and Archives Canada Cataloguing in Publication

Hughes, Susan, 1960–
    Virginia / written by Susan Hughes.

ISBN 978-1-55453-306-0 (bound). ISBN 978-1-55453-307-7 (pbk.)

I. Title.

PS8565.U42V57 2010   jC813'.54   C2009-904503-6

Kids Can Press is a *l'©r\js*™ Entertainment company

... somewhere in sands of the desert
A shape with lion body and the head of a man,
A gaze blank and pitiless as the sun,
Is moving its slow thighs, while all about it
Reel shadows of the indignant desert birds.
The darkness drops again; but now I know
That twenty centuries of stony sleep
Were vexed to nightmare by a rocking cradle,
And what rough beast, its hour come round at last,
Slouches towards Bethlehem to be born?

— excerpt from "The Second Coming" by William Butler Yeats

Part One

The Announcement

Chapter One

She could barely get the words out. And when she did, she didn't recognize her own voice.

"Who are you?" she asked.

"Who do you think I am?" he answered, with a grin.

✠✠✠

It was Saturday afternoon, late August, and hot — blazing hot. The last few days had been too hot for me to do my usual hour-long run, even first thing in the morning. I lay on a recliner in my backyard wearing a tank top and shorts, baking in the sun.

Except for the extreme heat, it was like any other normal summer day. But I guess every weird, bizarre, extraordinary event has to begin somewhere, and if you follow the trail back far enough, maybe you'd find the seeds of it starting to sprout on a normal day like this in a relatively normal neighborhood like mine.

I lifted my legs one at a time and eyed them. The heat gave everything an unnatural brilliance. I'd forgotten my sunglasses inside, and it was too bright to tell if my skin was burning under the sunscreen I'd slathered on. It was too bright to read. I flipped shut one of the fashion magazines that my older sister, Katie, had left behind when she moved out and let it slip from my fingers onto the grass.

My mind drifted to thoughts of high school, and instantly butterflies fluttered in my stomach. The week after next, I would start grade nine. I was excited that the teachers would be treating me more like an adult and less like a kid, but I wasn't looking forward to being at the bottom of a school hierarchy again, down in the lowest grade. Plus, I didn't know many people. I didn't have a lot of friends. And now I'd be surrounded by new kids in my classes, kids whose names I'd have to learn, whose cliques I'd have to navigate through.

Our next-door neighbor Mrs. Carlton turned her sprinkler on. The water made a pleasant swishing sound, and I imagined it falling on me, cooling me. A crow called from the tall pine tree that leaned over our back fence.

At least in high school my marks would finally start to matter more. I wasn't the smartest student in the class, but my grades were good. I pushed myself, did all my homework and studied hard. I was disciplined, especially with my running. After track had ended in the spring, I'd continued training all through the summer because I knew it would help me make it onto the high school cross-country team this fall. Also, running kept me feeling in control, helped me get my mind off the things that I couldn't do anything about. And when I sank into that place where I felt like I was drowning, running helped me float back up and find my way to the surface again.

Staying in control. It's important. And maybe that's why people try to look for signs of what lies ahead, or believe in God. Maybe that's why some people read their horoscope or try to interpret lines on palms. So they can stay in control. So they can use these signs to make sense of the world, to make the right choices, to stay safe or even stay ahead of the game. I guess others decide they just don't want to know what might happen, especially if it's something bad coming their way. They stick their heads in the sand, turn away from any indications that things aren't quite right, ignore the butterflies that unsettle their stomachs when certain ideas, implausible, impossible, are spoken, are set in motion.

A lawnmower started up somewhere in the neighborhood, ran for a few moments, then stopped abruptly.

I was melting in the heat. Five more minutes, I decided. And then I'd go inside.

My mother had been gardening. Now she stood in the shade at the edge of the flowerbed. "Ivy," she said.

I opened my eyes and looked at her.

"Ivy, it's too hot to be out here."

She wiped her forehead under the wide brim of her straw hat, shaking her head at me, a trowel dangling from one hand.

I didn't move, didn't respond. She flapped her hand dismissively and headed for the house, focused on getting her drink.

Sunlight seared through my eyelids as if it could burn a hole through them. A drop of sweat rolled from my forehead to my cheekbone and then slid slowly down my cheek. Other drops were pooling in my belly button. I shifted my legs again, unsticking them from the recliner's nylon covering.

The crow called again. When I first came outside, I had counted nine black birds, four in the pine tree and five in the maple tree in our neighbor's yard. Were they all still there? I couldn't open my eyes to check. My eyelids were leaden and my limbs without feeling.

The heat lay on me and purred.

I may have fallen asleep. When my father leaned out the porch door, calling, "Ivy, phone for you!" I had to reconstruct myself, drag myself up, up and out from wherever I'd gone.

"I'm going grocery shopping. See you later," he added.

Lightheaded, I sat on the edge of the recliner. Then I launched myself forward, somehow remembering how to put one foot ahead of the other.

The grass was hot; the kitchen floor tiles were cool on my bare feet. I placed one hand on the lemonade pitcher, and the chill of the ice entered my palm. My other hand, sweaty, held the telephone receiver.

"Hello?" I said.

"Hello. Ivy?"

"Yeah?"

"Hi, Ivy." There was a pause. "It's Virginia."

"Hi, Gin," I answered. I couldn't keep the surprise out of my voice. "How are you?"

I had known my neighbor Virginia Donato since she and I were seven. We used to play together a lot when we were kids. But I was stunned to hear her voice. We hadn't really talked in ages. We'd gone to different elementary schools, but we had been at the same middle school together for two years, and although we'd said hi to each other in the school hallways once in a while, she hadn't called me in a long time, not for a few years at least.

"Fine," Virginia replied. "I'm fine." But she didn't sound fine. She sounded distracted, as if I'd just interrupted her. As if she'd been in the middle of a conversation with someone else.

I waited, uncertainly, slightly uneasy to be hearing from her. There was a silence.

I felt a drop of sweat starting to trickle down my back.

Still Virginia didn't speak. "Virginia? So, what's up?" I asked lightly.

"Um, Ivy, I wonder if you could come over and talk to me." Her voice sounded odd, thin and breathy. I didn't remember it being that way. "It's important," she added.

I hesitated. This was even more strange, that she'd choose to talk to me about something important. We'd been ... well, friends, I guess ... but never really the best of friends. But I felt I owed her that much, and anyway, I was sort of curious about what had become of her. I hardly ever saw her on the street anymore. Her older brothers and sisters seemed to drive her everywhere she had to go. She kept to herself at school. And she seemed to have few friends, fewer even than me, maybe none.

"Well, okay. When?"

"Could you come now?"

"Now?"

"Yes, now would be good," she said.

It was weird. Hearing her ask for something so directly, it struck me that Virginia had never asked me for anything before. When Virginia and I used to play together, she had always wanted to do whatever I wanted. She had sort of flitted around the edges of my ideas, my little bits of organizing, my imagination. It wasn't like her to be demanding. This must be pretty serious after all.

"Okay," I agreed. "I'll come over in a few minutes, Gin."

"Thanks," she said.

And so it began.

✟✟✟

"*What are you doing here?*" *she asked. She knew she should be afraid, and she was, a little. He was a stranger, after all. A stranger here, in her own bedroom.*

Part of her knew she should scream and run, that she should call for help.

She was alone, and he had come in somehow.

He was here, in her bedroom.

Chapter Two

I went upstairs and changed into a T-shirt. My hands shook slightly as I brushed my hair.

I couldn't help it: I was nervous about going to Virginia's house. It was stupid, really. Mr. Donato, Virginia's father, had always been friendly to me. The few times I'd seen him, he'd beamed a big smile in my direction. Then he'd lifted my chin with his finger, looked into my eyes with great seriousness and asked me something ridiculous — "Have you remembered to feed your elephant today?" — just to make me giggle.

But he had been dead for a while now. He had had a heart attack in their backyard about four years ago.

Mrs. Donato had always been very sweet to me, happy that her youngest daughter had found a friend. I knew she'd be nice to me if I saw her today, even though she had pretty much vanished from view since her husband died. I had seen her only one or two times getting in or out of what now seemed to have become their family car, but never sitting on her front porch or working in her garden, like she used to. Even my father had mentioned it recently, when my mother had been complaining that she had no one to do anything with. "You could spend some time with Maria Donato," he suggested. "You used to talk on the phone with her a lot when the girls were younger." She had shrugged it off, but he had turned to me, reflecting. "I haven't seen Maria in … years. Not since Gus passed away."

I set the brush down and stared at myself in the mirror. Tanned face. Curly hair, forever tending to frizziness. Fourteen years old. Would any of Virginia's siblings remember me if I ran into them? I swallowed. I didn't *want* to run into any of them. They were one of the reasons I was apprehensive about going to Virginia's house. It was as if the parents had vanished, and the kids had taken over the place. They had always made me nervous, ever since I first met Virginia — at least the older ones had. The younger of her two brothers, Joe, he seemed okay, I guess. Normal, anyway. But the other siblings ... It was partly because I was shy, and they had seemed so much older than me, not adults yet, not then, but definitely not children either. I hadn't known what to make of them. I could hardly even tell the three girls apart. Teresa, Donna, Anna Maria. They all blurred together — tall, thin, plain. They were always busy, always talking with an edge in their voices, their faces hard and intense, as if they were being driven toward something necessary but maybe not pleasant. I would have preferred it if they had completely ignored me, but sometimes they would glance at me and something in their eyes would flicker, and then a thin line would cross their face, like a smile, but not quite.

And Paul, the elder brother, well ... he was the one who made me the most uneasy. I'm not sure why. The other Donatos looked pretty much like one another, but Paul's hooded eyes, high cheekbones and shock of black hair set him apart. He had this almost ... reptilian face, kind of primitive, snakelike. And what was weird was that it sort of made him more compelling, this almost-ugliness. I remember being seven or eight and feeling instinctively that I should stay away from him, but at the same time, hoping that he'd look at me, because there was something about his eyes ... And then a few years later, when Katie dated him, I felt confused. Mainly I thought she was crazy, but some small part of me understood why she might find him a little intriguing.

I shivered in the heat.

I found my mother sitting in the shade on the back patio in a high-backed chair, a gardening magazine on her lap. A tall glass was on the white wicker table beside her.

"I'm going over to Virginia's house," I informed her. I had learned the hard way a long time ago that if I didn't tell her where I was going, and she suddenly decided she needed me, she just might call all the homes of every kid who had ever been a friend of mine, hunting me down, embarrassing me with that slurred voice: "Hello there, dear, it's Joan calling, Joan Morell ..."

If she had been capable of being a real mother, she would have known I hadn't been to Virginia's house in years. She would have known that the two of us didn't really talk to each other anymore. She would have been surprised that I was going there now. But of course, she wasn't capable of that, and so she didn't say a word. She didn't even raise her eyes from the magazine page. She just nodded her head, her straw hat dipping its plastic flowers, and waved her fingers loosely at me. I left, fighting down a desire to slam the door behind me.

When I got to the Donato house, I was sweating, even though their house was only eight doors down from mine. The heat was that intense.

Like ours, the Donatos' house was old, red brick and two stories high. Unlike ours, however, theirs had an extension on the back, which gave them a few more bedrooms. It also had a hedge running around the whole front yard. The Donatos had planted it a few years ago, around the same time they had the high fence built around the perimeter of their backyard. The hedge had grown tall enough so that it already sort of hid the front of the house. The combined effect made the house seem sealed off, isolated.

Virginia was sitting in a chair on her small front porch. Seeing me, she lifted a hand, then let it drift gently back down onto her lap.

"Hi, Virginia." I sank down onto the top step and leaned against the iron railing that encircled the stoop. This summer

I hadn't once seen Virginia out on her porch as I'd walked home from babysitting in the evenings. Instead, it had been taken over by her brothers and sisters and their visitors. The visitors came frequently enough for me to begin to recognize them — two men in brush cuts and suits, maybe in their twenties, often pacing with long legs and short steps across the tiny porch, like caged-in animals, and sometimes a woman, legs crossed under a skirt, arms folded. I'd hear their low voices murmuring, see them suddenly huddle, their heads bent in close conversation with Virginia's sisters or her oldest brother.

I looked up at Virginia. Actually, I hadn't seen her any-where this summer at all. Maybe she'd been away. Her fair hair was quite long now. Virginia's skin, always more pale than the olive-ish complexions of her sisters and brothers, looked like it hadn't been touched by one ray of sunshine all summer. Had she been indoors somewhere the whole time?

Her gaze flitted over me. "Hi, Ivy," she said. Virginia's light sleeveless dress lay against her slight form. Her feet were bare and thin.

I shifted on the hard cement stoop. "So how are you, Gin?" I asked. "I haven't seen you in ages. How've you been doing? What did you want to talk to me about?"

I studied her carefully as I spoke. Something about her was different, but I couldn't quite place it. Not her hair. Not braces. Not glasses ...

Virginia looked down at her hands in her lap. She didn't speak.

That wasn't different, though. The indefinable something about Virginia that had set her apart from everyone else, that had often irritated me, had remained the same. It was like she wasn't ever quite in step. It was as if, to be with her or talk to her, you had to hold your breath or still your heart a beat in order to travel in sync with her pace.

"Gin," I repeated.

She wasn't slow. She just ... wasn't like everyone else.

I knew I should be patient. I owed it to her. And so I would be.

But something else other than impatience was making me edgy. The thought of running into her sisters or older brother? Uncomfortable memories of my relationship with Virginia herself? A hollow feeling settled in my stomach.

I just wanted her to talk to me, and then I'd leave.

A worried expression flitted over Virginia's face as she stared into the distance. Her hands twitched where they lay in her lap, unnatural and stiff.

"Gin," I said again. I moved to sit closer to her, at her feet.

Finally, she turned her head slightly, looking down at me. The rest of her body seemed immobilized, as if, rather than it supporting her, she was caring for it, gathering it around her as if it were precious, fragile, and might shatter without extreme caution. She was forcing a smile.

My shoulder was at her knee, and I could look up full into her face. I put my hand on one of her hands. It felt the way it looked, rigid and tense. I squeezed it. "Come on, Gin. Tell me."

She shook her head slightly. "It's not something terrible," she said to me, and she laughed a little, but uncertainly.

"That's good," I replied. "So what is it then?"

Virginia opened her mouth as if about to speak, and then, incredibly, began to blush. The pink rose up across her chest. It bloomed up her neck to her jaw, spreading to her cheeks. She looked away self-consciously, with another gentle laugh, and I realized that her pale face, suddenly suffused with color, was beautiful.

"Virginia ..." Now I spoke the word in wonder.

Misunderstanding, she spoke quickly to reassure me. "All right. I'll tell you. But it's difficult. And it's going to sound a little crazy." She paused. "I haven't told anyone else."

"Okay."

I pressed her hand again and waited.

Virginia's face took on a determined look. She was steeling herself. She glanced at the front door, then over her shoulder. She looked me in the eyes again.

"It happened a few nights ago," she began. "It happened here."

My pulse quickened.

"I was up in my bedroom ..." she said. "Ivy, you won't believe it —"

And just then the front door of the Donato house flew open. Virginia's brother Joe came bursting out. He was looking back over his shoulder, shouting something about a basketball game, and he was yelling, "I don't know, I don't know, Teresa," one hand pushing open the screen door, swinging a sports bag, and the other waving back at his older sister. He was moving forward like a bullet the whole time, and his knees or his sports bag rammed into me just as I realized that he hadn't seen me and had started to stand up and move out of the way.

I had been about to yell "Watch out," but then I was in the air, nothing under my feet. For an eternity, I was flying, heading for a crash at the bottom of the cement stairs, thinking that I should try to break my fall with my hands if I could only get them to move, get them in front of me, and then somehow, amazingly, I felt an arm around my hips, my waist, capturing me in mid-flight. Part of me was held, the rest was continuing to fly forward. Was I falling, flying or rescued? My hands, my arms were flung out in front of me, my head too, and my legs, and then they too were halted, and I was being set down, not falling, not flying, but sitting now on the edge of the porch stoop, and the moment of uncertainty turned back into time, turned back into now.

Joe had caught me.

I was hardly breathing, stunned. Joe was panting, sitting behind me, his one arm still tight around my waist, gathering me in, still saving me. My hips rested between his thighs, and my back folded into his chest. His sports bag had fallen far from the steps. His shorts, shoes, underwear, deodorant and shampoo had cascaded out.

A few more seconds passed, and then I began breathing quickly, my heart suddenly pounding, as the fear belatedly caught up with me.

He spoke into my hair, his words breathing onto my face, the smell of him soapy and sour. "Are you okay? I'm really sorry. I didn't see you there. Are you all right?"

Virginia was the youngest in the family, and I knew Joe was second youngest. He had been the only one Gin ever talked about with affection. When we were friends, she'd told me he was the one she went to when she needed help with anything. She'd called him her guardian angel. Now, I guessed, Joe had to be about seventeen or eighteen. Probably in grade twelve. In a few days, we'd be at the same school.

I managed to take a few more breaths and then say, "I'm fine. It's okay," but I had to fight to keep tears from springing to my eyes. I blinked hard a few times, looking down at the steps.

"I'm glad you're not hurt," Joe said to me, jumping up, and in a moment he had gathered up the items that were strewn about the lawn. Then, "'Bye, Gin," he said to his sister, and he headed off.

I rubbed at my eyes. When my shaking stopped, I swiveled around so that I was leaning against the iron railing again. Virginia still had a slight smile on her face. She was caught up in her own thoughts, gripped by whatever she had been about to tell me, reliving an experience. It was as if she hadn't even seen the collision right in front of her. Bizarre ...

So I urged her, "Gin, go on. You were saying that it happened a few nights ago," I prompted. "In your bedroom ..."

She smiled, recalling, and again, her face flushed with beauty.

Her eyes flickered back to mine.

She was about to tell me, was about to continue her story, when once more the porch door swung open. Instantly, a veil dropped over Virginia's face. Still she smiled, and she didn't release my eyes from her gaze, but now there was a wariness about her and a self-consciousness.

I realized I had been holding my breath. I released it, leaned away from Gin, looked up.

It was one of her sisters, but I couldn't really tell which one. She looked about twenty-two or twenty-three. Her clothes were simple and bland: a blue blouse, a beige skirt and black flat shoes. A cross dangled from a slim gold chain around her neck.

I had the crazy sensation that she'd been listening the whole time, standing just inside the screen door and eavesdropping.

Her hard face produced a grim smile. "Hello ... Ivy, isn't it?" she asked. "It's Teresa." She patted her palm on her chest. "We haven't seen you in some time."

"No. Hello," I replied awkwardly.

She stood looking at me for just long enough for me to realize that, oh, that had actually been a question, and she was waiting for an explanation of why I hadn't been here in a while, and why I was here now. But I had waited too long to respond. It would be embarrassing to try to answer her at this point, and besides, I didn't want to tell her the truth, that Virginia had asked me to come because she had something important to talk to me about. Suddenly it was obvious to me, as Virginia sat quietly under Teresa's stony gaze, that Virginia didn't want Teresa to know about it.

Teresa, sitting down, said, "It certainly is hot, isn't it?" She was toying with her cross with one hand.

"Yes," I agreed, too quickly.

And then a long, uncomfortable silence stretched out. I hoped Virginia would say something, but she simply looked out at the street, then lifted her eyes and looked up at the tree tops. Finally, she rose from the chair, her light cotton dress clinging to her. She moved carefully to the front door, placing her feet delicately, as if walking on a thin crust of deep snow.

"Ivy, I'm really hot," Virginia said. "I think I'm going to go in. But thanks for coming over." Her voice was flat, her words as careful as her steps.

"Virginia ..." I began, also getting up, but then I changed my mind about saying more.

"It probably is a good idea to get out of this heat." Teresa aimed a fake smile at me. "Good-bye, Ivy."

She edged her way around Virginia and went back inside, calling sharply over her shoulder, "Come on, Gin."

Virginia's hair hung down limply, a few strands caught in the corner of her mouth.

I stepped closer to her. "Virginia, what's wrong? Tell me, please." It felt like she was about to vanish for good. She had wanted to confide in me. After we hadn't been close in years, she'd called me over to tell me something. "Are you all right?" I whispered urgently. "Are you sick? Is there anything I can do?"

She shook her head.

"I wish you would just tell me right now," I continued. I put out my hand to touch her arm. "Just quickly."

But she was moving away, opening the screen door,

putting it between us. "No, it can wait." She tilted her head ever so slightly toward the interior of the house. "It will have to wait." As the screen door closed and she looked back at me, Virginia's face became thousands of tiny squares, a jigsaw puzzle remarkably and delicately constructed.

"I'll come over tomorrow," I promised, raising my voice as she disappeared into the darkness of her home, but I don't know if she heard me. And now there were thousands of empty holes left behind in the screen when her image vanished.

✛✛✛

*A*nd *yet putting it that way, thinking of him as a stranger, wasn't right. He wasn't unfamiliar. He was like someone she had once known, or always known. He was like family, or more than that even.*

What she felt was different from fear. It was more like ... She wasn't certain. She was amazed and mystified and overwhelmed and only a tiny bit afraid.

She knew that later she would think of him, would remember this visit, every detail of it, and would want to relive it, would wish that it had never ended.

"I have some news for you," he said. He sat down on the windowsill. He folded his arms and crossed his legs. "Are you ready?"

Chapter Three

I went up to bed early that night. First, I went into the kitchen for a glass of cold water. Mom's hat was on the kitchen counter. Her glass was beside it, empty except for a few bits of ice still melting in the bottom. She had shown up for dinner, but I hadn't seen her since. It might have infuriated me. Why bother having children if you don't want to spend time with them? It might have, but I wouldn't let it.

I drank the water down. Then I refilled the glass and headed upstairs.

As I passed my mother's darkened bedroom, her voice drifted to me from under her covers. "Close my door, please." I reached in and pulled it shut without replying.

I flopped across my bed, let my feet hang over the side, and stared up at the ceiling. The sky had darkened; the sun was down, but it didn't feel like the heat had dropped at all.

The crows were calling, their voices guttural and harsh.

I had never seen crows in our yard before this summer. I'd seen them around the city, I guess, but this summer, for some reason, they'd been gathering in either the tall pine or the spreading maple behind our house almost every evening, and some afternoons, too. At first, I thought that maybe they had a nest nearby, but I don't know. I still haven't seen one.

When they first came, they were difficult to ignore. They were really noisy. Dad said that's why a group of crows is known as a murder. *A murder of crows.* He says people associate them with death, and the loud cries they make sound like they're yelling "Murder."

A murder of crows. I didn't like that much. I preferred a tiding of magpies. According to an online article I read, that's what you call a group of birds that are similar to crows but with white edges on their wings and white bellies.

A tiding of magpies.

I knew I'd heard the word "tiding" before, but I couldn't remember where, or what it meant. I looked it up as well and found out that "tiding" means information or news. Because people have always believed that magpies and crows are prophetic — that they can help foretell future events, or bring us news of the future — a group of magpies is called a tiding.

Birds of prophecy. A tiding of magpies.

I loved the sound of these phrases, these ancient terms. I'd read more online about tidings and magpies, and I'd found an old English rhyme that described how to interpret seeing magpies. We don't have many magpies in North America, but we have lots of crows, so presumably the poem can be used here to count crows instead. The number of crows you see tells you what to expect in the future.

> *One is for bad news*
> *Two is for mirth*
> *Three is a wedding*
> *Four is a birth*
> *Five is for riches*
> *Six is a thief*
> *Seven is a journey*
> *Eight is for grief*
> *Nine is a secret*
> *Ten is for sorrow*
> *Eleven is for love*
> *Twelve is for joy tomorrow.*

I was amazed that there was a time when people actually believed that the things they saw around them, in their daily lives of air and dirt and drudgery and bird poop, could connect them with something more grand; that it meant they weren't alone here, floundering on this planet; that they could use these signs brought by crows and magpies to reach forward into what lay ahead, to make decisions now so that the future wasn't so frightening and unknowable.

Aw, aw. The crows were calling to one another again. Why weren't they asleep for the night?

It was hard to tell how many of them there were. If I knew, maybe I'd be able to figure out what would happen next, how life would unfold for me.

Yeah, right.

I took off my clothes, put on my pajamas and got into bed. Maybe there were eleven crows. Maybe there were twelve crows.

Maybe I didn't want to know if there were ten, or eight or only one crow.

Random things like the number of crows in a tiding outside my window did not really connect to the big picture of life. Neither did the shapes made by tea leaves. There were no signs of prophecy. There were no fortune tellers. The only one who could know the future would be God, if he existed.

If God existed ... My mind swung back to Virginia and the Donatos. She had been pretty religious. Her whole family had been. Especially Paul.

I switched off my bedside light. It was too hot to pull up even one light cotton sheet. An unpleasant memory blossomed in my mind. I had gone to church with the Donatos one day. When they moved into our neighborhood, they were the only family on our block to go to the large Catholic church at the bottom of our street. They went regularly, at least once a week, walking down and back every Sunday morning. A month or so after Virginia and I began playing together, she asked me if I went to church. I said no.

Her eyes opened wide, and she smiled. She asked me if I wanted to go with her.

Curious, I agreed.

That Sunday morning, when I stepped into the church, I was struck by the majesty of the building itself, the sun pouring in through the stained glass, the high wooden ceiling. I'd never been in a room so wide and tall, so solemn. The organ music reverberated throughout. I was mesmerized by the many bodies standing, sitting, kneeling in unison. I didn't understand anything that was said, but I liked following along, feeling included in something big and important, something solid and permanent. It felt relaxing, like I was floating, swept along with everyone else, lifted up in the palm of a great hand. It felt good.

We walked home, Virginia and I trailing behind the rest of her family. Everyone else went inside except her mother, who stood on the porch to watch me get home okay, and I said to Virginia, "I liked that. Can I go again?"

Virginia took my hand and led me inside to the kitchen, where her father and her brother Paul were sitting at the table, talking. Virginia was excited, smiling confidently, and I wasn't certain whether it was me, her father, her brother, or who it was exactly that she knew this would please. She even paused until everyone was looking at her, and then she said, "Ivy liked coming to church with us. She wants to go again. Can she? Can she come next week, too?"

Mr. Donato began to smile and even nod, and so did Mrs. Donato, who had followed us in from the porch. But before either of them could speak, Paul jumped up. I saw the look on his face, and I felt fear, embarrassment and shame. I wanted to run away before I had to hear what he was going to say. I think I even turned to go, but Virginia, still holding my hand, gripped it tightly, held me there.

"This isn't a game," Paul said. He walked over to me.

His eyes were open wide, like he was trying to keep them friendly, but they hinted at something deep and dark. "Ivy, one visit to church was for you to see and understand. But, no, this isn't a game."

He put his hand on my shoulder. I flinched.

"We don't go to church for fun. We don't go to church just because we feel like it. It's not just a pretty place with nice music. It's a serious place, a place where extremely serious things happen." He stood in front of me, tall, focused.

Mr. Donato shifted in his seat. "Paul —"

But Paul raised his hand, gesturing for his father to be silent, without taking his eyes off me.

"Ivy, I'm not saying you can't come again. In fact, we'd love it if you came again. Really we would. God would love it, too." He stared at me, with an almost hungry look. I believed him. I knew it was what he wanted. "I'd like you to come to church, Ivy."

Virginia had let go of my hand. I knew she was standing nearby, but Paul was looming over me, taking up all the air. He continued, "Do you want to get to know God? Do you truly want to learn about God, and his plan, and how to do his work? God needs you. God would like that ..."

Paul's blue eyes were alive with an intensity that felt like it might swallow me up. I think I wanted to pull away, but I couldn't. I think I wanted to shake my head, say "no," but I couldn't.

"Do you want to get to know God?" Paul repeated, in a low voice. Now he was crouching down in front of me, his eyes locked onto mine.

"Do you?" he asked, and now I wanted to do whatever he was asking.

I had felt warm and welcomed at the church service, but I suddenly realized that what Paul was offering was different. His God had a guard at his door, and it was Paul, and you had to get permission to come in, and then you might never get out again. It frightened me, but I wanted to do what he asked, even though I didn't really understand what it was. I didn't know why, but I wanted to get in and never get out again. The desire sparked in me and flared.

I think he saw it. I think he felt it.

Except now his father was interrupting. "Ivy, my dear! Of course you can come again if you want to. You don't need permission from Paul. 'Suffer the little children to come unto me,' is what Jesus said."

And his mother was shaking her head gently, with some bewilderment, and saying his name, "Paul."

And there was Virginia, putting her arm around me, and like a breath of air blowing gently, she said, "Ivy," and the weird longing to dive deep into Paul's bottomless pit was extinguished.

I shuddered even now, remembering the event. It had been a long time ago, and I hadn't thought about it in years, but it still had the power to disturb me. I was glad it hadn't been Paul who had come out onto the porch this afternoon.

I flopped over onto my stomach. A slight breeze came through my open window. In the silence, the crows called again.

I stirred restlessly. So Virginia was back in my life again. Her words drifted into my mind.

"It happened a few nights ago ..."

"It's going to sound a little crazy."

Had she been about to describe something good that had happened, or something frightening?

Thinking about her, I drifted off to sleep uneasily. There was something about Virginia that seemed formidable, like nothing could harm her. But there was also something about her that needed protecting.

✛✛✛

She *didn't know if she was ready.*

"Maybe you should sit down," he suggested gently.

She was trying not to be overwhelmed. She remained standing, trying to keep her balance.

"You have news for me," she said slowly, describing what was happening. "But I don't know who you are. I don't know what you're doing here. I don't even know that you aren't here to … to hurt me."

She had run out of air, out of breath.

He nodded. "I see," he said. He shifted his weight slightly, getting comfortable. "I understand what you're saying," he repeated.

He looked at her. "But I do think you know who I am."

Chapter Four

When I phoned Virginia before breakfast, it was Joe who answered the phone. I didn't recognize his voice.

"Is Virginia there, please? It's Ivy calling."

"Oh hi, Ivy. It's Joe. You know, Joe the klutz."

Blushing, relieved that he couldn't see me, I stammered, "Hey, that's okay. I mean ... you don't need to ... it's okay."

"I should have been watching where I was going. I'm really sorry I ran into you like that."

"It's okay. Really."

"So you want to speak to Virginia?" Joe's breath vanished from the line. For a moment, I remembered his body turning away and walking from me, his sports bag flung over his shoulder, the back of his head and the shape of his neck.

"Hello?" Virginia's voice sounded just like it had yesterday, odd, breathy, thin. I was seized by the image of a yawning abyss, a dark pit. At the edge of it stood Virginia, stepping out blindly, about to plummet.

"I want to come over and talk to you," I explained firmly. "I'm going to come over now. Okay?"

I waited, but she didn't answer.

"Virginia? So is it okay? If I come over now? We didn't get a chance to finish our conversation yesterday. Remember?"

It was as if she was only partly there. It was frustrating. Why was she being so difficult?

Click.

It sounded like someone had picked up a phone on this line. Dad had already left our house, and Mom was never up this early. Was it someone in Virginia's house?

"I'm not dressed yet," Gin replied. "I just got up."

Was someone listening in? Was it Joe? I tried to choose

my words carefully. "Gin, I really need to talk to you," I said. "I'll be there soon."

She answered vaguely, "Well, okay," and we hung up.

I dressed quickly, choosing thin cotton shorts, a faded T-shirt and sandals. The heat had not evaporated overnight. In fact, it was as hot now as it had been when I went to bed last night. Dad had opened the kitchen windows before leaving for his morning bike ride, but as I waited for my slice of bread to toast, I didn't feel a breath of air move through them. The curtains at the kitchen windows hung limp. The world was still.

I heard a crow call, over and over. Or was it two crows, one calling and one answering? *Aw, aw, aw. Aw, aw, aw.*

I spread avocado onto my toast and then added a few slices of tomato, leaning on the kitchen counter as I ate. I wrote a note telling Dad where I would be.

Then I walked to Virginia's through the heavy, sullen air.

The uneasy feeling came back as I saw her house down the street. I remembered the first few days after Virginia and her family moved into our neighborhood. My mother had latched onto Mrs. Donato right away. I could see now that it was probably because she realized there was an opportunity there to get me out of her way, so that she could do her thing.

And so she began to arrange these little play dates. At first, I went to Virginia's house. But I felt uneasy when I wasn't at my own home, like something bad was going to happen, like my mother was going to forget about me and not come and pick me up, or drift away into the sky like a big balloon without anyone to tug her back down. So Virginia started coming to our house. I didn't like her a lot, but she was quiet, and she'd go along with what I wanted to do.

And then, about the third time she came over, I was upset because I had wanted my real friends, my school friends, to come over, but my mom had said no, they were too noisy, and they ran all around the house and made a big mess, and they lived too far away, and she was too tired to go and get them and drive them home again and clean up after them, and couldn't I just play with Virginia because she lived so close by, and wouldn't I just do that for her? Why couldn't I go over to Virginia's house? Why did we always want to come over here? Why did I always have to make life so hard for her? Couldn't I just be a good girl and stop fussing so much; weren't all little friends pretty much the same anyway; how could one friend be so different from another, and if one lived closer, then that's the one we were going to have over, and it wouldn't make any difference, and I could just get used to it ...

I stopped for a moment on the sidewalk. I didn't want to be thinking about all these things. One visit with Virginia and bad memories were being stirred up.

I looked up and down the street. There was someone walking a dog, someone else putting out a sprinkler on a lawn. I felt stupid just standing there. I bent down and fiddled with my sandal.

My thoughts were stuck on that day. I didn't want to remember the rest, but the film was rolling on. Gin and I had been playing house. It was my idea. We were in my room, and we'd made a tent, clothes-pinning sheets from the bed to the radiator. Underneath we were pretending my stuffed animals were guests who had come to visit, and we were offering them lunch, so we'd got out all the plastic cups, plates and cutlery. I'd decided we'd use real water in the plastic tea pot, and we were hurrying down to the bathroom to fill it up.

Virginia was excited, but she said, "Do you think your Mom will get mad?" or something like that, and then we both went flying into the bathroom. I was saying, "No, she won't even know," and there was my mother.

She scared Virginia. She scared us both. I definitely hadn't expected to see my mother there, in the bathroom, with the door unlocked. She was sitting on the side of the bathtub, her head hanging between her knees, her hair cascading down on either side of her face.

I froze, and Virginia did, too.

I looked at my mother uneasily. She must have known we were there, but she didn't look up.

"Mom?" I said uncertainly. Weirdly, I was afraid I might be bothering her, interfering with something.

She slowly lifted her head and looked at me, and then at Virginia. There was no expression on her face. None. Not a flicker of recognition as she saw us. Not a flicker of surprise. Nothing.

And then she put her head back down between her knees.

There was a bottle, almost empty, balanced on the closed toilet seat lid.

Virginia and I stood there for another few seconds, staring, stunned.

The bottle. At first, I didn't know what it was or why it was there in the bathroom with my mother, but then I could smell it, the sharp tang of the alcohol. I noticed a glass lying on its side under the sink. And I understood. I was only eight, but I understood, and it flushed me with shame.

I remember grabbing Gin's arm, pushing her out of the bathroom in front of me and then pulling the door closed behind both of us. I ran past her into my bedroom. I dropped to my knees and crawled into our tent. I was crying with fear and with disappointment and mostly with embarrassment because I had seen it over and over again, seen my mother absent, distracted, turning away from me, looking past me toward something she was more interested in, and I'd known there was something not right, but now suddenly, when I saw the bottle and the look on her face, I knew what was wrong. For the first time, I knew that she was drunk. I knew being drunk was bad because it made you talk slurred and tell dumb jokes and maybe drive the car wrong and kill people, but worse than that, I knew that it was something people did for fun with other people, like at a party, but that this was Saturday afternoon, and she was alone, and she was sitting in the bathroom, and she didn't look like she was having fun, or telling jokes, or about to drive anywhere, and I knew it wasn't the first time. It explained so much about her, about us, about our family. I'd had some hope in the back of my mind that one of the times when we all occasionally happened to click into place and felt like a real family, one day that connection might just lock in and last forever. Now the hope evaporated. What I saw explained a lot of the bad things about Mom, and it took all the air out of the room so that I felt like I was under water. It was hard to breathe, and I was gasping for air as I sobbed, and worse, my discovery of this humiliating secret had come with Virginia standing beside me.

I sat in the dark, in the tent, and I pressed my fists against my eyes, and I said, "You should go home. Go home, Gin," even though I didn't really expect that she was still there.

But she said, "No, Ivy. I'm going to stay."

And so I sat in the tent for a long time, until finally I could breathe again. And when I crawled out from under there, I saw Virginia sitting by the window, at my desk. She was gazing outside, but she had a pencil in her hand. She was drawing.

I went and sat by her. She looked at me, carefully. Then she smiled.

She handed me a pencil and some paper. She moved her chair over, so I could pull the other chair closer.

We drew together, taking turns, until it was time for her to leave for dinner.

I thought maybe Virginia wouldn't come back to play with me again after that day. I thought she might tell her mother what she had seen, and her mother wouldn't allow her to come back, or that she might be too scared or too disgusted by our falling-apart family to want to be my friend, and then I would know that our secret was so bad we could not be saved.

But the very next time my mother called the Donatos, Virginia showed up. She must have run right over as soon as her mother said, "Yes, go ahead, *piccolina*." And I was so relieved, I almost cried.

We never spoke about it, not once.

And I never again asked any other friends over to my house, because I realized that anyone could find out as easily as she had, and they could push everything over the edge I was teetering on. Only Virginia was allowed to come. Only her. Because I knew she could keep a secret. Because part of my eight-year-old self already knew that keeping a secret might cost something, and the price might be friendship no matter how I really felt about her, or whether my feelings might change, or whether we really had that much in common other than living down the street from one another. The price didn't matter. I was so afraid of what her knowing could mean that I would have done anything to let the secret remain buried.

I stood up again. The sky was hazy. Maybe it would rain and break the heat, I thought, turning down the walkway in front of the Donato house.

No one answered my first knock or my second. Where were Virginia's brothers and sisters? Except for Joe, who obviously had a life, the others always seemed to be constantly hovering, like crows around the castle walls. It was one of the reasons I had stopped seeing Virginia. They just made it ... uncomfortable. Plus, she didn't go to the same school as me until grade seven, and by the time we got to grade six or so, she had begun easing away from me, kind of evaporating out of my life. Maybe it had even started the year before, after her father died — maybe it even had something to do with that — although I didn't really think of it at the time. Obviously, my mother wasn't arranging our visits together anymore — she hadn't for ages. I'd phone once in a while, and more and more often Virginia would say she couldn't come over. Eventually, Virginia herself never answered my calls, and whichever sister did would always have a reason why Virginia couldn't come to the phone. It started giving me the creeps. Ever since Mr. Donato's death, they had become incredibly protective. They'd turned her into a bit of a princess, remote, fragile, surrounded by high walls and jealously protected. Treasured. As if they were saving her for something.

And more than that, there was something about her sisters and Paul themselves that was ... unpleasant. It was more than unfriendliness. They acted ... wary, like I was a spy or something, or like *I* was going to do something wrong. They were all still living at home, and it was weird that they didn't want to become independent, start their own lives. Only Joe was still in high school, and maybe one of the girls was still at university, but Paul was working for sure and probably the other sisters, too. Were they just trying to stick around and support their mother? I don't know ... Something about them seemed unnatural.

For a while, I still went over to speak to Virginia when I saw her at school, but though she was friendly, she didn't seem to want to talk much. Finally, we'd just smile at one another in the hallways, and that was it.

So we lost touch, but actually, it was fine with me. Gave me more time to run, to focus on my schoolwork. Made me feel more in control of my life, in control of our family secret.

Just as I was about to knock a third and final time, Virginia's mother opened the door.

Mrs. Donato had always seemed much older than my mother and the other mothers on the street. I guess because many of her children were so much older. But now, if I hadn't known her, I might have thought she was Virginia's grandmother. Her black hair was streaked with gray. Her whole shape had changed. Instead of being straight and slim, she was stocky. And stooped. Her breasts seemed to dominate her whole upper body. Her waist had vanished. She wore a polyester pantsuit, blue on top and darker blue on the bottom.

"Hello, Ivy, you're up and about early," Mrs. Donato greeted me, smiling in welcome, as if time had halted, and I was still a little girl dropping in to see her pal. "How nice to see you. Come in, come in, Ivy. Virginia will be so happy that you've come to see her. This is so nice, so nice."

I smiled back. It was easy to respond to her friendliness.

I stepped inside, but when I replied, "Hello, Mrs. Donato. How are you?" it felt phony, like I was pretending that nothing had changed, that time hadn't passed, that Virginia was still an eight-year-old drawing a sun circle with sticks radiating out from it and that we were still the really good friends we had never been.

"I'm just fine, dear," Mrs. Donato replied. "As well as can be expected, that is."

We stood in the hallway. She continued smiling and put her hand on my arm. "Ah, little Ivy. You used to come by all the time. And Virginia used to spend so much time at your house." Her voice was soft and gentle, with its slight Italian accent. "You were one of her best friends. And now we don't see much of you anymore. Virginia has so few friends come by. Why is that, dear? Why don't you come by more often?"

"Oh, I don't know, Mrs. Donato. Just busy, I guess." I blushed a little with embarrassment.

"I see, dear," she replied, patting my arm.

Then suddenly, I saw something change in Mrs. Donato's face. Her smile faded, and her brow furrowed, as if she were recollecting something disturbing. She leaned into me, her hand gripping my arm too hard. "It's almost time, you know," she said in a low voice, urgently. "Has anyone warned you, dear? They've been preparing for a long while. I've seen them." Her eyes shifted, darting toward the kitchen, to the walls, to the front door. "They don't know that I see them, but I do. I know what they're doing."

I stared back at her, nervously. What was she talking about?

"It's very serious. Very serious." She looked right into my eyes. "Someone is going to get hurt," she said.

And then one of Virginia's sisters came out of the living room, was with us in two quick strides. I wasn't sure if she had heard exactly what her mother had said, but she placed her hand on her mother's arm, and now we were linked, the three of us, Mrs. Donato's hand on my arm, her daughter's hand on her arm, and Virginia's sister was saying, "Mama, come and sit down. Come and sit down now," shaking her head at me, and patting her mother's back, saying, "Mama, you shouldn't be upsetting yourself. You should let Teresa or me answer the door. You know that."

The sister turned to me and said, "You're Ivy? Do you remember me? I'm Anna Maria." She wore a short blue skirt and a white blouse, with hair swept up into a bun and fashionable, tinted glasses. She would have been pretty except that the expression on her face was pinched, and her lips were a thin line. "Ivy, I don't think this is the best time for you to see Virginia," she continued. Mrs. Donato looked puzzled, and I was puzzled, too, because I couldn't believe that my arrival was responsible for upsetting Mrs. Donato, and I wasn't sure what it had to do with my seeing Virginia.

Anna Maria was trying to steer her mother toward the living room, and it felt like she was trying to shepherd me along toward the front door as well. She repeated, "Ivy, I think it would be a good idea if you came back on another day …," and now her voice had a bit of an edge to it.

Mrs. Donato was nodding, and murmuring vaguely, "Okay, dear. Okay," and it seemed for a minute that she was allowing herself to be maneuvered away, but then, after a few guided steps, she seemed to catch herself, regain focus. She stopped, straightened and shook off Anna Maria's hand, gently but firmly. Mrs. Donato said, "I'll go and sit down in a minute, Anna Maria, but I'm going to go up to Virginia's room and tell her that her friend is here. There's nothing wrong with Ivy visiting her now. It's nice for Virginia to have a friend stop by." She gave my arm a little squeeze and headed toward the stairs.

The muscle in Anna Maria's cheek tightened. She put her hand out again, placing it on Mrs. Donato's arm, saying, "Mama, it's not really …," and Mrs. Donato again shook it off, this time not so gently, saying, "I'll just tell her that Ivy is here."

This was the Mrs. Donato I remembered.

Anna Maria stood and watched, her arms crossed. Mrs. Donato started climbing the stairs, her hand tightly gripping the banister, her legs heavy and slow. Waiting, feeling incredibly uncomfortable, I slipped off my sandals, just for something to do.

I could hear voices murmuring in the kitchen, but the rest of the house was very quiet. It felt oppressive. I was beginning to wish I hadn't come. This house and Anna Maria were giving me the creeps.

Then, when her mother was near the top of the stairs, out of earshot, Anna Maria turned. She studied my face closely. "I'm not sure what Mother might have said to you a few

minutes ago, just after you arrived ..." She paused, as if I
might tell her. The words rang in my ears, unforgettable —
*I know what they're doing ... it's very serious ... Someone
is going to get hurt ...* She shrugged. "She isn't herself today.
She hasn't been herself for some time."

She looked at me, hard. "Perhaps Virginia has already told
you. It's very sad. Quite devastating for all of us. Sometimes
our mother seems rational. Sometimes she says things that
are absolutely impossible to believe. It's very difficult. It's as
if she slips in and out of the real world, the world she shares
with us. And the other place she goes seems to be full of
people who want to hurt her, who want to harm others. She
can't tell these worlds apart sometimes. She can't tell *us*
apart sometimes."

Anna Maria looked toward the top of the stairs. "She's
also been having heart problems. She's on medication, and
it's possible some of this confusion is being caused by the
drugs. We're not sure. Virginia —" she stopped, looked at her
watch again. "I have to go. Good-bye, Ivy." Anna Maria
wheeled around on her heel and went into the kitchen, closing
the door behind her.

I stood alone in the hallway, my head spinning. Mrs.
Donato had made a serious allegation that might or might
not be a genuine warning, but Anna Maria had suggested
she was delusional. If that was true, why was she so nervous
about what her mother had told me?

I turned to stare at the picture of Jesus. It had been
hanging on the wall of the hall at least since I'd first come
here, when I was seven. It had faded a bit, but seeing him
was like recognizing someone I'd known a long time ago.
His brown eyes were like pools of melted chocolate; his
long, slender hands pressed together in prayer; his hair
shoulder-length and wavy. I remember asking Virginia if
Jesus had really looked like that, and how did anyone

know? I had asked why the picture was there, in the hall-way. And as if she were reciting something she had heard repeatedly, she told me, "We see Jesus before we go outside, and it reminds us to try to act properly."

Mrs. Donato was calling to me from the top landing. I headed up, and we met halfway. "Virginia is in her room, dear," she said.

I cleared my throat. I knew I had to find out more. "Mrs. Donato, is everything all right?"

She turned her startled face to me and in that instant, with the same delicate bone structure, the wide cheekbones, the blue eyes, she could have been one of her daughters. "Oh, yes, yes. Nothing to worry about. Was Anna Maria telling you? Just a little upset with my heart. Only a small problem," she said, waving her hand dismissively.

"That's good," I said. I went on carefully, "But what you … what you mentioned in the hallway to me when I arrived?"

Mrs. Donato frowned. "Hmmm, dear. I'm not quite certain what that was."

"You said, 'It's almost time.'"

"Oh, yes, that," Mrs. Donato recalled. Her brow cleared. "'It's almost time.' That's what Paul says. He seems so certain. He tells me he's doing all he can to make it happen, although what he can do, I don't know. Actually, between you and me, Ivy, I think he may have some of it wrong. It's not what I was taught, not what I believe." She gave a little laugh. "I don't know if anyone can rush the Lord." She gave another laugh. "Anyway, Paul says he can, and he is, and Teresa, Donna and Anna Maria, they all agree, of course. They say it's almost time. And what harm can it do, their new ways of believing?" She patted my arm and confided, "I just keep on with my old ways. I know Jesus will keep us safe if we do right by him."

"But Mrs. Donato, you said someone might get hurt …"

She paused, considering, and then suddenly her face did look old, and her voice sounded defeated. "Paul says Jesus will be here soon, and Paul, well — when he makes up his mind, there's no stopping him. He's always been a passionate boy. Fervent. He didn't like to listen to his father. Now, with his father gone ..." She shrugged. It was as if she didn't see me, as if she were talking aloud to herself. "It's very difficult. He's living here, under my roof, but he's a grown man now. I must be supportive — he's my son — but only to a point. And when that point is reached, I must let him go ahead on his own. I try to show support, but really, I stick to my own faith. Him? He has found something new. I pray for him, though. I pray for my son."

I felt a shiver of fear. I didn't have a clue what she was talking about. Not a clue. But the tone in her voice, flat and hollow — and the way she spoke — sounded ominous to me. Impulsively, I whispered to her, "But is someone going to get hurt? Mrs. Donato, what did you mean when you said someone might get hurt?"

Mrs. Donato just patted my arm again, and with a confused smile, squeezed past me on the stairs. "Off you go now, dear," she said. "You remember the room? You're a good girl, Ivy. You'll have nothing to worry about, as long as you believe and keep going to church."

"Yes, Mrs. Donato."

I waited while she descended, looking down at her.

✠✠✠

*H*e *was right. She did know.*

And suddenly she wanted to cry. Suddenly she was crying.

She put her face in her hands, and she sank to the floor before him.

Chapter Five

My mind was whirling. What was she talking about? "Paul says Jesus will be here soon"? That didn't seem so bad. Unbelievable, but not bad. What could that have to do with people getting hurt? Maybe Anna Maria was right: Mrs. Donato was having some medical problems that were affecting her perception of reality. Plus, she was living in a house, barricaded from outsiders, with overly protective children who had some major control issues. That was a reasonable explanation. Mrs. Donato's state of mind was probably a family matter and none of my business.

On the other hand, maybe these were the things Virginia wanted to talk to me about: her mother, and her totally oppressive sisters and brother.

The door to her bedroom was open, and I poked my head through the doorway. "Hi, Virginia."

"Come in, Ivy." Virginia was sitting in a chair by an open window, her knees pulled up to her chest, her chin on her knees. Her hair hung about her like a veil. "Please shut the door."

Virginia's room was pristine. The floor was bare; there was no sign of any dirty laundry, even the books on the shelves of her bookcase were neatly aligned. Her dresser top was decorated with two framed photos — one of her mother and one of her father — a few china horses and a jewelry box. Her desk was tidy, too, and she'd taped up some pencil sketches on the wall by her bed — mostly soaring birds.

I took the chair from her desk, placed it next to hers and sat down. "I haven't been here in a long time," I said, stating the obvious, trying to get it out there and over with.

"No," she agreed.

"I like your drawings," I offered with a smile.

She smiled back. "Thanks. I've always liked birds."

We just sat for a few moments, looking out the window together. I could see Joe working on Mrs. Donato's tomato plants, but what startled me was the view of the fence they'd put up around their yard. I knew it was there; I could almost see it from my own bedroom window, and I could see it when I walked by and looked down their driveway. But from up here it looked forbidding, absurdly tall. In addition, they had stopped trimming back the trees that grew along the property line. Now branches draped across the top of the fences, creating an even greater barrier. Their backyard was like a secret garden.

My eyes tracked back to Joe for a moment, and then I noticed something else: there was a gate between this backyard and the one behind the Donatos'. It was large and had a big padlock on it, and the yard behind also had a fence, identical to the one in their yard — same wood, same ridiculous height. It ran across the back, between the properties, and up the sides of the yard, just like the Donatos' did.

I turned to Virginia, about to ask why the gate was there, but her mind seemed to be somewhere else. Her gaze was blank; her body holding the same unnatural pose that it had yesterday. Who was this girl? I could easily see in her the eight-year-old with whom I'd played house, played hopscotch and traded ghost stories, but I really didn't know either girl very well, not then, and not now. And yet here I was, the person she'd chosen to ask for help.

I tried to get her attention. "Gin," I said, "Anna Maria told me about your mother's heart problems. Is she going to be okay? She seems a bit … confused about things."

When we were little, I believed that Virginia was really close to her mother. It had made me jealous, just seeing them together. Looking back, I guess any girl's relationship with her mother would have seemed close, compared to my relationship with my own mother, but it did seem that when Gin's father died she became even closer to Mrs. Donato, while her sisters became closer to Paul.

"My mother's fine," Virginia answered, frowning. "Didn't she tell you that she's fine?"

"That's what she said," I replied hesitantly. "But she also seems a bit ... well, both vague and ..." I started again. "Virginia, she told me something kinda disturbing."

"Ivy, she's fine," Virginia repeated casually, almost impatiently. She waved her hand just as her mother had done, brushing off my concern. "She's older than your mother, remember? It's just a touch of ... She's just a little weak right now. She says it's nothing to worry about."

Okay, I'd forget about it for now. I'd focus on finding out what was bothering Virginia.

"So, Gin, what was it you wanted to tell me?" I leaned forward on the chair. "What's up with you? I really want to hear what's happening."

Slowly, she smiled. "Ivy, you seem so worried. I told you it's nothing bad. You don't need to worry."

"Okay, that's good," I told her. "So why don't you tell me, then?"

A look of uncertainty crossed Virginia's face. "Listen, you have to promise not to tell anyone," she said. She brushed the hair back from one side of her face, put it behind her ears, then did the same with the other side. She lifted her chin.

"Okay. I promise."

Gin paused. She said warningly, "You're going to think I'm crazy." She wasn't smiling.

I shook my head. "No, I won't."

"I trust you, you know," she said.

"I know."

"Are you ready?" she asked.

Virginia continued in a low voice, as if reciting from a legend, as if it had happened long ago to someone else. And in a way, I realized when she was done, it had.

"I had a visit. It was a few nights ago. I was alone in my bedroom, in this room," she said, gesturing with one arm, "and in the window, there appeared a ... a presence. I could see him, but I wasn't sure what he was. I was afraid but not afraid. It was broad daylight. He was right here, in front of the window."

I opened my mouth and then clamped it shut, afraid that if I said aloud what was screaming through my brain — "*What?!* What are you talking about?! I *do* think you're crazy!" — she would stop talking.

"I asked him who he was, and he wouldn't say. He didn't come toward me. He just leaned against the window-sill. I couldn't tell how old he was. He seemed familiar, but I knew I'd never met him before. How could I have? He was ... He was magnificent." Virginia grinned and touched her cheek, looking out the window.

I breathed slowly and purposefully, full of questions and a sick feeling of dread, desperately waiting for her to finish and almost afraid to hear how this would end.

"But what was he doing in my room? How did he get there? At first, I wanted to know, but the longer he stayed, the less important it became."

It was as if Virginia were talking aloud to herself. Her pale face was flushed and a look of intensity animated her now.

✛✛✛

She wanted to smile back at him, and so she lifted her head. She gazed at him.

"I was sent here," he began. "From On High.*"*

He spoke the last two words as if they began with capital letters or were in quotation marks. Then he tilted his head and looked at her carefully. She nodded, waiting, not ready to begin to imagine.

"I'm here to bring you tidings." He uncrossed his legs. He turned slightly, lifting one foot up onto the windowsill. He looked at her expectantly. "Tidings of great joy," he added.

Her mind was empty, although she felt the breath of wings moving through it. She had let logic slip away and was only watching him and listening and meeting his eyes. Her gaze remained blank.

"Doesn't ring a bell?" he asked.

She had never felt so alive. Suddenly, she knew what he was going to say next, and then he said it.

"You have been chosen," he explained. "You."

✝✝✝

"He said I had been chosen." She stopped, her lips apart, happy, as if she had explained.

I felt weak with fear. The tale was bizarre, incomplete, dangerous.

"Gin, what are you talking about? Are you serious? There was a guy in your room?"

Words wanted to pour out of me, but I didn't even know where to start. It was all so confusing. I couldn't move past the fact that someone had been in her room; a man had appeared in her room. How could there be someone in her room and she not scream for help? How could she think everything was okay? What was wrong with her? What had he done to her?

"I knew it," Virginia laughed. "I knew you'd think I was crazy." The calm look on her face didn't waver, but I remembered how she had been yesterday, her phone call to me just yesterday afternoon. She had been distracted, concerned, wanting to confide in someone. This *had* done something to her, something that had made her want to speak to me. And now my words suddenly were flooding out — accusations, questions.

"Gin, who was this guy? Who was he really? What was he doing in your room? How did he even get in?" I searched her face for answers. "Tell me truthfully. Are you making this whole thing up?" I leaped up and peered out the window. "There's no way anyone could get in without coming from inside the house or by climbing in using a really long ladder. Is that what he did? Did he come in your window? Did he walk in through the front door?" I asked insistently, my voice rising.

Virginia leaned back in her chair, crossing her legs on the seat, folding her hands in her lap. "Ivy, how he got here isn't really important," she said, dismissively. "You haven't heard the whole story yet. What's important is that he *was* here, that he came to *me*."

There was a note in her voice that caught at me. Could it, incredibly, be pride? What was going on?

"Gin, no one can just *be* here," I told her sensibly, trying to stay calm, trying to talk about this swirling story in a logical way, trying to grab hold of a concrete detail. "He must have got in somehow, through the window or through the door. Did he break in? Was anyone else here at the time? Where was your family?" I crouched down in front of her. "What did he want? Did he touch you, Gin?" I asked. Then more softly, "Did he hurt you?"

"No." Virginia colored and drew back slightly. "Of course not. You don't understand ..." she answered indignantly.

"Listen, Gin, this is scary." I stood up. "This isn't all right. I'm not sure why you haven't told anyone yet. I think we should tell the police."

I was frightened, and the most frightening thing was that she wasn't.

In fact, her indignation changed, oddly, to amusement. Virginia smiled tolerantly and shook her head. "No, no, Ivy," she said mildly. "Calm down. I told you I'm not hurt. I'm fine. He didn't touch me. He wouldn't. You don't understand yet. He said that now I had to make a choice. I wanted to agree right away." Virginia looked at me earnestly. "But he wouldn't let me. He's going to come back and get my answer. So you see, everything is all right."

+++

*H*e gazed at her, silent now. His face had become serious. He had finally stopped moving, was wholly still, had become a vessel for something else. He was a messenger and he was also the message.

And something inside her began to shift. A feeling, in her stomach, beneath her ribs, began to shiver delicately, to swell. Gently, fear combined with joy. It was impossible that the miraculous could happen to her, but she felt it. She knew what it was to be chosen.

She smiled. It would be momentous.

"You must make a choice," he went on.

+++

"What?! Gin, you can't let him come back," I told her emphatically. I sank down beside her chair. I took hold of her hands, their bones tiny and birdlike, squeezed them gently. I felt like shaking them, shaking her into the panic I was feeling. "Virginia, I don't understand."

"Ivy, I'll try to explain. Let me tell you more. Sit down again and listen."

She withdrew her hands from mine, patted the chair beside hers. I sat.

"Ivy, we haven't been very close in the last few years," she said softly. "We're not *best* friends or anything. But we know each other well. We've known each other a really long time."

I nodded.

"He ... this presence ..." With wonder in her voice, Virginia said, "You need to open your mind, Ivy."

She looked at me, waiting, and I nodded again, but how could I open my mind as widely as hers? Her mind was so open she had flown away through it.

Then, "He's an angel, Ivy," she said, speaking so quietly I almost didn't know if I had heard her correctly. She held up her hand as if to stop me from arguing, from denying, but there was no need. I was speechless. "He's an angel, or whatever word you want to use to describe a messenger from God. He didn't have wings or anything, of course. And he didn't have a halo or a white cloak," she continued thoughtfully. "But he was undoubtedly an angel. I realized that as I listened and watched. I felt it."

She placed her palm on her chest. Her fingers splayed, like a flower opening.

"That's why it's all okay. That's why nothing bad is going to happen. He appeared, and we talked. He told me I was chosen. I don't know why it was me. He didn't explain that part. But he told me I was chosen. Me."

Virginia's voice shook. I was amazed to see tears come to

her eyes. She lifted her hands to cover her face, and she bent forward, her thin shoulders curved and her head bowed. "Ivy, it might just solve everything."

Images collided in my mind. White wings, halos, Webster's clouds, firefighters climbing ladders, black crows flapping, cherubs with bows and arrows, hearts with arrows sticking through them.

"Virginia," I finally managed to say. "What do you mean? What is it you were chosen to do? What is it you have to choose?" And as I spoke, there was a sigh of air. The curtains around Virginia's window lifted gently on either side of her, rose and settled, and I heard the leaves whisper. I could see, behind her, the first rain begin to fall. The drops, fat and slow, plowing through the sizzling air.

✠✠✠

*S*he nodded. *She thought that she would decide now. She wanted to say that she could decide now, that she didn't need to wait, but he put up his hand to stop her.*

"Take some time," he recommended. "It is forever. You must be sure. Completely sure."

She agreed because she would do anything that he asked. And yet she looked at him with wonder, and she had to ask: "Is it really possible? How can it be?"

She crossed her arms, stroked the skin with her fingertips, feeling flesh, the downy hairs, the reality of her life.

"Nothing is impossible," he said simply, and she knew it was true.

✠✠✠

Virginia lifted her head. Carefully, she placed her hands back in her lap. Her eyes seemed to be swimming, some tears not yet spilled. She was still and glowing and so familiar, and yet at the same time so far away from me that I hardly knew her.

"I've been chosen to have a child," she said in a low voice. "A child that will come from God."

✝✝✝

He had half-turned, as if leaving. He smiled gently at her. His eyes locked onto hers, and he looked straight into her and was the first and only one to recognize her and see how she really was, who she really was. And it seemed impossible to deny him anything if he would promise to return.

She asked, "You'll come back again?" knowing he would, but wanting reassurance.

"Oh, yes," he replied. Pleasure flooded his eyes. He laughed, a deep low laugh, and leaned away. "I'll come back. I'll need your answer," he reminded her.

Chapter Six

"What?!" I gasped. Was she out of her mind? Was she joking?

"It's true, Ivy. I've been chosen," Virginia repeated. She got up and went to the window, closed it, her back to me. And then suddenly I wanted to giggle. Of *course*. That was it. She was joking. She had to be. This was ludicrous, ridiculous. Hilarious.

An angel came to her? She'd been chosen to have a child, from God? I wasn't religious, but I knew this story. It was Christmas all over again. That's how Jesus was born. An angel had come to Mary and told her that she would have God's child, and then ... well, the rest is history, or not, depending on what you believe.

Virginia had to be kidding. Sure, she was a Christian — a Catholic — but she couldn't really believe this had *actually* happened, could she? It was a story. The virgin birth was definitely a symbol of ... something — I wasn't sure what — but it had to be about as connected to reality as the number of crows flying outside this window was to the actual future. And here was Virginia telling me that something that couldn't possibly have happened the first time was going to happen again.

She saw my smile. She saw my disbelief.

Virginia folded her arms but gave me a forgiving smile. "I didn't *think* you'd believe me at first," she said. Her hair lifted as a breeze swept through. "I know it must sound funny because you didn't see him with your own eyes. You weren't actually in the same room with him. You weren't approached by him."

Remembering, she stopped, and a look came over her face like she was sinking inside herself, melting. "You have no idea what he's like, what it was like to be with him. He was ..." She paused.

For a few moments, neither of us spoke. She was not joking. She was speaking with passion and sincerity. Oh my God. She really believed what she was telling me.

"Seeing him, being with him, there was no way for me *not* to believe it. It was real, and it did happen. When he was with me, what he was saying was real and true, and this could change everything; it could fix everything, and so I have to hold him in my mind and remember how it was. In the end, it wasn't a question of belief at all."

"Virginia ... I'm glad you're telling me," I said carefully. "Because I think I can help you sort this out. I think I can help talk things through with you, figure out ... some of this. Figure out who we can go to next, who can help," I finished lamely.

Virginia shook her head. "No, Ivy. I don't need help. That's not why I'm telling you. You promised not to tell anyone, and I believed you. You can't tell. If you break this promise ... it would be like betraying something monumental" — she chose her next words carefully — "something beyond both of us. I think ... I think something bad would happen."

I felt a sudden chill. I understood that she wasn't threatening me, but rather trying to protect me, warning me of consequences. In her mind was an image of some terrible future that might engulf me. A shiver of real fear rippled through me. Her angel had settled solidly in my imagination for a moment, bringing with it a sense of grace and peace. Now, whatever pain and suffering hovered in her world stabbed at me with its fierce possibility. I pushed down the sense of dread. "So if you don't want my help, then why are you telling me?" I asked.

Her face lit up. "It was my own idea," she explained. "It's so someone will know, right from the start, someone other than me. So that one day, later, when the baby is born and the truth of who he is becomes known to everyone, the story can be told from the very beginning. You'll be a witness. You'll be able to tell it all truthfully, and then everyone will believe."

Her words hung in the air. Thoughts were colliding in my mind, but I was speechless. The rain was drumming down harder now, hitting the window and sliding down, a sheet of water. Already a coolness had crept into the room, relief from the heat. There was a crack of thunder, and Virginia was bathed in a sudden light.

When Teresa opened the door to the bedroom, I was almost relieved.

"Mama wants you, Virginia," she announced abruptly. She stared at me unpleasantly and folded her arms.

"All right, Teresa. Thank you," Virginia said, dismissing her.

Teresa left the door open as she exited the room. "Come *now*," she told Virginia, over her shoulder. "Mama wants you right now."

"Thanks for coming, Ivy," Virginia said. "Sorry about …"

"No, it's okay," I replied, getting to my feet. I was grateful to be leaving. I couldn't find any more words to say to her. None. I felt stunned and inadequate.

Virginia reached out and placed her hand on my arm. "'Bye," she said easily, freeing me. "Thanks, Ivy."

I ran home through the rain. I stood for a minute on my porch, dripping, and I looked back at Virginia's house. From the outside, it looked the same as almost every other house on our street, but on the inside … On the inside, there was something disturbing going on. I watched the rain fall and pictured Virginia sitting by her window, looking out into the nothingness of the breeze, watching her curtains billow gently in and out, trying to hold the angel in her mind, feel his reality. Then it came to me, the note in her

voice that I had heard earlier and thought was pride. I had
been mistaken. It had been there again as she spoke of him,
and now I recognized it. It was love.

✛✛✛

*A*s *she breathed a sigh of relief, he rose to go. The air
rushed into her lungs, alarmed her with its richness, its
potential for transformation.*

*She realized how it would be without him, the emptiness
that awaited her. She wanted to reach out but couldn't.
She wanted to cry, "Wait, please don't leave me," but
couldn't. She was overwhelmed, uncertain about what she
was permitted to feel, to say.*

*He was leaving, and she didn't know how she would
breathe, how her heart would continue to beat, how her
bones would support her, for she had fallen.*

Part Two

The Preparing

Chapter Seven

I didn't see the crows all the next week. The heat had finally broken with the big thunderstorm, so maybe the change in weather had sent them off to other parts. When you consider how noisy they had been and how they had been stalking us all that unusual summer, hopping about in our backyard trees, it was amazing how easily I got used to not having them around. After a few days of silence, my eyes stopped flicking to the treetops every time I entered the kitchen or walked past my bedroom window.

It turned out to be a busy week. I had spent half of July with our neighbors the Hendricks at a lodge up north babysitting their two kids, Bailey and Barrett. They'd persuaded me to spend my last few days of summer freedom tied to their children as well. I didn't mind making some extra money, and it helped to distract me from worrying about Virginia, wondering what I should do, whether I should tell anyone, who I should tell. My mind would return to her words and then begin circling around them again, like the crows circling around the trees before land- ing, except my mind never seemed to land, never seemed to find firm footing, as if the idea itself was so unthinkable it couldn't be grasped. Was there any chance she was really pregnant? If it was true, if she was pregnant, it would be obvious soon enough. And if so, how had she got that way? Was there a chance someone had actually come into her room, had raped her? Or had it happened somewhere else, with someone she knew, and she just didn't want to admit it? However it had happened, I couldn't figure out why she would make up an explanation that was this crazy.

I'd be in the park watching the kids in the sandbox, and I'd see Virginia's face, the look on it, the rapture, the delight. I'd try to find a way into that, some way to understand, and then I'd be enveloped by a strange, lifting sensation. Briefly, I'd let myself float freely there, in the possibility of faith, where an angel had come to Virginia and something sensational was going to happen. Then Bailey would ask for help building a bridge, or Barrett would cry because his sandcastle wasn't working out, and abruptly I'd return to the reality of creating a structure with twigs and stones, or filling a bucket and flipping it over, just so.

I knew that Virginia and I needed to talk again. And preferably not at her house. I didn't feel comfortable there and thought that maybe if we were out somewhere more neutral, she might be more reasonable and easier to connect with.

I called her at least twice a day every day that week, but she never picked up any of my calls. Not only did she not pick up, she was never available when I called. "She's out," Teresa would tell me. Or "She's in the bath," another sister would report.

On Friday, it had been five days since we'd talked in her bedroom. I called once more. It was Anna Maria who answered this time. "It's Ivy. May I talk to Virginia, please?"

"Oh hello, Ivy." There was a pause. "She can't come to the phone right now. I'll tell her you called."

I was realizing that I'd never get through this way. I'd have to just go over there and knock on the door, no matter how uneasy it made me.

Leaving my bedroom, I passed Mom. She was upstairs on her knees, cleaning out the linen closet. Towels and sheets were piled up around her on the floor.

For a moment, I thought about telling her. What would her reaction be? Maybe she'd be able to tell me what to do.

"I'm going to Virginia's for a little while," I said. Would she ask about Virginia? Would she say anything about how we had played together as children? Would she ask about Mrs. Donato?

"All right, darling." Of course. No questions about the past. No interest in the lives of others. No interest in my life. Of course.

I walked over to the Donatos' house. There was a man sitting on their front porch, one of the two I saw there frequently. He looked up as I climbed the stairs.

"Hello," I greeted him and knocked on the door.

He nodded. "Hello." Smiled pleasantly. He uncrossed his legs and buttoned up his jacket. I waited awkwardly for someone to come to the door, shifting from one foot to the other.

"Little cooler now," the man said.

"Yeah," I agreed. I felt him watching me.

Joe opened the door. "Hi there," he said.

"Hi," I replied, with a smile, relieved that someone had come quickly. Then I was suddenly worried that I'd sounded too happy, that Joe would think I sounded so happy because I was happy to see him, and I was wondering when I had last brushed my hair, and I had to stop my hand from reaching up and straightening my shirt, and I was extremely aware of the man sitting nearby on the porch, listening. I struggled to keep from glancing back at him.

I realized Joe was waiting.

"Is Virginia in?" I blurted out, blushing. I curled my hands tightly into fists and put them behind my back.

"Yeah. I think so. Come on in." Joe held the door wide.

I stepped inside, and we were standing close to one another, and I realized he was tall now, about a head taller than me. "Why don't you go up to her room? If she's home, she's up there. She's always up there." He gestured toward the stairs, and his arm brushed against mine.

"Thanks," I said. Heading toward the staircase, I looked down the hallway and into the kitchen. There was a girl waiting for Joe, holding a coffee mug and biting a fingernail, and a river of disappointment rushed through me. When I was partway up the stairs, I heard the living-room door open. Glancing back, I saw someone looking up at me from the doorway, probably one of Virginia's sisters — I couldn't really tell — but I saw wide eyes staring, watching me ascend, and a shiver ran up my spine.

I knocked softly on Virginia's closed door.

"Gin? Gin, are you in there? It's me, Ivy."

"Hi, Ivy. Come on in."

I don't know what I was expecting, but it wasn't what I saw. When I opened the door, Virginia turned and gave me a big smile. She was sitting at her desk, drawing. She looked happy, healthy, normal.

I returned her smile, my mind backpedaling. Maybe she hadn't said what I thought she had. Maybe I had misunderstood. Maybe it was all a bad dream.

"Gin, I was wondering if you wanted to go outside for a walk," I suggested. "It's so nice out. Not steaming hot anymore."

She hesitated. "I don't know if I'm allowed to," she said, and my eyes widened.

Then she blushed. "That's not what I meant," she said quickly, trying to take it back. "I don't mean I'm not allowed to; I just mean ... I don't know if I should ..." She looked embarrassed.

"Why not? I don't understand," I said.

"Ivy, I just think I need to take extra care," she said, in a low voice. "What if anything were to happen to me? I have to be careful."

And as she spoke, everything about her changed. It was as

if a veil descended on her, or was it something being stripped away? Her face softened. Her smile became luminous. Her whole posture altered; she drew into herself, recomposed herself and seemed to connect with something that she was balancing inside.

"I'm so glad you're here, Ivy," Virginia said to me, reaching out her hand. "It was so hard to tell you, but I think it was the right thing to do."

I stepped forward and took her hand. It was as soft and light as feathers.

"Gin," I said. I crouched beside her. "I'm worried about you. It seems like your sisters don't want me to speak to you. Every time I call they say you're busy. It's like they're trying to ... control you."

She laughed. She waved her hand, dismissing my concerns like she had her mother's heart problems. "It's fine," she said. She wanted to move on. She wanted to talk about her angel.

"Okay, so let's talk about what you told me. Gin, I'm going to ask you a tough question." I put my hand on her arm. She looked at me, expectantly.

"Were you ... raped, Gin?" It was such a harsh word. It was difficult to say it aloud. "Is that how you became pregnant?" Virginia immediately began shaking her head, but I plunged onward. "Gin, it's okay for you to tell me. I can help you. I can help you try to sort things out ..."

She held up her hand to stop me. "Ivy. I haven't been raped."

"Gin, if you have been, it's okay to tell me —"

"Ivy, no. No, I have not been raped," she said definitively.

"So maybe a boyfriend ... Maybe ..."

"Ivy, *no*. I haven't been raped. I'm not even pregnant. Not yet," she said. "Nothing's happened yet." There was a faint tinge of ... something ... in her tone. Embarrassment?

Disappointment? She pushed her hair behind her ears.

Relief swelled in me like a balloon. "Are you sure, Gin?" I insisted.

"What do you mean, am I sure? Of course I'm sure," she said, frowning slightly. "I think I would know. I'm not twelve, you know."

"Then ... then there hasn't been anyone ... no one has ..." I was stammering now, but determined to completely erase the possibility.

She gave me an odd look, her head crooked to one side. "Oh," she asked interestedly. "Is that what you thought? That I got pregnant somehow, and now I'm making up a story to try to explain it?"

"It's possible," I said, defensively. "Lots of girls ..." and then I realized it was better to stop there. Virginia had got up and walked away a few paces. She stood with her face turned away from me for a moment.

I didn't know what to think. Maybe she was trying to compose herself. Maybe she was trying to find the strength to admit she'd been assaulted, that she'd been scared and hurt, had been in the wrong place at the wrong time, had been walking alone and been attacked. Or that maybe some boy she'd met had taken advantage of her, had misinterpreted something she'd said or done. It was possible. It wouldn't have been her fault, but she might think it was. Or maybe she was just afraid that if she told, he might find out and come back. Hurt her again.

"Gin, if you have, if you have been raped, you can tell me," I repeated quickly. "We could ... we could find a way to make it okay. I could help you. If you've been raped, you need to tell someone, you need to tell *me*, and —"

"Ivy." Virginia's voice was flat. She turned around. "Ivy, I have not been raped. I already told you that." She looked at me sadly. "Why are you turning this into something awful?" she asked. "What is making you so afraid to believe what I told you?"

"Afraid?" My eyes widened. "Afraid?" I laughed, a short exhalation. "Pardon me, but I'm not *afraid* of believing you. I think it's normal to be a bit skeptical when someone tells you they've seen an angel. I'm not afraid of anything you're telling me. I'm just thinking that your claim is pretty extraordinary, and maybe there's a more natural explanation for it." I folded my arms in front of my chest. I was breathing hard. "I'm happy you're not pregnant, Gin, but I'm worried about you. Thinking you've seen an angel isn't normal. Thinking you're going to become pregnant by some divine being is not normal either."

I looked at her defiantly. I was frustrated. I wanted to shake her back to her senses. But I was also ready to go if she ordered me to leave her alone.

But she didn't. Instead she walked toward me with her arms wide. To my surprise, she hugged me.

"I'm not crazy, Ivy," she said softly. "But I can see how you might think that. You know, it's hard for me to believe too. It's quite an honor, and I don't know why I've been chosen. I don't know what I've done to deserve this."

I returned her hug, but then I pulled away from her, resting my hands on her shoulders, and my words were direct. "Gin, listen to yourself. I don't know much about angels, or God, or religion, at all. But Gin, it just seems so … impossible. It just couldn't happen. It would have to be a miracle."

Virginia was framed in her bedroom window. She didn't speak.

Into the silence came the sound of crows cawing. The birds were back. Four of them, black and large, flapped across the Donatos' backyard on languid wings.

Virginia and I looked into each other's faces. I could see her blue eyes, the wisps of hair that fell in front of her ears, the slight scar on her chin that she got the day she fell out of the pear tree we had climbed in her backyard. She was as real and human as me, as ordinary as me and as young and full of life as me.

"I can't find a way to logically explain it," she said, shrugging. "And I've been thinking about it ever since it happened. It's been hard to think about anything else," she admitted. "But I've realized something important. When the angel was here, when he was talking to me, I knew it was real. I knew he was real, and what he was saying was true."

I gripped Virginia's thin arms with my hands. Despair welled up in me. "Gin, it's not possible. There has to be another explanation. It's very hard to make sense of this."

"It *is* hard," she agreed. "But you know what, Ivy? That's my point. Maybe it doesn't have to make sense to us. Maybe it's impossible for us to try to imagine God's plan or to try to figure out what's behind the duties he asks of us." Her face serene, she smiled. "And so I've stopped trying to figure out why it's happening, why it's happening to me, now, here. It's not hurting anyone, and it's what God is asking of me. So all I need to do is make up my mind about whether I can do what he asks. I don't have to understand it. That's what faith is all about."

Virginia took my hand and led me to her bed. We sat down across from each other, cross-legged. We should have been pouring our hearts out about a boy at school or complaining to each other about a math test. But then we weren't close enough friends to do that. We should have been friends. But we weren't really.

"Gin ..." I paused. I didn't know where to begin. My stomach seized up, like it used to do when I tried to talk to my mother about things that really mattered. She'd nod and her eyes would glaze over, looking at something I couldn't see, some alternative reality that only she had access to. "Gin," I tried again, taking her hand.

But I couldn't say anything. I couldn't get past her name.

And so she talked. I had taken her hand, but she turned it over, held my hand in the palm of hers. Spoke to me soothingly, gently, as if I were the one who was in trouble, who was afraid, as if I were the one in need of help.

"Ivy, it's okay. Really, it's okay. You don't need to worry about me. Everything is fine. Everything is more than fine." She squeezed my hand. "I know you don't go to church. Or at least, you didn't used to. You don't now, do you?" she asked, mildly hopeful. I shook my head. She smiled. "You probably don't even believe in God." I shook my head at that, as well. "But I do. You know I do. And so you'll have to trust me when I tell you that this is something to be happy about. This is an amazing opportunity. It's something few people ever experience. The chance to serve God directly. To help his mysterious purpose."

As she spoke, her words seemed to revive her belief and allay any doubts she might have. A flush came into her cheeks, and she smiled again. "It's come at just the right moment, just in time." She paused, considering. "Ivy, I don't know God's purpose but I do know there are things happening, things being planned, bad things, really bad — and I think they go against what God wants for the world." Her voice had softened, as if she were afraid someone might overhear, or as if she wasn't sure she should be confiding in me. "I think that's why the angel has come. I've been given a chance to do something about that. This could change everything."

"Virginia, what do you mean?" I asked. "What bad things are being planned?"

Virginia shook her head.

She couldn't say? She wouldn't say?

A hunted look had come into her eyes. "Maybe I shouldn't have said anything about that," she wondered aloud. She wasn't looking at me. "Maybe it wasn't a good idea to tell you. Ivy, promise. Promise me you won't tell anyone anything about this."

Now she was staring at me.

"Gin, you haven't really told me anything!" I laughed in frustration. "I wish you *would*. But you *haven't!*"

"Ivy, promise me." The translucent skin on her face tightened. It seemed to draw the bones closer to the surface. Her cheekbones, her brow. "Promise me. If you don't, I won't —"

"Gin, don't say that. Of course I promise." Another promise not to tell, but this one was easy. I still didn't really know anything! I felt caught, worried about these hints of danger, but I first needed to focus on what was more critical, the crazy thing going on with Gin. And yet, ironically, the truth about her, a girl who was sitting holding my hand, seemed more elusive than these glimmers of information about dark deeds.

Maybe if I laid it on the line, addressed it straight on.

"Gin, I don't think I believe in miracles. Maybe you believe you saw an angel. I can't argue with what you believe you saw. Of course, I'm worried that you think that all this is possible — the angel, the pregnancy — but to tell you the truth, if you're not actually pregnant *now* — and I know you're not — then I'm not too worried that you'll really be getting pregnant. I don't think you'll be ... made pregnant ... somehow, by God ... and then carry his child."

She didn't say anything.

"Because if this were true, if it were — think. Think of what it would mean." Virginia's eyes brightened, alive with faith and belief, and looked back at mine, a steady gaze. "A baby. You're fourteen. You haven't even started high school. You're ..." I threw up my hands, my mind floundering. "How could you have a baby?"

Virginia leaned forward and put her hands on my knees. "A baby!" she answered, love making her voice weighty and deep. "How could I not?"

I needed to leave. I felt overwhelmed by our conversation, by everything she had implied.

After a moment, I smiled at Gin and told her I had to go for a run, and she smiled back and followed me downstairs to show me out. But I said good-bye uneasily, pausing at the front door, not wanting to go without getting some reassurance from her that nothing would happen before we talked again, that she was safe, that she wouldn't do anything crazy.

"So, are you going to be okay?" I asked her, but it felt to me that she had already made up her mind, whatever that meant.

"Yes," she said firmly.

And then Joe's friend was leaving, too. It was awkward. She arrived at the door with him, and she reached up, pulled his head toward her and kissed his cheek just as he was turning toward me to say something. It was a weird feeling, having his eyes on me while he was being kissed by someone else. Joe sort of smiled, but I think it was for her. "Hey," he said to me, but I had already turned away.

"See you," I told Gin. "Maybe tomorrow."

"Maybe," she agreed.

In her voice, in her face, I could see that something had ended for her. She had told me. She had made her decision. Now, it seemed, all she needed to do was wait for it to happen.

✠✠✠

*I*t *exploded into her imagination, vivid and fresh. It often did. Two events, separated by a five-year gap, but in her mind, they combined into one, and together it had seemed the end of something and the start of something. Nothing had been the same since then. Happiness had ended like a cup of water suddenly emptied, knocked over and drained.*

She didn't want to think about it, but once there, it took her over. Reluctantly, she worried it round and round, like a loose tooth, unable to ignore it, driven to try to dislodge it, to try to undo the damage that had begun right then, on those two evenings.

The first had been a barbecue in their old neighborhood. She was there, and Joe, and Anna Maria and Paul. And Mama and Papa, too. She was five, and Mama was pregnant. Her friend Sarah was tugging at her hand, saying, "Come and play. Come on, Ginia." But she shook her head. Something kept her sitting by Mama's knee, sipping a cup of lemonade, and while the other kids ran and shouted and did cartwheels, she felt her mother's fingers playing through her hair. It was then that Mama had told her, "God has given us another baby. Your papa and I thought our family was complete, but God knows best. He wants to give us another gift. He wants to give you a little brother or sister."

She tried to remember how she had felt, finding this out. She strained her imagination replaying this one scene over and over again, worrying that perhaps she had not been glad, worrying that perhaps she had felt something fierce and unbidden grip her, a jealousy or anger that seared through her, that was the cause of Mama lifting her hand to press her fingers instead against her belly, stroking the unborn child.

But no matter how she tried, she could never be sure. She could never console herself with the thought that she had welcomed the idea of a younger sibling, that she had turned to her mother and smiled, met her mother's gaze and acknowledged the will of God.

She remembered months passing, and then waking up one morning, and Mama being gone. Her auntie told them, "Your mama has lost the baby," and she, at five, thinking how could that be possible? How could Mama have lost the baby when she was carrying it so close that it was impossible to even sit in her lap anymore?

And then another barbecue five years later, here in this neighborhood, in this backyard. She knew Papa was there, of course he was, but when she thought of him now, tried to picture him there in her mind, she could only recreate a shape without any features — no eyes, no mouth, no nose. She had only been ten. When she thought of him, she saw him wearing his black suit, collared shirt, black shoes. Because she had seen so many photos of him since, all dressed up, that was the way she always pictured him, even though she knew he wouldn't have been dressed like that for a barbecue. But, that's what she saw. A man without a face in a black suit, a man she had loved wholeheartedly, completely, unswervingly.

And at this barbecue, it was just their family gathered in the yard, their immediate family and maybe an uncle and a cousin or two. Her mother was in the kitchen, cooking the pasta and preparing the salad; and Donna and Anna Maria were there too, helping. Paul, sitting beside Papa on the deck, restless, looking at his watch, probably, or biting a hangnail, staring at the sky, wanting to do something, wanting to be in charge, had insisted, "Let me help. Just let me do it, Papa." It had been happening more and more frequently, Paul offering to take over, Paul wanting to have his say, Paul wanting to influence. But this time her father had clapped his big hand on Paul's shoulder, keeping him in his seat. She thought she remembered him grinning, although other times he hadn't. Other times, in the living room, sitting with his friends, he had told them, "Paul's a man now, yes, but he's still my son, and this is my house," and his face had looked serious, determined. But on this day, her father, grinning, had gone to turn the meat, the air cool and fresh, and as he stumped down the back steps, where she sat reading, twisting to let him past, he had kissed his finger and touched it gently to her nose, her face tilting then to catch a kind word from the busy man she adored, and he had said, "You'll always be Papa's good little girl, Ginnie."

When Papa fell, he was holding the barbecue tongs. He must have let go of them as his arm flung out. Joe found them later resting on the flower bed.

And so that was that, the two events, forever linked in her mind, forever fused into one. Two gentle touches — one Mama's and one Papa's — and one ugly thud.

So then what? So then the baby was lost, and her father was gone, and Mama grieved and grieved and then accepted that grief into her life as a permanent placeholder, filling in two empty spaces with its abundance: the one a crib empty at the foot of her bed, then arms empty of a baby, then the emptiness by her side where a toddler might have played, where a new little girl might have grown and

*turned into a young woman; the other the emptiness
beside her in bed at night, the empty seat beside her at the
kitchen table, in her pew. The grief filling in the emptiness
in her heart, the place where otherwise there would have
been love.*

*Mama had said, "God gives, and God takes away." And
somehow she filled these absences, both of them, the little
girl who wasn't there and the man who was gone, so that
they became overwhelming and overflowing, so that the
house was even more crowded, and sometimes Virginia
felt lost.*

*With their Papa gone, Paul had taken over, choosing to
guide them away from Catholicism and along the new
way. She thought of this now, remembering, and her chest
tightened uncomfortably. Mama had objected at first.
Virginia recalled the few strained dinner conversations, the
tension. It had made her nervous and upset.*

*"This is so far from what we've been taught," Mama had
said. "This is not Catholicism."*

*And Paul nodded his head. "Exactly, Mama. That's the
point."*

*Mama shook her head, stared at him. "Son, I'm scared for
you. By whose authority do you know these things, do
you set up this new church?"*

*Paul relaxed, got up and came around and kissed Mama
on the cheek. "Mama, it will be fine. It is by God's
authority. All of it. I've told you. It is by God's authority."*

*Fairly quickly, the fighting had ended, but Mama had
changed. Her focus had shifted inward, and though Mama
still cooked and cleaned and showed up at school for open*

house, Virginia felt she couldn't get her full attention. Mama was floating just out of reach.

And from then on, with Papa gone and Mama not standing in his way, Paul surged forward, trying to drag them all in his wake. He was the leader. He knew the path. He knew what was to come. He shed his old religion, and he knew that they must move in THIS direction, and it would happen THIS way, and it must be SOON. He knew that God was impatient, and they could HELP, some more than others, even if it seemed dangerous and fraught. No one was to worry, because he would take responsibility, only him, and only his hands would be bloodied and cleansed in the world to come. And so feel no shame, and act only as he directs and all will be well, and tell no one.

She heard all this, and she worried and worried, doing nothing.

Chapter Eight

There was a pot of water on the stove. A lettuce, a cucumber, some small tomatoes and an onion were on the counter. Garlic cloves. A tin of tomato sauce. Some dried pasta. Once again, it seemed my mother was not going to finish preparing the meal. My turn tonight again.

I went upstairs and tapped on Dad's office door, peeked in. His fingers stopped, poised above the keyboard of his computer. "What's up, hon?" he asked.

"I'll finish off making dinner. We'll eat in about twenty minutes," I told him.

"Oh. Sure," Dad responded. He'd probably been at his desk all day. He worked on contract for a big computer company, writing programs. He worked at home every day, and often on weekends, depending on the contract. Occasionally, maybe once a month, he had to go in to the main office for a meeting, which he did reluctantly, putting on a clean shirt and a jacket. Luckily, no one ever came here to see him. The mess in his office would have scared away even the most open-minded employer.

Dad's eyes flicked to the clock near his bookcase, checking whether he had enough time to finish what he was doing before dinner. If no one called him for meals, he might never emerge from here, I thought. What was there to draw him out? He and Mom never went out in the evenings together anymore. They hardly even talked.

They did "disagree" though, and often about my father's work. Especially in the last few months. I guess it would begin quietly, but then the sound of Dad's voice would finally rise from his office to my bedroom, as I lay in bed trying to fall asleep. By the time Dad was loud enough for me to hear, it would be almost over.

"I can't, Joan. I have to do this."

A silence, during which I assumed she was giving her response, which I couldn't make out.

Of course, it was never really an argument. It was a "disagreement." He saying one thing, she another, neither finding a place in the middle to meet.

"Sure, go alone, if you want to."

More silence. A long silence.

"I have to do this tonight. If it's not finished, I won't get paid, and you know we need the money. I'm sorry."

But his voice didn't sound sorry to me. It sounded like, by this point, he was happy to have her go, like going with her might be the last thing he would ever want to do. It was awful. Almost as awful as the few times that I'd caught them kissing in the hallway as if they hadn't intended to, as if they had each been thinking about something entirely different and suddenly, in passing, they had reached out for each other. They would see me and look startled, as if they were as surprised as me.

Unlike my mother, Dad was pretty good at remembering he had a daughter, however. Two daughters, in fact. Even though Katie hadn't lived here for almost two years now. I know he missed her; I did, too. Things were really different without her. Katie had always seemed to be yelling at Mom or slamming her palm down on the kitchen table, making the cutlery clatter. She would find Mom's bottles and pour them down the drain. She would hide her car keys and stand there, arms crossed, defiantly refusing to reveal their location. She would get down on her knees in front of Mom and weep, wrap her arms around Mom's knees and sob, trying to extract a promise that she'd quit.

Dad joined in as well, sometimes threatening, sometimes shouting, sometimes accusing. I would turn my face away and with my eyes follow the trail of wallpaper vines that wound their way in an endless maze up the walls. For years, the house shook.

Now it was just the three of us here. Now the house was quiet. And sometimes Mom was discreet about her drinking — hiding the evidence, going for weeks without drinking in front of us — and sometimes she wasn't.

As I made dinner, I thought about Virginia. Thank God she wasn't pregnant. At least she wasn't pregnant. I would have had to tell someone. I would have had to do something, fast.

I heard the crows call. I couldn't help myself — I put down the salad spinner and went to count them. Nine. I ripped the lettuce leaves into pieces and tossed them into the salad bowl, repeating the rhyme in my mind. *One is for bad news, Two is for mirth, Three is a wedding, Four is a birth, Five is for riches, Six is a thief, Seven is a journey, Eight is for grief, Nine is a secret.*

A secret. That's for sure. It couldn't be a coincidence that Virginia and her mother had both alluded to "really bad things" that were going to happen. What were they? Was it connected in some strange way to this fantasy that Virginia had concocted for herself?

I washed the little tomatoes, cut them into quarters, threw them into the salad bowl.

My hands paused. What if what Gin said about the angel was actually true? Was there even any point in considering that?

I washed a cucumber and began slicing it thinly. Could I totally reject the possibility that what she said was true?

The knife slipped. Blood began to ooze out of my thumb.

One night about two years ago, I had also cut my thumb with a knife. The four of us were eating dinner, and I was slicing at some fat on the edge of my steak. The others were finished, and Mom was standing up from the table and giving us an ultimatum. The knife slipped and nicked my thumb as Mom was telling us that she knew her drinking was causing tension and hostility in our home. I stared at the blood oozing from my thumb, ignoring again the feelings welling up in me, wanting to know why Katie and I weren't enough to make her happy but not wanting to ask in case the answer made me feel even worse than all this did, in case I began crying and couldn't stop, ever, tears mixing with a river of blood.

She went on to say that if we couldn't stop nagging her about it and accept that this was the way it was, that this was who she was, that this was the best she could do, then she'd leave. To stop the fighting.

She said it so matter-of-factly, so calmly. She didn't look like she cared which decision was reached. She just looked tired.

At the time, I actually thought this was a good thing. It seemed to make sense to me. To just let her be. But Dad started shaking his head. He couldn't believe it.

"Joan! You don't mean that! You wouldn't go! This is your first attempt to resolve this issue? To walk out on us all? You haven't even tried to stop drinking! You haven't gone to a rehab centre. You haven't applied to any programs! You haven't gone to AA, not even one meeting. In all these years, Joan!"

Mom didn't waver. She said, "I'm sorry, but I can't. I'm not strong enough to change. This is it. This is the only way it can be, for me."

I remember Dad staring at her, looking like his heart would break. She added, vaguely, "I've actually packed a bag," waving a hand toward the upstairs bedroom.

I wondered if Dad might be about to cry. Why didn't he

say anything more? Why didn't he tell her that she could stay, that we'd all leave her alone? Then he did begin to cry, still just staring at her.

One large drop of blood had seeped out from the cut on my thumb. It grew even larger. I watched as it wobbled, then slid down the side of my thumb, leaving a red streak.

Katie jumped up then. "Unbelievable!" She almost spat out the word. "You are really unbelievable, Mom. You'd do it, wouldn't you? Leave. Just to get what you want without having to argue about it, or listen to someone you love try to talk you out of it. Well, I can't stay here and put up with that. I can't live here and watch you kill yourself." Her voice was harsh, thick with emotion. "You stay. You do still have one more daughter to raise, after all. And I know how important it is for you to live up to your responsibilities," she added sarcastically. She swallowed, hard. "I'll leave."

"Katie, please!" Dad burst out, but Katie had gone. Eighteen, and flown away in her last months of high school, gone to a low-rent apartment that she had shared first with a friend, and then with Russ, the boyfriend she had met in college. Flown away to try to make a bad situation better, to try to keep a mother around for her sister.

I missed Katie, but I understood why she'd done it, why she'd gone. And she was doing okay. She was working part-time and taking night school courses at a really cool community college. She was very talented and creative, and she'd won a partial scholarship in the fashion design program. Katie was a go-getter, very hands-on. She could never stand by and do nothing, especially not when it came to Mom. For me, well, I guess it wasn't as difficult as facing the alternative.

I stared at my thumb, watching as the drop of blood bulged.

"Oh, thanks for starting dinner, Ivy." It was Mom, entering the kitchen behind me.

I put my thumb in my mouth, then stuck it under the tap for a moment.

"What happened?" Mom asked.

"Just cut myself. Nothing serious." I resumed cutting the cucumber.

"Sure?" she asked.

"Yeah."

She lost interest. She went to the cupboard and took down a glass. Of course.

I refused to notice. I added the cucumber pieces to the salad bowl, tossed the salad.

Then she took down two more glasses. She put place mats on the table and arranged the glasses. She added cutlery.

While I turned my attention to the pots simmering on the stove, Mom took the salad bowl, added tongs and placed it in the center of the table.

"Choice of salad dressing?" she asked, gazing in the open refrigerator.

I couldn't answer. She was behaving like a regular person, speaking in a normal tone, asking a standard question. She had emerged from her cocoon of drink and wandered into the dinner hour in the life of her daughter and husband. It wasn't fair. It was so simple, and she made it look easy. For a moment, I let it wash over me, the relief of it, and almost instantaneously felt regret. Because as I took that full deep breath of relief, anger also escaped, overwhelming everything else. It made me want to scream. There was no normal anymore. She had taken that from us. I couldn't even feel good making dinner with my mother because normal was something weird and strange, and so unexpectedly pleasant that it made me furious to be reminded of all the other times when it wasn't like this and when it wouldn't be like this. Feeling good about it required months of it, years of it, so that it was so common, so taken-for-granted that I didn't even notice it. Why should I have to grab for these tiny fragments of how life should be? Why did she have to do this to me?

I was shaking. But she hadn't noticed. She was still looking in the refrigerator. "Ivy?" she said, and I didn't want to let her know this about me, how angry I was. It was too personal. She would think I cared. And so, "French. French dressing," I told her, my voice level and controlled.

Mom poured the dressing on the salad and tossed it with the tongs. "Almost done," she announced.

"I'll get Dad," I told her. And she picked up the gin bottle, examined it, and put it down. Empty.

She bent to a bottom cupboard and took out an unopened gin bottle, and as I turned to go she opened it and there she was pouring it into her glass. Virginia had asked me about miracles. Now that would be a real miracle. Mom having dinner with us without a drink in her hand. I was as likely to believe that would ever happen as to believe that an angel had propositioned Virginia in her bedroom.

✛✛✛

She remembered: Several months after their father died, Paul called a meeting in their home. He had invited a small group of people to attend, most of them around Paul's age. She didn't recognize any of them, but they seemed to be friends with Anna Maria. Paul was greeting them all at the door by name, and so was Anna Maria.

She watched them shake their hands: "Hello, Pam, Jack. Hello, Frank. Hello, Bridget, Lynne. Janie."

The men and women all smiled and ducked their heads. They looked the same. They acted the same. They all gave little smiles, and they made themselves small. They nodded and took many tiny steps. Perhaps they were the meek, and they would inherit the earth. Or maybe that was a disguise behind which they were hiding.

They came inside and sat in the living room. Teresa, Donna and Anna Maria had put out folding chairs, borrowed from somewhere. They had known just how many they would need. No one sat in Mr. Donato's chair. No one had sat in it since he had died.

Paul had told Joe and her to attend. He showed them where to sit, in the front row, side by side. It reminded her of her father's funeral, of how they sat knee to knee. Then, she had sat between Mama and Paul. She remembered, on her left, Mama's hands clenched in her lap, squeezing, the fingers intertwined; on her right, Paul's shiny black pants, his hands pressed onto his thighs as if he were not able to wait, was just waiting to rise and begin ... something, the next thing. And she knew she should be thinking about Papa, except that she couldn't because Mama was now weeping, shaking with grief, tipping sideways onto Teresa's shoulder, and Paul was taut, wound up like a steel spring about to explode, and then it just happened. She floated up. Maybe she was raised up, or maybe she simply opened her palms to what was above, and then she was looking down on the service, looking down on her father, and from here, where there was space, her tears were free to fall.

That had been four years ago. Her father's photo was on the fireplace mantelpiece, and she looked at it as everyone else was seated. Then Paul brought Mama into the room, on his arm. Now it reminded her of the beginning of a wedding. She had only been to one, her cousin's. Her uncle had walked her cousin down the aisle proudly, showing off his veiled daughter.

Here in their living room, Paul had stood Mama in front of the empty seat that was for her and gently helped her to sit. She had smiled, flattered, beaming at her son.

When Paul stood in front of the assembly talking, telling them about his plans, about what God wanted from them, Mama's smile faded. Virginia watched Mama's face harden in disapproval because she did not believe as Paul did. But then Mama's eyes wandered away to some other place, her face softened again; she folded her hands in her lap and waited. And Virginia wondered where Mama had gone and marveled that she could set her mind adrift so easily, disconnecting.

"I have made a decision," Paul told them. She looked at the faces of the other listeners, rising up to his, like little baby birds in a nest, mouths open, seeking, hungry. "Several of us, including three of my very own sisters" — he looked at them, acknowledging them, and they leaned in toward him as if greedy for his approval, thirsty for his praise — "feel we need to move closer to God's intentions. We cannot do this within the existing Catholic church. We do not believe we can do this within any *existing church. Not the way God wants us to.*

"God has expectations of us, and he is calling us to act. And we will.

"We will leave behind the old. We will form a new con-gregation, and we will form a new church with a new meeting place, based on a new belief."

Paul looked so sure of himself. There was authority in his tone. Teresa was nodding. "I have chosen you to be part of this new adventure. God has chosen you." He spread his hands, including them all, welcoming them, reaching out to them, embracing them. "I will be the leader, and there will be Elders, three of them. Together, we will guide this group forward until the End, and the signs that the End is near are many."

Donna and Anna Maria were nodding, too, as if they had already heard this. As if they were pleased, certain that it was good and true.

She heard the words, but she didn't fully understand them. She felt relieved to be included, because she wasn't certain if she might be overlooked, but at the same time, she was nervous because there was an undercurrent of something, excitement or fear or guilt, and maybe it was wrong for Paul to be saying he would be the leader. What if everyone got mad at him, or began arguing, or said, "Who do you think you are?" And why wasn't Mama listening when it was her job to look after her youngest daughter still, make sure she was safe and make the right decisions on her behalf?

"The End will come, and we will meet God, but there has been too much waiting. God needs us to contribute."

She saw Teresa pat Mama's hand, and Mama turned to her vaguely and nodded. Donna wiped her eyes. Joe was staring at the ground, frowning.

Contribute? *She wondered what that meant. She looked around, and no one seemed mad or angry. No one ever seemed to defy Paul. No one except Joe, who had drawn a line that he wouldn't cross. Nothing could pull him across it, not even Paul's outstretched hand, his harsh tone or his unnerving stare.*

She looked at Paul and could not tell if she was proud of him or afraid of him. She tried to think of her father, but all that came to her was the forever image of him gliding through the air, black suit, arms out, barbecue tongs in one hand, floating and then sinking, gone from her.

Papa was gone, and now Paul was like a father to her. That's what everyone told her, and Paul thought so, too, and so did Mama and the girls, but Joe didn't think so. And she didn't think so either. Paul wasn't her father, and it was wrong to pretend he was. He didn't deserve it. Papa had cared about them and loved them and looked after them just because they were his family, and she didn't understand how she knew, but she did know, that though Paul loved them, too, he loved beyond them and wanted more and might give them up for that. She knew this, and she saw that Joe had carved out some space for himself somehow, and she wanted that for herself, too, needed it.

So she had yelled at Paul that he was not her father, and she would not do everything he said, so that he would know, but she wasn't sure if it would change anything except that he might dislike her now, the way he seemed to dislike Joe, and it made her sad, because despite everything, she loved Paul. He was her brother, and she would do almost anything for him. But that wouldn't be enough for him because she could see him clearly, and she could see that he would demand it all.

"I, as leader, have bought the house behind this one — with the help and support of my family, of course," he added. Paul's tone had changed. Now his voice was light, as if it were making suggestions. But these weren't suggestions. They were directions. "We will have our

meetings there. It's a good investment for my family, and it will be more convenient, more intimate.

"Please join us. If you wish, there will be more opportunities to become involved, more ways to do God's work." Then he cautioned, "You are all welcome. And there may be others invited as well. It may become necessary. But this is a private undertaking, and it will remain private. It must. Please tell no one."

The air stilled.

"This is between us." He gestured at his people. "Between you and me. The more levels of discretion, the better."

She felt the sudden electricity in the room. What had happened? What did he mean? She didn't understand. She was only ten and a half.

Chapter Nine

I counted the black birds that I saw through our kitchen window, sitting on the treetops, as I reached for the ringing phone that Sunday afternoon. One, two, three ...

I heard my sister's husky voice. "Hey, Ivy, just a warning," said Katie. "I thought I'd come over for a short visit. Russ, too."

"Oh, good." I tried to sound enthusiastic, but she laughed, and I knew I had failed.

"Don't worry, sis. I can't *not* come. You know the rules. I have to check in at least twice a month. Make visual contact. Maybe it'll be okay this time."

I think she really meant it. She had left, given up on being Mom's watchdog, unable to stand by and do nothing when Mom was right in front of her every day. Now she lived at a distance, tried not to think about Mom because it made her so frustrated and mad, but I knew she still couldn't give up hoping that things might improve, that Mom might stop drinking. She dropped by, sometimes more than twice a month, even though it seemed almost painful to her, but it was like she had to see for herself, see if there was any change, even though there never was.

I missed Katie. We hadn't been close, but we had been able to count on each other. I knew how much she cared about me, how much she still cared. And yet even between us, as between all people, there were enormous, empty, unknown spaces. They were the spaces that we each lived in alone, the times that we were apart. Never could they be filled in completely, joined one to another seamlessly, not even with endless words or explanations. It was frightening in a way to be so separate. It was frightening to know that not everything meets the eye, that every person carries around his or her own impenetrable mysteries.

I was happy Katie was dropping by, even though she'd be disappointed once more.

We said good-bye, and I gave the message to Dad.

"Great," he answered, smiling, conflicting emotions rushing across his face, pleasure mixed with anxiety. "I'll tell your mother." But he didn't get up right away. "Ivy, it'll be all right." His concern was flickering from one daughter now to the other. Then, without even a breath, he began the never-ending campaign. "You know, if the two of us can ..."

I knew, I knew, I already knew. And I didn't want to know again. I didn't want to hear about what we had to do, how we could make it together. Before he could say it all again, to get himself through it, too, I left the room. I headed for the front door, slipped on my sandals and stepped outside.

I sat on the front porch, alone, and emptied my mind of everything. I concentrated on just waiting.

After about fifteen minutes, the unmistakable sound of a motorcycle drew near. I watched as Russ and Katie parked in front of the house. They each pulled off a black helmet and unwrapped themselves from each other and the machine they rode.

Katie came bouncing up the walk.

"Hey, sis," she called. She shrugged off her brown leather jacket, shaking her long brown hair into place. I had never realized it when she was living with us, but she was really pretty, especially when she wore clothes she'd made herself. Her narrow face surprised everyone with its large, luminous brown eyes. It had been a long time since I had seen those eyes fill with tears of anger or sadness. Not since the day she left.

"Hi," I answered brightly, standing up.

Katie drew closer, and we hugged. It was so good to see her.

Russ was close behind. "Hey, Russ," I greeted him again. We rapped our fists together, our friendly way of getting out of hugging.

Katie was still hanging onto me. She had her arm draped over me, and it felt terrific. She was the breath of fresh air that made everything seem good again.

As she planted another kiss on the side of my head, I suddenly had a brainwave. I could tell *her* about Virginia. She had known Gin as long as I had, although because of their difference in ages, they had never been friends. Katie knew Gin's family, her brothers and sisters. She definitely knew Paul, even if it was a long time ago. Katie was level-headed, older than me and more experienced. Plus she would never tell a soul if I asked her not to. She and I had grown up knowing how to keep secrets.

"Come on in, sweetheart," Dad called out to Katie from the kitchen.

I managed to whisper into her ear before she went in. "I need to talk to you alone before you leave."

"Sure," she agreed.

Katie and Russ didn't end up staying long with Mom and Dad. That wasn't unusual, but the visit probably set the all-time record for shortest time between arrival and departure.

"We've got news," Katie announced, placing her hands on the back of Dad's chair and kissing the top of his head.

I happened to be looking at Mom, who was leaning against the kitchen counter. I saw her face go white and her mouth jerk once in an ugly spasm.

"Darling ..." she started to say, instantly turning her

face into a controlled mask of calm, and a band of tension tightened around my stomach.

Katie's voice was light and determined. "Mom, let me speak first before you bring down the angels of doom." Her hands rested on Dad's shoulders. He turned his head and twisted slightly, trying to see her without dislodging her friendly grip. "No, I'm not pregnant, so don't worry about that. Russ and I have decided to get married, though, just the same. Because we love each other, actually."

She kept the smile stamped on her face as she met Mom's eyes. Then Katie turned and looked at Russ, and her expression changed, softened. She lifted one eyebrow in a signal that I knew meant, "Now watch what comes next."

I was proud of her. It had taken a lot of courage for her to make this announcement. But I was scared for her, too — for all of us. I wondered if she couldn't have waited, if she couldn't have put her own needs to the side for a while longer. The decision she had made might blow everything apart. It could be the beginning of us spiraling into the black hole at the center of our family. Because we all — all four of us, Katie, me, Dad and Russ — knew what would come next.

But then Katie spoke again, quickly, nudging her words into the intervening few seconds of silence.

"You know, we've decided. We're not here to ask you to make a decision for us. We're not asking your permission. We just wanted to tell you. We thought maybe you'd be happy for us." But this last sentence was spoken so softly, I think I might have been the only one who heard it. Or maybe I imagined it.

I didn't try to speak, and Dad didn't get a chance to say a word.

"Darling Katie," said Mom, her voice level. She crossed

her arms, but she didn't take a step forward. She remained where she was, still leaning against the kitchen counter. "This sounds like another one of your wild ideas."

I listened to her, wondering. It was odd. She was the center of our family. We circled around her, treading water. Anyone watching would have thought she was what was holding us together in our synchronized pattern, when in fact she was the one who was drowning and almost taking us down with her. It was only our superhuman efforts to stay afloat, to keep our heads up, that kept her up, too. She struck out at us, grasping instead of supporting, and we, too frightened to watch her sink, refused to give up contact.

"You know I have to say what I think, even though I know you aren't going to like it," she went on, as if we might admire her for that.

"Joan," Dad said, in a warning tone, but it was Katie who patted his shoulders with her hands, pressing down to keep him in his seat, saying, "It's okay, Dad."

"It's nothing against Russ. You know that, Russ," Mom said, looking at the young man, who gazed steadily back at her. "But Katie, you're so young. Too young to be making such a big decision. I know, I'm not one to talk about making decisions. Look at me, marrying at eighteen myself. But maybe that's just what makes me the best authority on the subject. I thought it was the right thing to do, but I was too young. Much too young."

I sighed. This was old news. We had heard this since we were kids. Marrying at eighteen, divorcing at twenty. Then meeting Dad, and wishing she had waited to get married. Like a modern cautionary tale. Like if she repeated it often enough, it would become a talisman we could hold against the world.

I didn't listen to the rest of what she had to say, although

I knew it would end in "How could you do this to me?" and her putting her hands over her face and weeping. I don't know what it was. Maybe I was tired of feeling anxious about her, angry at her, sorry for her. She sapped every situation dry. All the emotion and energy drained from us toward her and left me feeling empty, helpless, a failure. Sometimes it was better just not to engage. To observe was bad enough.

And sure enough, there was Dad getting up finally, despite Katie's hands, and heading over to Mom, poor Mom, and putting his arms around her, wiping the tears from her eyes. And Katie, with her engagement news, was left standing with her hands resting on air, receiving only a glance of regret from Dad that almost turned to accusation as it floated across the room toward her.

✛✛✛

Paul hadn't said secret — he had said private *— but she knew that was what he meant. A secret place. She liked the idea of a secret place.*

She wondered if she would be allowed to play there when no one was using the secret place behind their house for meetings. Maybe Ivy would come, if she told her it was something special. When she asked Paul, he squatted down on his haunches right in front of her. He held her by the upper arms. She knew he wouldn't hurt her on purpose, but he was squeezing too hard, as if he didn't notice, as if some secret part of him would do whatever it took to make her obey. "No, Virginia," he said firmly. "You can't go there without me. Do you understand?"

She nodded. But that wasn't enough. He made her promise on the Bible.

The next day, when Joe asked her where she had got the bruises on her arms, she looked at them, surprised, and told him, but she didn't tell him why, didn't talk about the secret place. Paul had said not to go there, and though he hadn't made her promise not to talk about it, she knew he meant that, too.

It was okay about not playing in the secret place with Ivy, because even if she invited her, Ivy probably wouldn't come. They were almost eleven now, and Ivy hadn't come to her house in almost two years. When the girls did play together, she usually ended up going to Ivy's house. Almost always Ivy's mother phoned and asked, pretending it was Ivy's idea. She loved the way Mama's eyebrows would lift in delight, knowing her little girl was about to be invited out, was popular. Frequently in the beginning, and now and then since, Mama and Ivy's mother would chat for a few minutes. Mama was patient with Ivy's mom, listening a lot, saying "Uh-huh" often, or "You poor dear." Sometimes the calls went on a long time, and Mama would look at her, wave her away, so she didn't have to wait, wave her toward Ivy's house, like a bird dashing water off its wing.

And she would run all the way to Ivy's house through the backyards because their hedge hadn't been planted then and no one had fences built in their yards yet.

But that day, the day after Paul had said no, she had planned to use the secret place as a lure, to entice Ivy over. She hadn't seen Ivy in three weeks. Ivy's mother hadn't called, and something in her knew that whatever Ivy had seen in their friendship was almost gone. But she had called Ivy and asked her to come over, although she almost never did that, and she had told Ivy that she had something special to share with her. Now she dared not take Ivy to the special place, or even tell her about it. She dared not even go herself. So she decided she'd share with her the Fátima story instead.

They sat down together, and she told it, a story about secrets.

"There were three children, and they lived in a little village called Fátima in Portugal. They were shepherds, and their names were Lúcia, Francisco and Jacinta. This happened a long time ago — about a hundred years ago." Her voice was sing-song. She tried to tell it correctly, the way her mother had told it to her, over and over again.

"An angel appeared to the children three times. Then Mary, the mother of God, appeared to the children. She came six times. She was clothed in white and brighter than the sun," she almost chanted. "She gave them messages of hope. Also she told the children three secrets."

She looked at Ivy and paused. Surely, she would ask what the secrets were. But Ivy didn't say anything.

"She also told them that she would perform a miracle. And she told them where and when. She said it would convince everyone to believe the children had really seen Her. The children told everyone in the village. On the day, and at the time they said, the sun danced in the sky. Thousands of people saw it."

Ivy was looking at her, intently. "Did they tell you this at church? Is this true?" she asked.

She smiled. "My mother told me, and yes, it's true," she replied proudly and continued. "Also, the children saw a great light, and in it they saw the sadness of God."

She rushed onward, "Ivy, guess what? Mary told Lúcia, one of the shepherd girls, that Jesus wanted to make use of her. That he would use her to make Mary known and loved." She tried to say it just the way her mother did, with great respect and wonder. "She said the other two would die sooner, and she told them when, and it didn't bother them at all. Imagine, Ivy! Knowing when you were going to die! So they told others, to prove that they had really seen and heard Mary, and they did die when she had said they would." She paused for dramatic effect. "Francisco died first, two years later. Jacinta died next, before she was ten."

Gin shivered. The story took her breath away.

Ivy was standing up, restless. "That's a good part. It sounds a bit like a ghost story," Ivy said. "When did your mother tell you this story?"

"She's told me it lots of times. She tells me at night sometimes, when I'm falling asleep."

"Oh, like a bedtime story," Ivy said.

"Sort of," she said, "except that it's true."

"How do you know it's true?" Ivy asked.

"Because my mother said so. And ..." She thought for a moment, and this was just as important, "I just believe it."

Ivy considered this for a moment. "I don't," she said, and then gave a quick nod. "Okay, so let's go out in the backyard now. Let's do something that I want to do."

"Oh, but there's more," she protested. "That's just the beginning of the story. I can tell you more about the three

secrets. *The ones Our Lady told the children. They were ... prophecies.*" *She said the word carefully, with respect.* "*They told about things to come on earth.*"

"*That's okay,*" *Ivy told her.* "*I don't want to hear anymore right now. Maybe you can tell me some other time. I think I have to go.*"

She was disappointed, but she hid it behind a smile, and Ivy said good-bye and headed for the bedroom door, giving her a little wave.

Chapter Ten

"I'm happy for you, Katie." I wrapped my arms around my sister.

She hugged me back, and I felt like it was me being comforted, and not me giving my congratulations. As Mom and Dad's voices began to rise, we left the kitchen and went out and stood on the front porch.

"What was it you wanted to talk to me about?" Katie remembered to ask. I could guess how urgently she wanted to get away. Russ was standing on the front walk with his bike helmet in his hand, swinging it back and forth.

I hesitated.

"No, it's okay. I have time," Katie reassured me. She glanced at Russ. "He's okay to wait, too," she added with a smile, then called to him, "Russ, I just need to talk with Ivy for a few minutes."

I was uncomfortable. It suddenly seemed too bizarre, too impossible to describe what Virginia had told me without it seeming crazy, even comical. Plus I *had* promised Virginia not to tell, and Katie was in a hurry. It could wait until I was more certain about what was going on.

But I did still want to pick her brain for information about the Donatos. Katie was leaning against the porch railing, patiently.

"Katie, there's something ..." I faltered. I wasn't sure how to begin without getting into the whole weird tale. "There's something going on with Virginia. Remember her? Virginia Donato?"

"Sure. You used to be good friends with her for a while, didn't you?" Katie asked.

"Uh-huh. So recently she called me and kind of asked for help. Advice, I guess. About some family stuff."

Katie laughed, and I smiled back. "Yeah, it *is* a bit ironic. Her asking *me*, the girl with 'the perfect family.' Anyway, she mentioned some stuff about her older brother, Paul," I said vaguely, "and I remembered that you went out with him for a bit, didn't you?"

Katie laughed again. "I *did* go out with Paul," she said, cocking an eyebrow at me, "but I didn't think you knew that, although you and Virginia were actually friends at the time. Mom and Dad never did, that's for sure."

I laughed. "I think you told me. It was a secret."

She smiled. "Dad would have killed me."

I waited. *Because Paul was so weird? So intense?*

"He was so much older than me!" she explained, with another smile. "It was about ... four years ago, I guess, so I would have been about sixteen, or maybe not quite that, and Paul was ... well, he's quite a few years older than me, five, I think, so he would have been twenty or twenty-one. I seriously don't know why he asked me out. I was way too young for him." She shrugged. "Which is probably one of the main reasons I said yes when he asked me. Although ..." she considered. "There was always something about him. He was unusual, attractive in a kind of ... non–boy-next-door way." She grinned wickedly, and I managed to grin back.

"Go on," I urged her.

"So, it was spring, near the end of my grade ten year, and he came up to my locker. I was surprised to see him there. He hadn't even gone to my high school, and he'd graduated a few years earlier and was working for his dad. Mr. Donato ran a specialty paper product business, and Paul was learning the ropes from the ground up. He was working in sales at that point, and I think he was doing well. With those eyes and that look of his, anyone would have found it hard to say no to him. So there he was at my high school — and I think he said he was putting up posters or distributing flyers in between sales calls, something to do with an event his church was planning, I think. And he was down the hall from me, and he saw me and recognized me, said hi, and then, just like that, he asked me to meet him for a coffee after school that Friday. I was so stunned. I hesitated because he seemed … he seemed to expect I'd say yes, like he knew he was irresistible or something. So that I almost said no. But actually, he *was* kind of irresistible." Katie admitted this with a little laugh. "And I told myself it was all quite innocent — though it actually felt the opposite; it felt risky, somehow — and I knew it would be totally outrageous to go out with a twenty-year-old, right?" She nudged me playfully. "So I agreed.

"We only went out five or six times, though. Paul turned out to be … a bit too intense. And we didn't really have much in common." She shrugged.

We stepped off the porch, moved into the sunshine.

"You knew his sisters though, right, and his younger brother, just from seeing them around our neighborhood, didn't you?" I asked. Maybe she'd noticed something back then that I wouldn't have, something from the past that could help me understand what might be going on there now.

"I guess so, but not well. They kind of kept to themselves a bit. I think when they moved here, they were all going to Catholic schools for a while, and then … I guess it was some time after their father died, the kids who were still in school moved to the local public schools …"

She thought for a moment. "Let's see … Donna is about the same age as me, right? And the other boy, Joe, is younger, closer to your age." I flushed hearing his name. Katie didn't notice. "And there are two other older sisters, too, but I don't remember their names. They all still seem to live at home — I've seen them going in and out of the house over the years — but they're still just as ... shadowy ... now as they were then." She looked at me curiously. "But don't you know them? You used to go over there when you were younger, didn't you?" My sister sat down on the porch steps. She threw her head back, letting the sun bathe her face.

Russ saw Katie sit down. He hung his bike helmet on the handlebars of the bike, and lay down on the lawn, hands behind his head. He closed his eyes.

I was too agitated to sit. I stood in front of Katie, explaining that Virginia had mainly come here to play, but that I had been there recently, and I found her family incredibly overly protective of Virginia, as well as ... a little creepy. "The house seems ... oppressive, somehow."

"Hmm, well, I was only in their house once — no, twice." She paused, remembering. "But it seemed fairly normal to me. I guess they had some crucifixes, and there was a picture of Jesus hanging in the hallway. Paul's room, though —" She grinned. "Yes, I *was* in his room, but only once, and it was a very innocent visit! I do remember that it had lots of religious stuff around."

"Katie, lots of people have religious pictures and symbols in their homes."

She raked her fingers through her long hair. "Yeah, I know, I know. But this was different. This stuff in Paul's room, all the religious books he had stacked up everywhere ... it all just seemed too much. Like it wasn't just part of Paul's life, but it was kind of taking over his whole life, it was taking over *him*. It's hard to explain." She said, shrugging again, "On our dates, Paul talked and talked, and he mentioned his college night courses, and his job at his father's company, but mostly he talked about himself, his church and religious stuff. And not just what he believed, but he went into great detail about these spiritual decisions he was trying to make, and he was incredibly intense, and I don't know why he would think I was interested. I hardly even knew him. But he went on and on, overwhelming me with all this … content, and it seemed really complicated and sophisticated, and I was impressed that he was passionate about it all, although I didn't really understand most of the issues. I couldn't really follow."

I frowned.

"Yeah, I know. He was clearly full of himself. Like there was nothing else in the world more important than what he was doing, and what he was thinking and what he might do next. It might change the whole rotation of the planet! And he seemed driven, like it was his duty to help others see the bad things they were doing so they could change and be with God, like he was following some plan, moving toward some goal that had to do with helping people unite with God. It was as if every single thing he did was spectacular, of momentous consequence. So, needless to say, he didn't ask me anything about myself, at all. Lowly little me." She grinned, stretched her legs out and crossed them at the ankles. "He definitely seemed to think he was pretty special."

I grimaced. "Ugh."

She raised her eyebrows. "But you know what's funny, Ivy? He actually *was* pretty special. Despite being so completely narcissistic, there was something totally alluring about him. It scared me because there was something in him that appealed to something in me that was … I don't know … lazy and vulnerable, maybe — his ideas that everything was black and white, evil or good. The world just isn't like that, is it? We know that, you and I." She grinned at me and gestured back toward the house. "The world has lots of grays. You can love someone who drives you crazy, right?"

"Right," I agreed, groaning.

Katie looked toward Russ, who was probably wanting to

get going, and I asked, hurriedly, "So what happened? Is that why you only went out for a short time?"

"Well, no, not really. I was actually kind of into him. Wild, huh? Despite all the religious stuff, the narcissistic stuff, he was really … interesting." She laughed. "I would have probably kept dating him, crazy as that sounds, but then a few things happened. On what ended up being our last date, he was really upset, and he went on and on about how his family had always belonged to the church down on the corner — but one of his sisters had met some people who were challenging what the church was teaching, and she had introduced them to Paul. They liked him a lot, he told me" — she raised her eyebrows — "and he actually agreed with their ideas and really thought this was the way to go, a completely new way to … connect with God, or something. His parents and he had argued and argued about it. He wanted to hook up with these people, and they were enthusiastic about him, but his father was completely set against it."

Katie twirled the end of her long hair around a finger thoughtfully.

"The Donato kids — well, the girls and Paul, that is; I don't think Joe was really this way — all had this thing about their father, this attitude toward him that was …" she spoke slowly, picking her words, "not just respectful, but more than that. It was a bit medieval, like he was the supreme authority and did all the thinking for them, and they just accepted what he said. That's how Paul explained it, anyway. I actually asked him about it, and he said, 'It's our family tradition. He's our father, the male head of the household, and so we honor him,' and my mouth dropped open, probably, because it's just so autocratic and so patriarchal. Don't they know we've moved into a new millennium? But he didn't exactly notice, or care, what I thought." Katie grinned. "Yes, you can see that my relationship with this guy was definitely *not* going to last long!"

I smiled back at her, my feminist sister.

"Anyway, so this argument, this going against 'his father's will,' was a really big deal. And then suddenly, soon after that, Mr. Donato was gone. Do you remember when he died?"

I nodded. Of course I remembered. I'd been ten, and he was the first person I'd ever known who had died.

"Paul and I had begun dating at the end of April, and his dad died one night in June. In his own backyard, barbecuing. Paul and I had plans to go out after dinner that night, after he ate with his family, and I'd had my evening swim team practice. And so I went to the house and rang the bell. My hair was still a bit damp from my shower, and while I waited for someone to come to the door, I was worrying about what he'd say, but I was trying to show I didn't care ... You know."

I nodded. I did know.

"One of his sisters opened the door, and right away I knew something was wrong. Her eyes were red, and she looked distracted and upset, like she wasn't sure what to do once she saw it was me. She sort of blurted out that their father had had a heart attack and died just a few hours ago, in the backyard. That he'd been taken to the hospital by ambulance, but it was too late. That Paul and Joe had just come back from there. Then she just kind of turned away, and I stepped in. From the hallway, I could see Mrs. Donato sitting in an armchair in the living room — she was wearing a red dress, and someone had draped a sweater around her shoulders, but she was shivering anyway. Her eyes looked empty." Katie swallowed hard.

"All the children seemed to be in there, around her. Paul was crouched down in front of her, his hands on her knees.

He was looking up at her and talking. I could hear his voice, low and compelling, but not his words, and everyone else was very still, and they all just listened, and his mother gazed down at him ... and then, from just inside the doorway, I saw Virginia. She was sitting on the bottom step of the staircase. She was cradling that picture of Jesus — the one that I'd seen hanging in the hallway. She was cradling it in her lap.

"I called out her name, softly, and she looked up at me. And I was about to step in, to go to her, when one of Paul's other sisters, I think it was Donna, came out to me, hurrying. She must have heard me or seen me, and she ... kind of intercepted me. I said I was so sorry about Mr. Donato. She looked at Virginia, and she looked at me, and she said it would be all right, that they'd all be all right, and it was clear to me that I should leave. Paul was still there, with his mother, and I don't think he'd seen me. So I asked his sister to tell him I would speak to him tomorrow, and then I left."

Katie's voice was trembling.

"Wow," I said. "That's really sad."

She nodded, and we went together down the front steps. I squinted, moving from darkness to light, shaded my eyes.

"I saw Paul one more time," she explained as we walked toward Russ. "He never did call me again after his dad died. I went with Mom and Dad to Mr. Donato's funeral, and of course I saw Paul there, but he and I didn't speak. And then one day, I ran into him on the street almost a month later. He wasn't embarrassed. He just coolly explained how he was really busy now. He had got more involved with the new religious group. He told me details that I didn't really care about, as if he thought I'd be really interested. And at the same time, he gave me the feeling that he didn't really think I was good enough for him. Or, no, not really that ... more like I wasn't important enough.

That the other things in his life, and him, were more important." She smiled. "And yet even when he was saying all that to me, even then, there was energy coming from him, energy that kind of drew me in, let me listen patiently to everything he said, nodding, and if he'd said, 'So let's go out again,' I would probably have said sure."

"If *who* said, 'Let's go out again'?" It was Russ, and he was grabbing Katie around the waist and kissing her face, her neck, making her laugh, making her scream, "Russ! Cut it out!"

Then Russ was climbing on the bike and getting it started up. "Ready to go, Katie?" he suggested.

Katie looked at me. She gave me a hug good-bye. "You know, something strange happened in that family when Mr. Donato died. I can't explain. I'm only looking in on them from a long way away. But when he died, it was like an iceberg tipping over, things being wrong end up. Paul had lost his father while we were dating. And yet that last time we met on the street, he didn't speak to me about his father at all. He didn't even mention him. Don't you think that's weird?"

"Yeah, I do," I agreed.

"He didn't talk about his dad's death, and yet it seemed to have energized him, as if he'd gained something instead of having something taken away. His eyes were even more electric. I didn't see Paul again after that, and so I never saw him grieve. I wonder if he ever did?"

For a moment, neither of us spoke.

It was Russ good-naturedly revving the engine that prompted our good-byes. "Sorry, Russ! Thanks for being so patient." I waved at him. "Thanks, Katie." I hugged her once more, quickly, before letting her go. "And congrats again on the great news."

"Thanks, sis," she responded. "Hope some of that helps. I did go on and on a bit, but it was kind of nice to share it all with you." She blew me a kiss as she ran toward the bike. "See you later!" And Katie was gone, sailing away on the back of the motorcycle, her arms wrapped around her fiancé.

†††

She had gone to the Sunday meetings at the church behind their house and looked at her brother standing at the front of the room, facing their small congregation, and listened to him give his sermons. It had made her uncomfortable. He was eleven years older than she was, but he was her brother and her mama's son, and she wondered how he had become so confident, so certain about himself and everything he was saying, how he had learned to speak so well and with such power. It seemed to come naturally to him. It was like there was something inside him that poured out, and his face lit up, and his eyes flashed, and at first she believed everything he said as he was speaking the words because he seemed to become someone other than her brother, someone with a special relationship with God, someone who could see things and understand things, someone who could show the way and make it easy to just follow. His voice soared, commanding and demanding, and he was her brother, but all these other people were looking to him, and he was explaining what was right or wrong, and he said that God had told him things and had asked him to make preparations, and who could not believe?

But then, after months of Sundays, her belief wavered and her unease grew. She wondered if Paul really did have a special relationship with God, and she wondered how he knew the things he was saying, and when she was listening to him preach, sometimes the words caught at her and carried her with their passion and intensity, and sometimes they didn't. She wanted to believe what he was saying. She wanted to just give in and accept what he was saying, because it would be so much easier just to believe her brother, but he was telling them things that the priest at their old church had never said. Paul was explaining that his role was to point out the wickedness of others, to be the watchman, to ring the alarm. His role was to show them that God was coming, and their actions might prevent them from being with God. He said that this world was on its way to annihilation, which meant destruction, but this was exciting and something to look forward to because all the good people, like Paul and her sisters and of course their mother, would go to be with God then. But first, to get to that, the Bible said there had to be worse and worse things happen in the world. It was just something they had to go through. Those events were starting to happen. Paul read the newspaper, and he knew.

At their old church, no one had said these things. No one had mentioned the End of the World and how close it was, and she wasn't sure why, if these things were true. She wished she could just believe, but maybe these things weren't *true*.

Also Paul was making loud promises to God about what he would do for God, about how he would try to help him raise the sword, and maybe God would think that she was promising too, but she wasn't, not these things anyway. Paul led the prayers in church, praying to God, speaking for all of them, and perhaps God had forgotten who she was, perhaps he might not know her anymore. She started praying to God on her own, in her bedroom, to set things straight.

As the months passed, she began feeling that somehow it was wrong for her to continue going to Paul's church. It felt like being there meant she was agreeing with what she heard. She really didn't know why something in her was keeping her apart from Paul when others were so drawn to him and his beliefs, but sitting in his congregation, accepting his words, made her feel more and more uncomfortable. She felt she might be betraying something important to her.

And yet she was torn. Not going would be almost like abandoning her family. The new church was becoming something that was realigning their home, something that joined them, like another family member but even more important, and it had settled right in the middle of them all ever since Papa died, and everyone had shifted to make room, to give it the best spot, everything else making way. Everyone but Joe, that is.

Joe had never gone back to church since that first meeting. Paul had tried to persuade him to go, then demanded that he go. They were in the living room, and Teresa told her not to go in, but she could hear their voices, raised, and Joe saying, mocking, "Papa would never have wanted this, and clearly I don't want it either. So what are you going to do? Tie me up and carry me into the church? You're taking this all a bit too far, buddy. You might be the head of the household now, but you can't force me to believe in your 'new church.' And if you want to keep pushing, I'll have to begin pushing back and that might not work out too well for you."

There was silence, and she thought probably Paul was replying. Then Joe continued, "Maybe I'll pay a trip to our old church and chat with Father Guillot, let him in on what's happening here. Maybe I'd have a chat with the accountant at the family business and see where some charitable donations are going ... That kind of thing." Joe's voice got louder. "Hey, I'm not threatening you, not really. I just don't want to be involved, Paul. I'm just asking you to leave me alone, and I'll leave you alone. That's all." A pause, and then, "Actually, that's not all. Leave Virginia alone as well. Grab her one more time, leave any more bruises, and ..."

Teresa had turned up the radio then, loudly. But afterwards, Joe didn't go back to the new church, and no one ever mentioned it. And a year later, she tried to talk to Joe about it, about how she didn't want to go to the new church either, but he wouldn't speak to her about this. "Talk to Mama," he said. But they both knew that was useless. When she tried anyway, her mother said, "Oh, Virginia. You must talk to Paul. It's really up to him. It's his decision, not mine." And so it was *useless.*

So she had made up her mind alone. She chose to give up Paul's church. And the next Sunday, she simply refused to go. She had thought it might be difficult, that they might force her, but it was easy. Perhaps her mother sensed what she was about to do, because Mama took her hand that morning and said, "Come on, Ginnie. Come with me. It's good for us all to be together."

But she shook her head and said no, she didn't want to.

Paul, hurrying to follow Anna Maria and Donna through the backyard (Teresa had been at the church for several hours already, preparing, as she did every Sunday

*morning), heard them and stopped in the kitchen. He
looked down at her, his eyes hard. She could see him
thinking, and she had a fleeting sense of danger.*

*"I'll stay in my room while you're there at the church.
I promise," she said. She told him she'd sit in her room
and read the Bible, say her own prayers. She told him she
wouldn't be alone. "Joe's here, sleeping," she reminded
him, "so I'll be safe."*

*Paul's eyes flickered. She knew he was wondering if she
had mentioned Joe's name on purpose, was using it as a
talisman maybe, and she wondered, too.*

*Paul said, "You must come," and she, not breathing,
replied, "No, I won't."*

*Mama left, with only a glance at Virginia. She was moving
slowly through the backyard, toward the fence gate. Late
for church now, Paul lifted his hand. She thought he might
strike her, because no one denied Paul what he asked,
no one but her and Joe, who both seemed immune to
whatever magnetism worked through him and inspired
obedience, right or wrong, in all others.*

*But he only made a sign in the air above her head — a
blessing perhaps? — and muttered, "I pray God does not
desert you."*

Chapter Eleven

Tuesday was the first day back at school and my first day of high school. I had been dreading it and all the changes it would bring, but it actually wasn't as bad as I thought it would be. It helped that the first hour and a half was an assembly at the end of which we were handed a map of the school and our rotation schedules. The rest of the day consisted of moving through the periods of day one, spending only half an hour in each class. In homeroom, period one, we got our lockers and more information sheets. Then the bell rang, and off we went to our next class, so we could meet another teacher and get some of our textbooks.

I saw Virginia once. She was in my English class, right after lunch. I tried to sit beside her, but someone else took the seat before I could get there, and the seat on the other side of her was already taken.

I kept an eye out for her after school but didn't see her, so I promised myself I'd drop by her house later. But I never did. When I got home, Dad was there working, and Mom was in the garden drinking. I made dinner, and we ate. Then Katie called and told Dad that she and Russ were hoping to be married really soon. They were trying to line up a date at City Hall, and they were looking for somewhere close by to hold a small reception. They would let us know when they did.

"Why the rush?" Dad asked lightly, but his face was tight, the muscles in his jaw flexing. When he hung up the phone, he leaned against the wall, his arms folded, deep in thought. He finally looked up and relayed the news to me in a matter-of-fact voice. When Dad said, "I guess I'd better go and tell your mother," I went out for a run.

I had trouble getting to sleep that night. Thoughts of Virginia filled every empty space in my head, crowding the active part that had to deal with real life, pushing, aggravating my brain like the throb of a hurting tooth.

The next day, I saw her in the school hallway. I insisted to her that I come over and talk with her on the weekend. She agreed so reluctantly that I worried she might not be there when I came by.

Fortunately, running practices began almost right away. Only when I was running did Virginia's secret move completely out of my mind that week. Not when I ran alone — that opened my mind to thoughts and ideas — but when I ran with the group at cross-country practice. The very first day of school, there was an announcement that practices would begin on Thursday and continue every day after school for three weeks. Everyone was welcome. The first cross-country meet would be held the second week of October, and it was open to all. Instead of try-outs, runners' individual standings at this first meet would determine who made the team and went on to compete in the next meet.

Of course, I was there from that first Thursday. The coach, Ms. Cooper, seemed very professional, and a large group of kids, girls and boys from all grade levels, turned out that afternoon. I knew at once that some would never make the team, but there were many others who were strong runners and took it seriously. A lot of them were in grade eleven or twelve, really confident, and seemed to be good friends with Ms. Cooper. They had obviously been on the team for a few years. She took a real interest in these kids, taking them aside often to make individual suggestions.

The juniors, those of us in grade nine or ten, were more of a mixed bag. It was obvious that some of the kids had never run more than half a kilometer before. But Ms. Cooper said how glad she was that so many of us had come out. She told us to do the best we could and said if we began training now we would improve a lot in even three weeks.

I had already pretty much decided that there were nine real contenders for a five-person team, and fortunately I was one of them. So were two of the three girls from my junior high who were trying out. I made up my mind to stick with them, pacing myself alongside Moira and Eleesa. Nicole started out at our pace but then began to drop back after a few laps.

Moira, Eleesa and I continued on, sometimes chatting as the kilometers melted away. Our coach encouraged that. "You should have enough breath to talk, otherwise you're going too hard!" she shouted as we pounded past. "It's not a race. You're training."

And so we spoke of the new teachers, the new students — just in a superficial way because we were tuned to our working bodies, silently assessing energy levels, endurance. And it felt great to be moving, to be strong, to be pushing myself to be the best.

On Friday, we were following a route through the streets. Ms. Cooper was leading us, and we were taking it slowly. I was relieved. I had spent two restless nights, and I was tired. It was hard to keep up with the others, and I wasn't chatting much. I almost stumbled when the conversation took an odd turn. Moira said, "So, do either of you know the story about that cute guy in grade twelve, Joe Donato?"

I inhaled deeply a few times. I was going to say that I knew him, that he was my neighbor, but Eleesa spoke first. "He's totally hot. He's dating someone, though, Moira, and she's in grade ten, I think. So hands off ... for now!"

I didn't say anything. But Jamie, tall, slim, and running near us, had overheard the conversation. "Well, I don't know. It would be weird to date a guy with some religious nuts for family," she chimed in.

"What do you mean?" Eleesa said. We were approaching a fairly busy intersection. The light turned red, and those of us in the back of the pack had to stop and wait.

I bent over and breathed deeply, appreciating the brief rest, keen to hear Jamie's response. Hands on hips, the grade ten runner swayed from side to side, trying to stay loose. "I heard the Donato family aren't Catholic anymore. They've like … gone AWOL. You know, End-of-the-Worlders, waiting for Doomsday to come," she said in a jeering tone. "Spooooky."

Eleesa frowned, wiping her face with her wristband. "You shouldn't joke about it," she cautioned. "Some people take it really seriously. My cousin goes to a fundamentalist church. He believes that some of the disasters that are happening now, like global warming and all these terrorist attacks, are all warnings that the world is going to end soon." She paused. "And I wouldn't call him a religious nut," she added defiantly.

Moira and I exchanged glances, and Moira said apologetically, "No, of course not."

Jamie sniggered. "Your cousin might not be, and Joe Donato definitely isn't. He's totally … into other things." She lifted her eyebrows, suggestively. "But his older brother is weird all right. Have you ever seen him? He didn't even go to our high school, but rumor has it that he sometimes hangs around there, talking up the grade twelve boys." She paused. "He's gay, maybe. Although some people say he's selling drugs, even dealing guns. Hey, maybe he's into all three." She laughed, gave a mock thumbs-up. "I think the principal has headed outside to talk to him a few times, but he takes off." The light changed. And as Jamie sprinted ahead to catch up with her friends, she added, over her shoulder, "Poor Joe, having to live all that down."

Eleesa and Moira rolled their eyes.

"Get a life," Moira muttered in Jamie's direction.

"It *is* possible he's talking to teenagers about something *other* than sex," Eleesa grumbled. "*Some* people occasionally think of something other than that."

The three of us began running again, following the pack.

That night, instead of falling sleep, I replayed the conversation over and over again in my brain. The two girls had dismissed it so easily, but the conversation made me uneasy, even slightly sick. This End-of-Worlder stuff seemed somehow to fit with Paul's unusual personality and the things Virginia and her mother had told me. Katie too.

My worrying thoughts morphed from abstract into actual images, from a black blur into a flock of black birds, circling round and round. And as I was drifting off, I began counting the crows. *One, two, three* ... Round and round they went. Lulled by them, I kept counting ... *eight, nine, ten* ... until I slipped dizzily into sleep.

✚✚✚

"*Virginia!*"

Paul snapped at her, loud and angry. She remembered. She was a little over thirteen years old. He grabbed her arm and yanked her back as she was trying to scoot past.

Tears stung her eyes.

"You told!" He squeezed her arm hard. "I told you not to tell. Not to tell anyone!"

"I didn't tell," she protested. "I didn't — and stop hurting me."

It was true. Whatever it was, she hadn't told. She didn't

talk about anything anymore. She wasn't sure what was okay to say and what wasn't, so she didn't speak about anything. She couldn't sleep at night because her heart fluttered and her palms sweated. She didn't know what was going on, and it was easier just to not think about it at all, not listen, not talk. She had lost her few friends, tired of shepherding them through the house only when Paul said it was okay because she couldn't remember when it was okay, and it was embarrassing to be creeping around and easier just not to have the friends come, even Ivy, who had been her oldest friend. And her mother was vacant ever since Papa died and the baby was lost, and she couldn't count on her mother except for food and clean clothes, and her siblings were bossy and overwhelming, and she wanted to do what they said because Paul knew the mind of God and was clear about it all. Even Joe, who had been her favorite, who had stood up for her, now looked at her as if from across a great distance, and she felt she was on her own, trying to make do, and strangers came and went, watching her as if she might betray something that was important to them all.

She knew Paul cared about her, because he cared about everyone on earth, and he wanted them all to rise to the Lord, rapturous.

But she had gone into the church house to find Teresa several weeks ago, and — no one knew this — she had heard more. She was standing outside the large room where Paul was meeting with the Elders and some of the people who always came and went. She listened as he explained that he cared so much for the people of the world that he wanted to hasten its end so they could ascend to their proper place, which was with God. He told the others that he was frustrated, and he said it was because God was

*getting frustrated. Things weren't getting bad quickly
enough. So he was going to help things along. He cared
enough to "take matters into his own hands," because
God's laws were primary and "everything was relative."
At first his words were careful and precise, but as he
talked, she heard them becoming grand and uninhibited,
and she knew there was a gap between his love of God
and his idea of right and wrong. It frightened her, because
he was meant to be pointing out the wickedness of others,
but didn't he see there might be wickedness in him, too?
He said he was going to "plan a grand finale, a great
exorcism, a great painful display of human disregard and
evil," which he hoped would be "the final nail in the
coffin and exhaust God so completely that he would give
a sweep of his weary hand and the End would come. And
there would be wailing and gnashing, and then joy finally,
and rising to heaven and eternal life." She wished she
hadn't heard this. And how would he do it? What kind
of plan would this be? It frightened her. It sounded scary
and violent, and who might be hurt? Certainly people
would be hurt, and she was confused because Paul could
not really be serious, because how could planning something this horrible be good, and wasn't Paul endangering
his own life, his own chance at eternal life, if he really
did this?*

*"Virginia, you told!" Paul let go of her arm. "I know it
wasn't Joe," he said now. "He's out of all this. I'm leaving
him out of it, and he wouldn't care enough to tell
otherwise." He considered her.*

"It wasn't me," she repeated, insistently.

*Paul stared at her hard, searching the eyes of his little
sister. Then he realized and said it aloud, "Maybe not.*

Maybe not this time. I think I believe you. But you might some other time. I can see that you would," he decided. Interest briefly crossed his face. "You're different, involved in some way."

Fear stirred within her, because he saw her truly, and she knew he was right. He saw that she could be dangerous to him. He saw that she had it in her to tell, to risk all for something, maybe even for him.

"It would really be best if you stayed completely out of this, too," Paul advised. "Don't see anything, don't hear anything, don't say anything. Don't tell anyone anything. It would be wicked to do so, and the wicked will be punished. This is a warning, Virginia, and it is for your own good, for your own spiritual safety. It's what God wants," he added. "The sword is coming against the land."

"I won't," she repeated. "I told you I won't."

And Paul left her then and went straight out into the backyard and toward his church, but neither of them knew if what she had said was true.

Chapter Twelve

Gin's voice was deep. It didn't even sound like her. She rubbed at her nose again, and she rubbed at the corner of one eye. She put her hand behind her head and felt her ponytail, checked that it was in place. She made all these normal movements, but they scared me. It was like something else was moving her arm, controlling her voice, floating behind her eyes.

We were in her bedroom. It was Saturday morning, and I had shown up at her front door, insisting to Anna Maria that I needed to see her sister about some homework. She let me in, but reluctantly.

"Ivy," said Virginia, irritably. "I don't see the point. I don't think we have time for this, to talk about my family. There are other much more important things to discuss."

She placed her hand on her belly and turned her back on me, walked to the window impatiently and stood there looking out.

I got up from where I was perched on her bed and went to stand beside her, trying to think of what to say next. As I looked down into the Donatos' backyard, my eye was drawn again to the gate in the fence between the yards. Why would anyone need to get from one yard to the other, to someone else's property? Maybe they knew the people who lived there? Were friends with them?

That seemed hard to believe. Other than the few men and women I'd seen on their porch, and Joe's girlfriend, no one seemed to come and go from the Donatos' house. They seemed much more interested in keeping people out than inviting them in.

I stared at the house on the adjoining property. Curtains were drawn in all the windows. There was nothing in the backyard — no toys, no tools, no flowers in the garden. It looked abandoned.

I was just about to ask Virginia whether anyone lived there anymore, when suddenly I saw a man come out of the back door of her house and head across the backyard. He reached the fence, placed his hand on the latch and pushed open the gate, looking back over his shoulder and then up at the house. I shrank back. I'm not sure why.

"Gin, who was that man?" I asked her. "Where's he going?"

Virginia didn't answer. It was as if she hadn't heard me.

When I stepped back to the window, cautiously, the gate was shut, and the man had gone.

"Gin —" I began again.

Virginia shook her head and moved from the window toward her bedroom door.

"Ivy, don't ask so many questions," she complained. "I wanted to share one thing with you. An incredible thing. And I've told you, and I think that's all you need to know for the moment. That should be enough. I just want someone to know, someone to know everything that is happening, from the beginning. I don't want you to *do* anything. I don't even need you to believe what is happening. I just want you to be an observer, a witness."

Out of the window I saw crows in one of the tall trees. One hopped off its branch, then opened its wings and was airborne. The black feathers shone in the sunshine, reminding me of the black robes of the priest who had stood at the front of the church, the time I had gone with Virginia.

"Gin, I'm glad you told me. But maybe you should talk to a priest. Have you thought about going to your church and speaking to someone there?"

Gin had her hand on the doorknob. "Yes," she said impatiently, "I thought of that."

"And?"

"There wouldn't be any need. I know what he would say."

"What?"

"He would encourage me to have the child," she said easily. "When God asks, you say yes."

She was so matter-of-fact. She believed she'd seen an angel. She believed she was going to have a baby, the child of God. It almost took my breath away to hear her talking about God like this, as though she knew him intimately, as if she knew the absolute rules that he had made and that were not to be broken. It seemed dangerous somehow, her nonchalance.

The words she used so casually represented huge, powerful concepts, and it seemed her life was poised on the tip of the structure she was building with them. Wasn't religion supposed to be something that happened on Sundays in a church, with singing and smiles and good deeds? How did this become so integral to Gin's world, so that every breath she took, every move she made, was reflecting on something vast, was linked to this larger presence?

"Besides, we don't go to that church anymore," she added. She'd calmed down a bit, moved away from the door.

"No?"

"Paul bought that house behind ours, on Turner Avenue." She pointed to the one across their backyard. "Paul and the others, they go there for services. It's …" She shrugged. "It's another one of their secrets. They've sort of made it into their own church. No one knows about it except the people that attend — and the people in my family, of course."

My eyes widened. *And now me,* I thought worriedly. "Gin, I won't tell," I said quickly, but she was waving that away before the words were even out of my mouth.

"No, of course not," she said, almost carelessly. "I trust you." She placed her hand on her stomach again. Now she was looking at me directly, speaking with more significance: "I'm trusting you with *all* this."

I nodded but didn't say anything. I hoped she'd just keep talking.

"Ivy, you know Paul has changed everything. Mama says he's just trying to do what he thinks is right. She says he has to follow his heart, even if it takes him away from his first faith, the Catholic faith ... Joe doesn't believe in Paul's new way, and Mama — well, I know she couldn't possibly. And I don't either. But it used to make Paul really mad. He would try to talk to me about the end of the world. He really wanted me to believe." Her voice was soft, like she was about to recount a fairy tale to a baby on the edge of sleep. "He explained to me how it was something to look forward to. We'll all be with God then. But before that would come a bad time. Bad things would happen."

She paused. "Paul says this is the End Time now."

I bit my tongue. The phrase made my skin crawl. What Virginia was saying seemed almost exactly what Jamie had said, what the rumors had been, that the Donatos were End-of-the-Worlders. The idea of looking forward to death, to the end of the world, seemed crazy to me, gave me the creeps.

Virginia went on in a sing-song voice, as if she were reciting Paul's own words. "Paul said that when things get really bad here on earth, during this special time God will lift up to heaven the dead who already believed in Him, and then He will lift up to heaven all those living who believe in Him. He will catch up all the people who believe in Him, and this is called the Rapture. For a time, the world will be left without Him. The people left behind will learn what life without God would be like, how horrible it would be. They will learn an important lesson, that they should believe in God and Jesus Christ. And then, Jesus will come and set up His kingdom on earth."

She sighed. "At first, I thought it was a story Paul was making up. I didn't think he meant it for real. Then I realized he did. It scared me, and so when he spoke about it, I just went somewhere else in my mind. He would notice and get mad. But he can't make me believe when I don't, can he? You can't just *make* someone. And so he's still angry at me and at Joe, too, because he doesn't believe, either, but at least Paul has stopped trying."

She didn't speak for a moment. Then she looked back at me. Her face hardened and then paled. "Ivy ..." she said nervously, "I think you should go."

"Gin, is this why Paul started this new church, this secret church?"

"Ivy. Really," Virginia said. "We can't talk about this anymore. Not here. I could get in trouble. And you, too."

The words leaped out at me. I saw fear in her eyes. A shiver ran down my spine.

"Okay, I'll go," I reassured her. "I'm going. But Gin, what could get us in trouble? Knowing some of your family believes the end of the world is coming?"

"No, no, not that, Ivy," Virginia said, impatiently. "It's what Paul is planning. That's what no one can know about."

"What is Paul planning?" I asked. Virginia was about to open the door, but I put my hand on hers, stopping her.

"Ivy, please stop. I can't tell you. I don't even really know. But if Paul heard us ... If any of them heard us ... If they thought we were talking about this ..."

"Okay, Gin," I said, hurriedly. "Okay, I agree. We won't talk about it anymore here. I promise."

I said good-bye and headed downstairs. Gin's fear seemed genuine, but then so was her belief that she was going to have God's child. Was what she was saying really true? But what could Paul be planning? The rumors that Jamie had repeated to me, the allusions to weapons and Mrs. Donato's warnings reverberated in my mind: *"Someone is going to get hurt."* Was she right? Was there really something to be afraid of?

Surely not if Paul's mother knew, and his brother and sisters. They wouldn't just go along with *anything* he said, would they? I hesitated.

Well, at least not Joe, I thought desperately. Even Katie had singled him out. He actually seemed slightly normal, and Gin had said he didn't believe. Although — my uneasy feelings grew — maybe he didn't know about these plans ...

Anna Maria watched me go out the front door, turning away before she saw me wave good-bye. I walked home, leaving Gin there, in her strange world. Leaving her in a place where the things you saw and the things you didn't see were equally real. I was trying to get her out of there, but she seemed to be trying to find a path within that place, where she had maybe become at home. From where I was, outside looking in, I could see how easy it might be to lose your way there, and how dangerous.

✝✝✝

W*hen she thought about what Paul had said, his plan for a "grand finale," it made her almost unable to breathe or swallow. It was hard for her to think about it. It was hard for her not to think about it. He didn't know she had heard. And so it was a secret.*

She tried to pretend to herself that she didn't know about it. She told herself all kinds of things: that she didn't really understand what it meant, that it was only words and ideas, that it wasn't anything specific or concrete. She told herself it didn't concern her, that it was too big for her, that it was none of her business. She told herself it would come to nothing.

But it circled round and round inside her head like a big, black bird. It was relentless. And she wasn't like her mother, and she wasn't like Joe. She wished she could accept or ignore, but she didn't know how, and it was overwhelming her, and she couldn't bear it. It loomed up and over her, and she knew she had to try to stop it. She had the idea that maybe someone would come and help her — someone or something. Something big and powerful. Something ... anything.

Part Three

The Demonstration

Chapter Thirteen

Her mother had told her about him. Told her many times. Since she was a child, Mama had told her about the angels, and especially about Gabriel. She said that Gabriel had appeared twice in the Old Testament. He was a messenger, sent from God to make announcements. Once he had been sent to explain to Daniel that his dream meant the end of an empire. Another time he had been sent to tell Daniel when Christ would appear.

That's how she knew that sometimes angels came to help people. They came to announce what was going to happen. The things that were going to happen were momentous, could change the future, could seem impossible. But they were real.

Daniel had seen Gabriel. Her mother had read the passage to her from the Old Testament, where Daniel says that Gabriel "flying swiftly touched me." Sometimes she had repeated this aloud to herself in a whisper, a shiver running across her skin.

Gabriel had also appeared twice in the New Testament. Mama read to her the verses when Gabriel foretells to Zechariah the birth of his son. He would be John the Baptist, the chosen one of God who tells the world that Jesus will come.

And of course, he had appeared to Mary. Everyone knew that. Even kids who didn't go to church, even kids who didn't believe in God or Jesus knew that. Even Ivy would have heard of that. It was part of the Christmas story.

When Gabriel came to Mary, he offered her a gift. And nothing was the same afterwards. Jesus had come and changed the life of Mary, certainly, but, most importantly, of everyone around her. With Jesus there, God must have felt optimistic. It was like giving everyone another chance.

But when Mama told her about it, she had made it sound so simple. Momentous, but dull. He had appeared, said a few words, Mary had listened and submitted and that was that.

She had been left feeling that Gabriel was barely there, that Mary was barely there, that they were cardboard characters, stand-ins for something greater — Gabriel for God and Mary for humanity. She had never imagined Mary as an actual person, so she had never stopped to think about what it might have been like for her. To Mary, it was real. Gabriel, an angel, had come to her, a human. It hadn't been written down in a book yet or told over and over, from generation to generation. It was the moment itself. Meeting Gabriel, hearing his voice, understanding what was wanted of her. The sacrifice, the possibility of salvation. The breath of the angel on her very face, on her very skin.

She shivered. It had not been simple or pure or dull. It was extraordinary. No one realized. No one knew how it had been. No one could imagine.

✝✝✝

Life went on. Even though our cross-country team hadn't been picked yet, we'd all been invited to compete in a race at Beaton Park on Wednesday. So on Sunday, I went for a practice run at the park with the coach and the rest of the girls.

That same evening, Katie phoned and left a message, telling us that her wedding was going to be two weeks from Saturday at City Hall, with a reception in a nearby community hall.

When Dad played the message later, Mom was livid, threatening loudly that maybe we wouldn't even bother to show up. I went to bed, but I couldn't sleep. I was making a list in my head — a long list. There were so many things I had to do. Help Mom, somehow. Talk to her again, maybe get her into some kind of program, get Dad to do it with me. Help Virginia, somehow. Bring her back from this strange place where angels could talk to her, where God had chosen her to bear His child. Find out what was going on with Paul and how it connected with Virginia. And, of course, help Katie.

I phoned my sister first thing after school on Monday.

"So the wedding's really going to be two weeks from Saturday? That's the big day?" I asked, excited.

"I know it's short notice." Her voice was determined, almost apologetic. "But I didn't want to give Mom any more time to influence me. I totally predicted her reaction to our engagement news, and I told myself not to let it bother me. She's just an out-of-touch drunk who can't even look after herself, let alone us."

I flinched at the harshness in my sister's words. "But Ivy, the very day after we were there, I found myself having doubts. Mom says a few words, and I begin to waver. I can't completely block her out. And yet I don't want any part of what seeps in. It's like she poisons everything. Just because her marriage to Dad wasn't the incredible love story that she wanted ... Just because she decided to stay home and look after us instead of having the career she wanted ... Those things *are* sad, don't get me wrong. But it's like she can't see past them to the other *good* things in her life, to us," she said bitterly. "It's like she's always looking back. As if the not-perfect marriage, the lost career, destroyed her ability to hope for the future, even though she still has Dad, and she could work at making things better, even though she could still find something fulfilling to do with her brains and her ambition! It's like she's denying what might be ahead, any goodness that might be ahead in the future. And she's denying it not just for her but for Dad, for you, and for me and Russ. She can't face more disappointment, so instead she tries to wreck things before they even happen." Katie took a breath to steady her voice. "And so I decided to do it right away, get married before things — before anything between Russ and me — began to fall apart. I won't let her ruin my chances."

There was silence on the line.

"Is she going to come to the wedding?" she asked.

"I'm not sure, Katie," I told her honestly. "She didn't really say. She just sort of ranted about the date."

More silence.

"Well, would you let me know what she decides, Ivy? I think I need to know before the day. Just to be prepared, one way or the other."

"Sure thing," I agreed. "I'll try to find out. But, hey, listen. Two weeks — two weeks from Saturday. You're getting married, Katie. Married! Is there anything I can do to help? Anything I can make? Sandwiches? Salad? You name it."

Now my sister's voice quivered for the first time. "Hey, it would be great if you and Dad could help set up for the reception, on the big day," she replied. "Thanks. That would be really great."

"Sure, we'd love to," I assured her.

She laughed, and it was good to hear it. I liked that happiness could bubble up so easily in her. I think she deserved that.

Then it was Tuesday. I needed to focus on my race. I needed to think about me. If I didn't, I thought I just might go out of my mind.

Wednesday dawned overcast. As I slipped on my sweats and my favorite T-shirt, my eyes scanned the sky. Endless gray. Five crows sat in the pine tree, close together, silent. By the time I got to school, it was drizzling.

We all met in the gym after homeroom and checked the posted lists to find out which car we were in. Parents had volunteered to drive us to Beaton Park. I watched with envy as the moms tried to suppress their excitement and pride, loading up their minivans with the nervous competitors. I had told Dad about the race but hadn't made a big deal about it.

The real surprise came when I was standing at the starting line with Moira, Eleesa, Nicole, and the one hundred and fifty others in our race.

"Ivy! Hey, Ivy!"

I turned, startled, my adrenaline keeping me taut.

"Go, girl!" It was Katie. She had come to watch me. Dad must have told her about the race. It felt great to have a fan here, just for me. I grinned and waved back at her. "That's my sister," I told Moira proudly.

Then Katie and everything else in the world dropped out of my head. The gun went off, and the race began.

Moira and I took off as hard as we could. So did half the pack. A few girls were knocked over, but Moira and I both managed to stay on our feet. After a brief bottleneck, we entered the woods. I lost Moira, and now the path twisted and turned, and I couldn't see exactly how many other girls were in front of me. The dirt felt good underfoot, but I reminded myself to watch out for roots or half-buried rocks.

After a few minutes, I pulled ahead of the girl in front of me. Then I began to accelerate, passing one girl, another, and another. A Thompson High runner kept her elbows out wide, deliberately making me go wide around her. She gave me a hard look as I went by, her face red.

When I hit the hill at the halfway point, I dug in, pumping with my arms until my lungs burned. Over and over again I told myself, *The pain is only in the moment. I can endure it for now. It will be over soon, when I reach the end.*

I passed another girl and then another. But still every time I rounded a corner, there was one more girl in front, arms swinging, knees high. I separated my mind from my screaming muscles, a skill learned from my hours and hours of training. I propelled my split self into the future, reminding myself there would be a time, soon, when this would be over.

Finally, I burst out of the woods to a surge of noise. There was the finish line, about 200 meters away. I could tell other girls had already finished, but there was only one runner between me and the tape, so this became my new goal, to pass this girl.

The crowd was clapping and shouting, urging us over the final, forever-long stretch toward the tape. My lungs were about to explode. Every step was an effort of willpower and experience. With only 100 meters to go, pushing, pushing hard, the race almost over, I called on everything I had left, any last secret stores of energy.

And somehow, I began to gain on her. She was slowing down, or I was running faster, or both, maybe. My legs felt numb, heavy. But I was beside my opponent, and the spectators were cheering, crying out the names of our schools.

Fifty meters to go. My stride lengthened. So did hers.

We were side by side, sprinting, and I couldn't breathe, and my lungs were burning.

And suddenly, the heaviness dropped away. I knew the pain was there. I knew it. But I couldn't feel it anymore. I stretched out again, and I thought I might just lift off, fly.

When she pulled ahead, just slightly, as we reached the line, I couldn't match her. This was fast, as fast as I could go, and she entered the chute first.

It was over, and my coach was at my side, congratulating me. "Ivy! Great run! Great job, Ivy!"

I felt good. I hadn't come first, but I had run a good, fast race. It had been exhilarating.

"Sixth place," intoned the race referee. A green ribbon. Sixth. I smiled, and then Katie was beside me, wrapping me in a hug. "Ivy, you did so well! Sixth, Ivy! You came sixth!" That made it even better.

And when Dad came into my bedroom later that afternoon, he was pleased as well. I had pinned my ribbon to my bulletin board, and we stood there together, admiring it and all my other cross-country ribbons — reds, blues, browns, yellows.

"What riches!" He smiled at me. My sixth place win had made him smile, and suddenly I wondered: *could* I tell him about Virginia? Could I tell him my suspicions about her brother? My father knew I wouldn't make up an outrageous story. If I told him all the details, wouldn't he agree that it was something worth investigating, that something bad might be happening in our neighborhood, among our friends? He would want to help Virginia. He would want to help the Donatos.

Wouldn't he?

Dad put his arm around me and squeezed. He said, happily, "I'll tell your mother. She'll be so proud," and it was ruined. I knew it was no use telling him about Virginia. He was almost as bad as her, living in a fantasy world that his faith had created; a world where a daughter won ribbons and a wife cared enough about that daughter to be proud of her. A world where something real, his wife's drinking, was made invisible, was not spoken of, did not exist. Virginia saw things that weren't there. My father refused to see things that were.

✠✠✠

*H*e *came again. Joy filled her being. How had she*
breathed while he was gone? How had blood flowed
through her veins? Perhaps it hadn't, and only this was
real, this being with him.

She gazed at him, and perhaps she should have said right
away, "Yes," and meant that she would do it, that she had
made her decision, that of course she would have the baby
as he had asked. But it felt like he knew, and that he had
always known and that this was what had drawn him to
her and what urged her forward to be enveloped inside all
he was, and so instead she breathed, "Who are you?" She
meant she wanted to know about him, about who he was
— not just an angel, an Angel, not just one among the
many, indistinguishable, but who *he was — so there*
would be more of him to cling to, more texture, ridges, to
grip, to fasten onto, when he left her.

He did not speak, and she did not speak, held in his gaze,
as if lifted from the bedroom floor, levitated and wrapped
in the warmth of his being.

And still he did not speak, and so she waited.

But then suddenly, like a whisper of feathers, like a sound
of notes beyond hearing, the notion slipped into her like
ice into blood that those three words might not be trans-
parent, might not be absorbed as instantly as air. He might
be angry. She might have offended him. And before the
thought turned to emotion, before the fear reached her, it
was with relief that she heard him boast (or was he simply
laying out the facts before her?), "I am chief of the four
favored angels."

A wind sprang up. His edges blurred, his skin shifting, ruffling.

"I helped bury Moses." The timbre of his voice altered, so it seemed less like words she was hearing and more like an echo of sounds, strange and wonderful. "I told Noah to gather the animals. I stopped Abraham from slaying Isaac."

She nodded admiringly. Each statement sparked a memory, something her mother must have told her, sitting by her bed, rocking her, soothing her fevers, slipping her into sleep.

"I dictated the Qur'an to Muhammad. And when Muhammad died, I brought words of comfort to his daughter, Fátimih." These things she hadn't known. She was surprised. The angel knew the God that was the Holy Spirit and Jesus, the God of the Jews and also the God of Islam.

And something was different. Suddenly the room began to throb. She had felt uplifted, but now it was difficult to breathe. He was even more than she had imagined. He flooded the edges of her understanding. Perhaps, she realized, he was unknowable. Perhaps he was not who she had thought, what she had thought ...

She looked at him, and she knew he was too big for the small, confined space of her bedroom. He might expand against the walls, crush her against them with his immensity, smother her.

Her heart pounded. How would it be? What would it feel like to be touched by him?

Chapter Fourteen

The race had only been over for about six hours, and already the sick feeling smothered me again.

An image kept moving through my mind, an image of a man walking through Virginia's yard toward the back gate. Virginia had said that her brother Paul had purchased that house and now it was his secret church. A secret church ... it was strange. Why would a church have to be kept secret? What was Paul up to? I just didn't get it.

I was supposed to be doing my homework, but instead I was only flicking my pen against my page, again, and again and again.

I was helpless. I couldn't do a thing for Virginia. She just wouldn't listen. And she wouldn't tell me anything more. She said Paul was going to do something, but she wouldn't tell me what. She said she didn't know exactly, and that it might be dangerous to talk about it. Her mother had hinted at something bad. Anna Maria's hovering, lurking, slipped in and out of my mind. My stomach clenched.

I flicked my pen against my page.

What was Paul going to do?

I wished someone else would come along and take charge. Virginia had a whole family, a mother, brothers and sisters surrounding her. I wanted them to look after her. It was fine for them to care about God and to start this new church, but why couldn't it just be simple and good? Couldn't they help Virginia instead of making things worse, instead of making me sit here, paralyzed, anxious, afraid to do anything but more afraid to do nothing?

Maybe just getting more information could convince me that there was nothing sinister going on, that Paul was doing nothing bizarre or undercover, and that it was okay to talk to Joe or one of the sisters, and try to get them to step in and do something for Virginia. Or maybe it could explain away this feeling of unease that I had.

So, okay, if I had to find out more, how could I do it? There wasn't anyone I could ask. I didn't dare go to anyone in her family yet. And my own family ... well, Mom was useless and Dad was too preoccupied with propping her up. Katie was planning a wedding.

There was only one thing to do. I had to investigate the house behind the Donatos' where Paul was meeting with his church people. It was the only way I might learn more, maybe find some clues to what was going on. I had to go and have a look.

I sprang up and slipped on a black sweater. It was about ten minutes after nine and had been dark for some time. I wasn't going to do anything crazy. I was simply going to walk around the corner and stroll past the house. That's all.

I didn't stop to ask myself how that could possibly help. I simply headed downstairs and out the side door.

I was nervous, but it felt good to be doing something. I gave a quick glance at the front windows of the Donato house as I went past, my head down. I told myself again that it would be all right. I was simply going for a walk. It was very innocent. Every day people walked by that house on Turner Avenue. That's all I was going to do. I didn't look suspicious, and I wasn't doing anything wrong.

At the end of our block, I rounded the corner onto Greer Avenue. Then at the next corner, I turned left again and headed up Turner Avenue. I slowed, trying to figure out which was the house directly behind the Donatos'. That was it. That one. Four-eleven.

It looked like any other house on the block, except there was only one light on, the hall light. I slowed even more as I got closer. The front curtains were drawn. No car in the driveway. The place looked as abandoned from the front as when I looked at the back from Virginia's second-floor bedroom window. Some junk mail lay on the front doormat.

Should I go up on the porch and try to peer in through the windows on the door? I'd better make sure the house was empty.

I continued walking slowly past it, looking down the walkway on the east side. No light on there either. I glanced at my watch. It was 9:20.

To be cautious, I carried on walking right up to the corner of the block and then turned and began walking back. I went past one house with a bedroom window open. Rock music wafted out. From another house on the other side of the street came the muffled sound of a dog barking. Shapes of people moved past lit windows, and the light of a television flickered against a wall.

When I was within six houses of my destination, several cars turned up the street, moving slowly. They pulled up in front of 411 Turner.

I slowed, bent down to tie my shoe. People got out of the cars, greeting one another in soft voices. Car doors slammed.

My heart pounded as I remembered I might have been standing on the front porch of the house.

I crossed to the other side of the street and kept walking slowly eastward. Another car pulled up, and more people got out. There were about ten altogether, assembling on the sidewalk. The men were wearing suit jackets. The women carried purses. They all headed up the walkway to the house.

I waited for a few moments, just to make sure no one else was coming in or out. Then I crept up the front walkway. I paused on the lawn. The same thought: Should I try to peer in the window?

Quickly, I tried to calculate whether it was worth running

the risk of discovery. The closer I got to the house, the more nervous I grew. Now that I was standing on the front lawn, my breathing was shallow, as if I were midway through a race.

What if someone else arrived while I was poking around?

I took a good look up and down the street. There was no one out, not even neighbors. There were no cars heading in this direction. I made my way to the front steps. The porch light threw a wide beam. I paused at the edge of it, glad that the curtains were drawn across the front window.

I couldn't believe how nervous I was. I was remembering Mrs. Donato's voice: *Someone is going to get hurt.* I couldn't persuade myself to move up the steps.

I had to get a grip. There's no real danger, I told myself firmly. So what *was* the worst that could happen? Maybe someone yelling at me. Paul probably wouldn't even recognize me anymore.

But Virginia's pale face and her frightened eyes as she spoke of her brother lingered in my imagination. I didn't want to risk him thinking I was prying. I didn't want him to see me, even if he didn't know who I was. I had a feeling he could find out anything he wanted.

I heard a slam from inside the house, from the hallway, and my mind was made up. I turned and walked away as fast as I could, cutting across the lawn, down the street, and I didn't look back, and I didn't slow down until I had rounded the corner again and was nearing my own house.

I slipped back in the side door, sweating and shaky. I felt I'd let myself down and let Virginia down, and so I made myself a promise: I'd go back on a night when I knew no one would be there, and I wouldn't just peer in the house, I'd find a way to get inside and look around. I'd do it for Virginia. I'd do it because I didn't know what else to do.

✝✝✝

*A*nd then the immense dimension of his shape and his capacity, nearing her, abruptly began to contract. It withdrew into him, and his manliness sharpened, defined itself into head, neck, body, arms, legs, his eyes focusing on her and boring into hers.

And it was like Paul, her brother who loved her, melting into Paul, her brother who was electrified with certainty that he must deliver the world to God soon, with fire and pain and terror if need be, because he was so certain there was no other way, and God would approve because how long, oh, how long could God remain patient, his gaze calm, his palms open, suffering the little children to come unto him? And she was afraid.

"You doubt me?" Gabriel challenged her, fierce. "Do you know of Zechariah? Have you read of this? I told Zechariah that his wife, Elizabeth, would bear a child. She was old, very old. Zechariah looked at me with fear, but he asked, 'How will I know this, because I am old and my wife is advanced in age?'" Gabriel shook his head. "I had told him what would happen, and he asked, 'How will I know this?' as if it was not enough that I was there before him, come just to him, telling him in my words. He should not have done that. I was announcing the birth of John, and he questioned me."

He lifted his chin slightly and lowered his eyelids. She realized he was addressing her, and not just her. She saw him tremble into something possibly dangerous, and his voice growled softly. "I told him I was Gabriel."

She believed. She only believed. She wanted to say it. She had not thought she could do wrong by him. She was his servant, ready to be whatever he asked.

"*Wasn't that enough? It should have been. 'For if God says it, it is possible.' This is what I told Mary. And she accepted my words. Zechariah was an elderly man. He was wise, experienced. He should have known. But he didn't. So to make it clear, I gave him a sign. I struck him dumb.*"

She wanted to tell him that his word was enough for her. It was. She wanted him to know so that he did not leave and never return, so that he did not strike her, except now she was wondering how an angel strikes. How would it feel? And to have that mark, that loss, it wouldn't be nothing, and it might be easier than the mark he had chosen for her, the bearing of a child.

He was glowing, giving off a white-hot aura that shimmered like heat rising from black tarmac on a sweltering summer's day.

"*It wasn't permanent. But it wasn't until John was born, his first and only child, a miracle child, that Zechariah could speak again,*" *he warned.*

It wasn't forever. A child would be forever. She tried to say, "I believe. I do," but he was speaking quickly now, in a rush, as if something more was needed, as if this wasn't enough, and he had to show her what he was capable of.

"*Once I was punished. I was asked to do something, and I did it, but I didn't do it precisely in the way I was asked. For twenty-one days, I was locked out. Turned away. Dobiel took my place.*" *He looked at her. "I was outside."*

He paused, and his silence emptied the room of air. She couldn't breathe, and he watched her. Evaluating her? Testing? And she would show him the truth, that it didn't matter to her, that even this, breathing, was overwhelmed in importance by his words, by what he was telling her, by who he was. She wanted to know more, ask for details about what had happened, what he had been asked to do, who Dobiel was. She wanted to know everything about him, but she opened her mouth and nothing came in or went out.

"I was placed outside. Away," he repeated. And she wanted to know what there was on the outside, and whether he had been afraid or lonely and what he had done there.

She wanted to ask if this was a threat.

She wanted to say that there was no need. That she believed, and he didn't need to show her what he could do.

But her lungs were still empty, and her eyes, she realized, were closed, and she felt herself beginning to sink, or was she beginning to rise? There was a pleasant whispering, the sound of hundreds of wings lifting and then falling. He was leaving. Again. Abandoning her. Or was he? Maybe this time he was taking her with him. Sinking, rising, lifting, falling ... She couldn't tell the difference, and how could that be? How could they feel the same, being left behind or being swept away, when one was devastating and one was all she longed for?

She struggled to breathe, to open her eyes, but when she did, he had vanished, and she saw nothingness.

Chapter Fifteen

I had planned to return to the house on Turner Avenue on Thursday night, just to have another look from the outside again, but Katie called at about 9:30, and I ended up talking to her for a long time, trying to get excited about her wedding plans, trying to be helpful and supportive.

I had thought I would go on Friday, but I was tired. I had tried to talk to Virginia at school both days, but she had disappeared right after class, looking pale and nervous. And then I had come home from school to find Mom pretending that the world was what she saw through a glass of gin, and Dad hidden in his study, pretending that reality was only what he saw on the computer screen and could be deleted or added to or pasted in somewhere else. I was so sick of being the only one who saw the breeze move through the leaves on the trees, the only one who put a hand on the doorknob and pushed it open and walked in and saw a family self-destructing and didn't try to turn it into something else, and the only one who heard the clock tick away every minute that went by, every minute of now turning into then. How could they tell a story that skipped over all this, that created some imaginary world, while waiting for what they wanted to be happening to come to them? How could they be living the same events as me but looking back on a different history?

Didn't they see that all our moments were creeping past, and if they looked at it now, only saw it now, connected these real moments one to another, that whatever they were facing, whatever they saw that they were so afraid of, so sad about, so suffocated by, could be our real story, and we could try to solve the problem that every good story has together? We could work on the rest of it, the rest of life together?

I was upstairs in my room when Dad called me from the front door. His voice sounded urgent, serious.

I ran.

An ambulance had pulled up at the Donatos' house. The siren wasn't wailing, but the red light was flashing. We watched as the two medics jumped out and hurried to the front door. A few minutes later they came back out with Virginia's mother on a stretcher. They loaded her into the back of the ambulance; Paul jumped in, and they drove away.

"I'm going to go and check on Virginia," I told my dad, pulling on my jacket and running over to the Donatos'.

Breathless, I knocked on the front door, but no one answered. Would Teresa be there? Or Joe? I knocked again. The door opened a crack, and Anna Maria looked out.

"Yes?" she said. She had a blank look on her face. Her eyes were red.

"Anna Maria, I saw what happened. I saw the ambulance ..." Stupidly, I asked, "Is your mom okay?"

"They're taking her to the hospital. They think she had a heart attack. Right here. Just a little while ago." Her voice was shaky. "Mama has been saying 'Maybe it's my time. Maybe God wants to take me now.' I don't think so. I don't think he'd do that. But perhaps it's one more sign to us that the Great Tribulation is near. We are at the beginning of sorrows."

I stared at her.

"It's one thing after another, just like the Elders tell us. Little things and so many big things. Wars everywhere around the world, terrorist attacks, so many deaths and natural disasters, tsunamis, hurricanes, global warming, global food shortages, water shortages, pandemics ..." She opened the door wider. "Do you understand? These bad things aren't actually bad, because they may mean the End

Days will come, and then the graves will explode and all of us, all Christians that is, alive and dead, will rise to heaven. The Rapture." She was speaking so quickly; I could hardly make out the words. Tears were streaming down her face.

Teresa was at the door, gently pulling on her sister's arm. "Come on, Anna Maria," she said. "Come back inside." She looked at me calmly. "We're fine, thanks, Ivy." She started to close the door.

I put my hand out to stop it. "Is Virginia there? Is she okay?" I asked.

"She's here. She's okay," Teresa told me, looking at my hand.

I removed it, and the door closed.

✚✚✚

She heard raised voices and running footsteps. She got up and hurried downstairs. Her mother was lying on the floor, on her right side. She looked uncomfortable. Her legs were splayed like scissors, and her dress was hoisted up around her wide thighs, as if she had been dragged down by her feet. Mama's hand was flattened against her chest. Gin couldn't see her face. Mama was facing the opposite wall.

Now Anna Maria was there, kneeling beside Mama, pulling her dress down, carefully putting a pillow under her head. She was stroking Mama's arm, murmuring to her gently. Now she clasped her hands together, praying.

Paul was pacing up and down, glancing impatiently at his watch, then at Mama, then at the front door.

Teresa was on the phone, one arm curled around her waist. Gin watched as Teresa noticed her standing there and then looked away. "Paul, Virginia's there," Teresa said quietly, urgently.

Paul hurried over to her. "Virginia, everything's okay," he said, reassuringly, and she felt his arm around her. He was turning her away from her mother, guiding her out of the room. "The ambulance is on its way. Mama has had a few more chest pains, but everything's okay."

"Wait." She stopped in the doorway. "How do you know she's going to be all right? Everything's okay? I don't believe you," she told Paul.

"Gin," he said, trying to move her into the hallway.

"No," she sobbed angrily, shaking herself out of his embrace. "She's my mother, too."

She looked back at the broken black bird on the floor. Her mother's chest was moving, heaving up and down, which meant she wasn't dead. Not yet.

What was happening? She didn't want her mother to die. "Where's Joe?" she asked helplessly. Joe would tell her the truth. He was the only one who ever did. What was wrong with everyone else? Why were they always hiding things from her?

Chapter Sixteen

It was driving me nuts, hovering out there on the edge of everything I did or said or thought, black and dark and frightening. I could push it away but only so far, and then it came gliding back in, closer and closer. Saturday came, and in the evening I went for a walk up Turner Avenue. I checked out the church house at 8:00. It was dark. I went back at 10:00. Still dark.

Then Sunday came. I knew there would likely be people at the church house in the morning, and maybe even the afternoon, a typical church day. So I didn't go by again until that evening. There were people there at 5:00, but by 8:00, the lights were out. At 9:00, still no lights.

Monday came, and Virginia wasn't at school. Was her mother still in the hospital? Was Virginia staying home to be with her? I looked at their house on my way home from school and it looked still. No activity at all, no one coming or going.

"Should I call?" I asked Dad at dinnertime.

"Maybe not yet," he cautioned. "They might need some time alone right now, some family time."

"But I could just call and find out if she's okay," I suggested, and I meant Virginia, but Dad of course thought I meant Virginia's mother, and he shook his head uncertainly. "Better not to intrude just yet," he repeated.

Incredibly, Mom spoke up. "Do you think, Ian? Perhaps it would be all right to see how Maria is doing, poor soul."

And I thought that would sway Dad, seeing that Mom cared about an old friend. But he seemed certain that it would not be appropriate, and I don't know if he was right or wrong, but I agreed to go along with what he thought was best. Meanwhile, the anxiety grew in me. Mrs. Donato's illness didn't mean that Paul wasn't still marching ahead with his plans, and I couldn't stop thinking that Paul and his plans might be connected in some way to what was going on with Virginia. One thing was certain. I had to get into that house, that church, and I had to do it soon.

I decided to do two more nights of surveillance, just to be on the safe side. So that night, and then on Tuesday night, I walked past again. At 8:00 and at 9:00, no lights. At 9:30, people arrived, pulling up in cars.

Now I felt pretty confident that there was a pattern. The church house seemed to be empty before 9:30 every night. So I chose that night, Wednesday night, because I had had the added comfort of seeing the church house empty before 9:30 last Wednesday.

After dinner, I couldn't concentrate on my homework. I kept looking at the clock. I knew it had to be after dark but not too close to 9:30. I wanted to be gone long before anyone got near the place. I was aiming for 8:30.

By the time I'd had dinner, cleaned up the kitchen and done my homework, I'd come up with a plan. It was simple, maybe too simple.

At around 8:25, I told my dad I was going to a friend's house to pick up some homework notes. I slipped out the front door. For a moment, I stood on the porch. Several cars drove by. A man talking on a cell phone walked his dog past our house.

I walked slowly down our front walk. The street was empty. It was a beautiful night, warm but not hot. There was a slight breeze.

I headed around the block. Near the corner, an elderly woman sat on her front porch with a white cat in her lap.

She was listening to soft music on the radio.

My palms were sweaty. I headed up the street until I was a few houses away from the property. With relief, I saw that only the hall light was on, and not the porch light.

I continued on until I was standing directly in front of the house. It seemed quiet. There wasn't any sign of movement in or around the house. None of the neighbors were outside.

For a moment, I hesitated. I was scared. I couldn't help imagining what it would be like if Paul caught me.

But then I took a deep breath, glanced around to make sure no one was watching and headed down the driveway, between the houses.

It didn't seem real. I almost didn't believe I was really going to do it.

But there I was, trying the side door. It was locked. I didn't want to try the back door because I knew someone might see me from the Donatos', so I tried the basement window at the side of the house, close to the rear. It looked like it hadn't been opened in a long, long time. Maybe it wasn't locked. Maybe it was so old and stuck that it didn't need to be.

I kicked at it a few times, hard then harder, trying to dislodge the paint that was keeping it shut but not make too much noise. Then I bent down and felt the window along its edges. I reached in my pocket and pulled out the pocketknife I'd brought along, just in case. I pried along the window, trying to free it. I banged hard with the heel of my hand, and one side cracked open. I hit hard against the other side, near the bottom, and it cracked open, too. I reached forward and pushed slightly against the window and it swung open, inwards, hinged on the top.

At that moment, too late, I realized there could be an alarm system. I tensed, waiting for the sirens, whistles and bells. Nothing. How stupid I was not to have even thought of that.

My heart started beating quickly. What else had I not anticipated?

But nothing, it seemed, was going to stop me now. It was going to happen. I was going to go inside the house. I felt like I was on autopilot. I felt like I had to do this, like I had no choice.

Squatting, I inched forward. I put one leg through the window, then the other, and turned onto my stomach. I scooted back until I was dangling inside the basement, my waist on the ledge between in and out. Words formed in my head: *Be careful.*

Slowly I wiggled backward, my feet searching for something to step onto. There was nothing. I was balancing on my elbows, feeling the crumbling of the bricks against my skin, and then, hoping I wouldn't fall far or damage anything or make too much noise, I dropped.

I landed on my feet on what seemed to be the cellar floor, but then fell sideways, my arms out into the blackness, flailing for a moment. When I regained my balance, breathless, my blood was pounding in my ears. I froze, blind in the cellar's blackness, waiting until I could hear again and breathe.

I gathered myself. I had to begin searching. I had to look around quickly.

I felt for the wall, and keeping my fingertips against it, walked slowly along one side, exploring ahead with one foot and then bringing the other to meet it. In the darkness, after several minutes, my fingertips discovered the underside of a staircase.

I inched forward, my hand feeling the side of the staircase and the rail. I was at the foot of the stairs, breathing heavily, and my hand went back to the wall as I searched for a light switch. There had to be one here — wasn't there always one at the bottom and top of a staircase? — and I found it.

I paused again. *Wait twenty seconds,* I thought. It helped to tell myself what to do, as if I were not alone, as if I were following instructions from someone who was not scared, who was in control, who was smarter, sensible.

I waited, counting to twenty, listening.

What time would it be now? I wondered, worried, wanting to hurry. *Probably not much after 9:00. Just seems longer because you're afraid,* came the calm answer.

There were no sounds.

I held my breath. I counted to three, just to be safe. Then . I forced myself to flick on the light.

The cellar was old and dusty. Cobwebs hung from the ceiling and decorated the one light bulb. An ancient furnace with octopus pipe-arms winding and twisting took up about a quarter of the space. A water heater rusted beside it. A pile of old bricks and moldy boards sat in one corner. A few boxes were piled up against the wall and covered in plastic. They looked dust-free, possibly recent additions to the basement, but otherwise, the space looked unused and neglected.

I took a breath and began to climb the stairs, up to the half-landing, where the side door offered possible escape, and then up to the door that would open onto the main floor. I turned off the light and stood listening for a few seconds. I didn't hear anything.

I put my hand on the doorknob and turned slowly, trying not to make a sound.

The door opened into a kitchen. The light from the front hallway shone through, helping me see. The kitchen still looked like a kitchen — it had cupboards and a stove, a refrigerator, a linoleum floor, but it looked like it served many people. There were cups lined up along the counter on a tea towel. There was an industrial size coffeemaker and a mound of teaspoons, a teapot and a large sugar bowl. The kitchen table had several wooden chairs placed around it.

I moved through the kitchen to the doorway and looked into what must have been the dining room originally. It and the living room now made up one large space with hardwood floors and white walls. There were lots of chairs and two couches set up at one end of the room. At the other end was an altar with an altar cloth folded neatly on top and two candleholders with tall white candles. There were pictures of Jesus in gilt frames on the walls and on the old fireplace mantel. The curtains in the front window were pulled closed. The door to the hallway was closed and curtained.

There was definite evidence of religious gatherings here, but it all seemed pretty normal. No sign of anything that should frighten Virginia or Mrs. Donato. Nothing dangerous. Jamie had mentioned a rumor about Paul selling weapons. Had I really thought there might be cases of guns stacked against the walls, boxes of grenades in the living room?

A little relieved, I looked at my watch: 9:10. I just had time to go upstairs. I had told myself I would be in the house for no more than half an hour.

I took another deep breath and headed into the hallway. Being in the light made me feel nervous and exposed. Quickly, I went up the stairs, not touching the handrail.

I stood in the hallway of the second floor. The floor plan seemed identical to the one in my own home. One open door showed me a small bathroom. When I opened the door to the hall closet, I saw towels and linens stacked neatly on the papered shelves. A half-used package of toilet paper rolls sat on the floor under the bottom shelf.

I opened the door to the small rear bedroom and stepped inside. The curtains made the room almost pitch black. I went over to the window and pushed them aside a bit, just to let in more light. With a start, I recognized the Donatos' house across the yard. Of course. And then I noticed Virginia. She was in her bedroom, and it was lit up against the dark sky, and it glowed, light pouring out of it. I shrank back, worried she might see me trespassing, but then remembered that I would be invisible; this room wasn't lit from within. I stared at her. I couldn't help it. She seemed to be sitting on her bed, speaking, gesturing to someone, maybe someone on the other side of the room, but I couldn't see anyone but her. She didn't move. Then she stood, and I couldn't see her face, couldn't tell if she was happy or sad, angry or delighted. She lifted her chin a little, tilted it, as if she might be laughing, and she clasped her hands together in front of her, like she might lift them to pray, or sing, or prevent them from trembling. I could have gazed at her all night. Something calm and serene entered into me as I looked at her from afar.

But then the voice inside me warned, *Hurry*.

I looked around the room. It was set up like a small office. There was a desk with a computer on it, a chair and a small filing cabinet against one wall, a bookcase against another. I peered closely at the spines of some of the books. Most were about religious subjects. There were several about finances, stocks and bonds, and stacked on one shelf was a pile of financial ledgers and binders.

I went to the desk, picked up some papers randomly and brought them back to catch the light near the window. Some were bills — an electrical bill, a telephone bill. One was a typed letter from a church in Illinios — something about a prayer meeting. There were several others that seemed like junk mail. I returned them to the desk and opened the drawers. Pens, paper clips, blank paper, blank invoice pads ... In the bottom drawer were several scratch pads and a stack of paper. I carried them all quickly to the window.

I flipped through the papers. They were photocopied pages, all copies of the same thing. On the top was a sticky with this year's date on it:

Youth Camp

Your teen has been invited to attend three 2-day leadership training programs this fall. We will travel to the site by small bus. Accommodation is 8-person cabins with bunk beds. Meals provided.

Campers will be involved in group activities that will help them find a deeper relationship with their faith and initiate them into leadership roles.

Dates:

Friday, August 28, to Sunday, August 30

Friday, September 11, to Sunday, September 13

Friday, September 25, to Sunday, September 27

Fees: $450
(includes 3 sessions, bus, food and accommodation)

Leader: Paul Donato

Elders: Frank Camdon, Teresa Donato, Janie Parke

Seemed pretty ordinary, pretty normal.

I quickly glanced at the scratch pads. The three on top were unused. The one on the bottom of the stack had half its pages ripped out. The remaining pages were covered in hand-written notes. Each one began with a date, again all from this year. They seemed like notes jotted down for a speech or a sermon.

Select group. Urgent appeal. God tells us to participate.

Standing and waiting is how some serve. Do you want to serve in this way, or TAKE ACTION?

God says It will come. The signs are all around us. But these occurrences are a burden to God. They do come from him; signs. God can = wrath. Impatience with us. How it must pain him to inflict us in this way ... needs our help. We can speed the End Days. Violence to serve a purpose of purity and justice.

I checked the date: March of this year.

I flipped the page. There was another: May 12. My eyes raced across the page, reading the handwriting.

It will take 8 brave souls. Courage. Which of you will serve?

Gathered you here because have seen signs within you of purpose and strength. Resolve. Willing to break away and do what is right.

Our congregation is already showing independence. Who can offer more?

Tell no one ...

And another: June 12.

Elite group.

Violence is not outside God's plan. E.g.s: floods, hurricanes,

*war, terrorist acts ... I believe. I will lead. Follow my
example.*

*We will be discreet because the laws of this country are
not always the same as God's laws. What this country
permits does not always coincide with what God permits.
Yes to risk, because it is for God. Yes to pain, because it is
for God. Yes to sacrifice ...*

We have obtained the means. Now, the method —

Training must begin. Who will commit ...?

A dreadful fear had entered me. I looked at the words. Did
someone — Paul — really say these words? Were these real
ideas? Had he actually formed a group that was planning
some horrible event? My hands began to sweat. I looked at
the date again. June. It was September now.

I flipped to the next page of the pad. Nothing.

I turned back to the notes and skimmed them again
quickly, my heart pounding. Phrases jumped out at me:

TAKE ACTION.

We can speed the End Days ...

Violence is not outside God's plan ...

What did it mean? Could it mean what it looked like, that
Paul was planning a violent act, because he thought God
wanted it?

This was truly crazy. He couldn't possibly be actually
suggesting this to other people living in this country, in this
community, other church members, some of them family.
No one would be nuts enough to go along with this for a
minute.

Quickly, I flipped through the stack of photocopies again, just to make sure I hadn't missed anything. I had. There was one loose paper at the bottom. On it was a list of names neatly handprinted in ink. I counted. There were fifteen names, all male. Each had an age in brackets beside it. Most were between seventeen and nineteen. Seven of the names had been crossed out.

Who will commit?

It wasn't possible. These couldn't be actual people thinking about breaking laws, hurting innocent people for some theoretical outcome? It just couldn't be.

I swallowed hard, my mind racing. What should I do? Pocket the page? But what if Paul discovered it gone? Try to remember all the names. Maybe it would help to try to find these guys, speak to them. But even if I could remember them all, how could I find out who they were? They were only first names with initials for last names. I was getting scared. I was feeling panicky. I didn't know what to do, there was no one to ask and time was running out.

All of a sudden, the obvious answer hit me. Was I losing my mind? I grabbed a pen and a scrap of paper and hurriedly copied down the names. Feeling time ticking past, I only recorded the ones that hadn't been crossed out.

I shoved the list in my pocket and glanced at my watch. It was 9:20. I had to leave soon. No, I had to leave now. I wouldn't even let my mind travel to where I was standing upstairs in this house, alone, and what would happen if Paul Donato and his friends in their suits walked in and found me.

I eyed the pad with Paul's jotted notes. Take it, or leave it? Take it, or leave it? My mind was spinning.

Calm down, I told myself. *Think about it.* Okay, take the notes and I would have proof, but proof of what? Proof that someone had written down some notes about what he might or might not have wanted to say, about what he might or might not have actually said, and who was that someone, anyway? This wasn't proof of much. And if I took them, and Paul discovered them missing ...

Okay, I would leave the notes. I wanted out of here.

I shoved all the pages back in the bottom drawer of the computer desk, breathing hard, then hurried to the top of the stairs. Panicking now, terrified, wanting *out*, I pounded down the stairs and raced into the basement. Hearing the *click* of a key in the lock of the front door, I practically threw myself down the basement stairs into the darkness. *Oh, why couldn't I fly?* Hands out, walking blindly, flailing, I scrambled from the stairs to the window. Knowing footsteps would be coming, pounding down the steps after me, telling myself that never, never, *never* would I do anything as crazy as this *ever* again, I found the window ledge. But how was I going to get out? There was no way I could reach the window!

Again, panic rushed up my throat and into my mouth, and I could taste it, because how was I going to get out? I had nothing to stand on, no way of climbing *out*. I hadn't even thought of this ahead of time. *How stupid could I be? What was I going to do NOW?!*

I looked around, but it was dark, and I couldn't see anything. Frantically, I made my way along the wall, stumbling, praying that I'd come across something I could stand on, and *Thank God!* I found the stack of wooden boxes I'd seen earlier. I tried to pick one up. It was too heavy. I dragged it across the floor, and it didn't make too much noise. Finally, it was below the window. But when I jumped up on it, I couldn't reach the ledge. It wasn't high enough. *Now what?!* I tilted it up onto its side, pushing hard, shoving. Whatever was inside shifted, clanged like metal against metal, and through the slats in the box I saw a silvery gleaming. My stomach lurched at what I suspected, but I couldn't stop and check. I had to get *out!* I stepped up onto the box, and now I could grab the ledge. The window was still open. So I pushed off with my feet and pulled up with my hands, and *bang!* the box fell over, but I was *up*. My forearms were on the ledge and then my elbows, and I scrabbled forward, twisting my upper body, the edge of the window scraping along my back.

And then I was out, panting, on my hands and knees. I was out and safe.

Gulping in the night air, I pulled at the window, awkwardly using the pocketknife to pry it forward, making it flush to the frame. With luck, no one would notice it had been vandalized.

I stood up. Done.

Then suddenly I had a sickening realization. Anyone going into the basement would know someone had come in. They would see the box on its side by the window. They would know it had been moved there.

I needed to get out of here. Now.

There was no way they would know *I* had moved the box, was there?

I moved down the driveway between the houses, flattening myself against the wall, looking at the front door to see if whoever had arrived was inside and checking to see that no one else was coming up the walkway or passing by on the street. All clear. I walked quickly out to the sidewalk.

I turned once, looking back over my shoulder at the house. The hall light and porch light were on. The light in the living room was on. And as I looked, a light went on in one of the rooms upstairs.

I wanted to run. I wanted to run home so badly. But that might have looked suspicious.

Instead, tears welling up in my eyes, heart pounding, I put my head down and forced myself to walk.

That night, the way home seemed incredibly long. I was scared. I was terrified. And one thing I knew for certain: this nightmare was not anywhere close to being over.

✟✟✟

*S*uddenly *she knew.*

It was him. He had done it.

He had done this to prove something to her.

Fear gripped her, shocked her. An angel had come to her! He had offered her a gift and given her a choice! He had been casual, polite, almost deferential. But when he thought for one second that she was questioning him, questioning his authority, he had seized her mother and shaken her until her heart hesitated. An angel had come to her, and he wasn't sweet and kind and understanding and gentle. He was fierce and demanding and potent and capable of ...

"You didn't need to do that."

Could she say that to him? Did she dare? Her chest felt constricted, as if there were a band around it making it difficult for her to breathe. She didn't think she should leave the house to go to the hospital. What if he came back, and she wasn't there? What more might he do before he understood that it wasn't necessary?

When would he come back? She wanted Ivy to be there. She wanted her to be a witness to this story, to this miracle. She had tried to plan it. She thought she could plan it, that she could conjure him, call him forth.

But she had not expected this display of his wrath. She had known he could do pretty much anything. Of course she would have imagined he could hurt people, including her, including her mother. She had known without him telling her. He had not needed to do it, though. She thought she was transparent to him, that everything she thought or felt was absorbed by him, understood by him. She had thought he would know of her belief. But she had been wrong. He had misunderstood. He had thought she doubted, but she didn't.

So there was no need for this. He could leave her mother out of this.

For a moment, she faltered. Because suddenly she wondered whether she could tell her mother. For if Mama knew this, if she knew her Ginnie had been chosen, she might sit up and her heart might heal at the miracle of what was being offered to her daughter, despite what Gabriel had done to her. She might think that all would be well, that Paul could rest because little Ginnie had been offered a way to save them all, her family and everyone else, because God had chosen to send another Child to redeem them, to walk the earth and live among men and perhaps save the world in this way.

The thought of confiding in Mama came, rebellious; and then, subdued, it went, because she feared it would anger Gabriel. If Gabriel had chosen to damage her mother, and she reached past the angel, glided right into the angel, through him, and out the other side to bring relief and healing to her mother, Gabriel would not like that. And she was not certain what he might choose to do then.

She shuddered. She would show him that she was his: obedient, willing. He could ask her to have God's child, and she would. He could ask her to rise, to walk, to fly, and she would do it, would try it. For Gabriel. Because doing it for Gabriel was doing it for Paul, for her mother, for her family. For Gabriel, she would do anything.

Chapter Seventeen

I sat on my bed, biting my nails. I rocked back and forth.

Over and over, I replayed the sound of the clanging in the wooden box in the church basement, the sight of the gleaming metal. Each time, I knew they were weapons. Maybe guns. Even thinking the words in my head seemed crazy, but I'd just broken into someone's house — me! — so anything seemed possible right then.

The phrases in Paul's notes were also running repeatedly through my mind.

TAKE ACTION.

Violence to serve a purpose of purity and justice.

... the laws of this country are not always the same as God's laws.

Anna Maria had said something about "the beginning of sorrows." And her list: so many wars around the world, terrorist attacks, natural disasters, global warming, pandemics. She had said these events seemed bad but they weren't because they were leading to something good. The end. Everyone going to heaven. Virginia had explained it this way too.

It was so glaringly obvious. It was all about the End Days.

Paul was planning something bad, something really bad, so that the good end might come more quickly. This was the "purpose of purity and justice."

His notes had mentioned something about speeding up the process, and he had weapons, boxes of them.

I knew it was impossible. I also knew it was true.

Virginia's words floated into my mind. She'd said that

she believed that the bad things being planned were going against what God wanted for the world. That she had a chance to do something about that. That it could change everything. She had to be talking about her angel and the baby. Somehow she'd connected these to Paul's plans. But how? And didn't going against Paul make things dangerous for her?

I was exhausted. I had to get ready for bed. I put on my pajamas and brushed my teeth. But of course I couldn't sleep.

I had to figure it out. All of it. I had to figure out exactly what Paul was planning and also try to protect Virginia.

I went back to my desk and wrote down everything I could remember reading in Paul's office. I reread each item. I stared at the words: *sorrow, action, violence, risk, sacrifice, 8 brave souls.*

I pulled out the list of names I'd copied and read it once, twice. Who were these people? Teenagers, obviously, but how had they become involved with Paul? And why?

I knew the words had to form a trail, one connecting to the other, pointing to an answer.

Again I looked at the dramatic, frightening words and phrases. Again I looked at the list of names. And then it hit me: the youth camp. I'd forgotten the youth camp. And with a thud, deep in my stomach, I was certain. The camp was a front for something illegal. At the camp, they had to be training young people to do dangerous and violent things. To threaten, or shoot, or bomb.

With a shiver, I quickly turned off my light and crawled into bed, pulling the covers up to my chin. Before tonight, I wouldn't have believed it, even though I'd heard news stories about secret camps where terrorists were trained to attack public places. But here? So close to my own house? It shouldn't be possible. It shouldn't be remotely possible that my neighbor, a young man brought up in our peaceful and democratic society, raised by loving and kind parents, was planning and plotting, with the help of others, a violent event of some kind. How had this happened here, almost next door to me? And what was I going to do about it?

Focus on the youth camp, I told myself. Try to remember everything I could about them. Okay, the dates. When were the camps being held?

I couldn't remember. *Concentrate.* What dates had been on the paper? I slammed my fists on my mattress. I should have brought back one of those notices. The dates were important. The event wouldn't occur before the last date on that list.

I wracked my brain. I was fairly sure there had been three weekend camps and they had been scheduled to fall over a two-month period. Had it listed August and September? Or September and October?

It was the middle of September now, so whichever one it was, there might still be time for me to do something. But what? Who could I speak to? Who could I turn to? I had no proof, nothing but strong suspicion and rumors to go on, and how could I confess that I'd reached my conclusions by breaking and entering?

I finally fell asleep, but not for long. Several times throughout the night I woke, struggled up from a dark, frightening place, felt relief, remembered the reality, and descended again into a more frightening sense of foreboding.

When morning finally came, I dragged myself awake, my sheets wet with sweat.

I lay there, feeling drugged with fatigue. Sunlight poured in the window. Uncomfortable dream images of cellar windows and black feathers sticking to wet wounds faded and were replaced with a recollection of the even worse conclusions I'd reached before climbing into bed. I flung off my sheet, rolled over onto my side and bunched up my pillow under my head.

Slowly, I opened my eyes, looked out at the blue sky. Staring at the world, I tested my theory again, repeated to myself my suspicions, played them out against the backdrop of autumn leaves, white puffy clouds and the cawing of crows. In the light of day, my conclusion seemed less solid, less possible, and I felt a vague sense of relief. Maybe there was no danger. Maybe I wouldn't have to do anything at all.

Or maybe I did have to do something. Maybe I had to get more proof, dig deeper.

A feeling of hopelessness surged over me. There was still no one for me to turn to. I rolled onto my back and stared at the ceiling. Definitely not the police. There was nothing to show, nothing I really knew. They would laugh and then probably arrest me.

Could I speak to Virginia? She would likely believe me. In fact, she might even know more than me about Paul's secrets, but I also remembered the hunted look on her face after she'd begun to confide in me about Paul, how she had begged me not to tell anyone else. Talking to her about Paul now, with her mother in the hospital and the wings of her angel even more firmly wrapped around her mind might just tip her over the edge. No, I wouldn't let this, let Paul, hurt Virginia even more. There had to be another way.

Could I go to Joe? An image of him bloomed in front of me. I lingered on it for a moment, then let it fade. No. Part of me longed to. A bigger part of me knew it was impossible. Knew it would be too embarrassing. That he might not even remember who I was. That I wouldn't have the guts to explain.

I pulled myself out of bed. It was far later than I'd thought. Eight a.m. It was hot in here; the sunshine searing the air, flooding my room.

I showered, dressed and began to sweat again. I brushed my hair, sitting in front of the mirror at my desk.

There was no one but me. No one to count on but myself. I sat and stared at the girl in the mirror. Who was she, after all? Could she find out what tragedy was being planned by a man who thought he was saving the world?

The girl in the mirror looked back at me, her eyes wide. Could she help her friend find her way back from the sweetness of being chosen by God to serve him?

I looked closely at the girl. I thought I knew her. She was the girl who couldn't persuade her own mother to give up drinking and really be with her family, live with them and love them. She was the girl who could see tragedy everywhere — and felt helpless to change anything.

I closed my eyes wearily. It was too much. The world should not be such a difficult place. The world should not be depending on me, a kid. Who could *I* depend on? Who would help *me*? Why wouldn't an angel come and stand over my shoulder, appear in the mirror behind me, point at me and say, *I'll tell you. This is what you must do. Listen to me. I have the answers.*

I longed for it.

Come to me, Gabriel, I thought. *Come to me.*

A breeze stirred, and my curtains billowed.

I leaned back in my chair, my eyes still closed. And for a moment, resting there, wanting more than anything to open my eyes and see something fantastic and all-powerful, something that could look after me, all this, and everything else that was beyond me, I could understand how Virginia might allow herself to sink into a belief that was so impossible.

Part Four

The Choosing

Chapter Eighteen

She saw something out of the corner of her eye, something moving, something in the air outside.

Was it him? Was he coming back?

She went to the window and looked out. She wanted him to come.

"What else do you want me to do?" she could say. "I'll do this. I'll have the baby. I'll do anything. I believe you. I believe everything you say. I know how powerful you are."

She would do what he asked, and the bad thing that had happened to her mother would be over, and none of the other bad things would happen.

✛✛✛

I sat in history class that morning totally distracted. I had brought to school the list of boys' names that I had copied down. The first thing I had to do was find out if any of them went to this school. It was possible, even likely. They might have ended up coming to Paul's church because they lived in the area.

But how could I find this out without attracting any attention to myself — or to them? If they were doing something subversive, even something illegal, they wouldn't want anyone nosing around, researching them. I had to be careful.

By second period, I'd had a brain wave. If any of the boys were in grade eleven or twelve this year, they'd be in last year's yearbook. If they were older, they'd be in earlier year-books. When the bell rang for lunch, I headed straight to the library. I asked the librarian, Mr. Frenway, for help, and he pointed me toward a shelf at the back without looking up from his newspaper.

All the yearbooks were there in a row. They went back about twenty years. I started with the most recent one, last year's. All the students were arranged by grade, alphabetically by last name. I started with the grade elevens. Nothing. Then I looked through the grade twelves. Bingo. There was one Cameron H — Cameron Handler. I stared at his photo. He was blond and goofy looking and making the peace sign.

How could I be sure this was the guy I was looking for? I read the comment under his photo.

Revelation 22:10.

A passage from the Bible. I was on the right track. I jotted it down, along with Cameron's last name.

I continued on, looking for Taylor P. I found two grade twelve students with that name: one a girl, Taylor Prentice, and one a boy, Taylor Packham. Under Packham's photo was *Ezekiel 3:17–19.*

I shivered. It had to be him. I wrote down Taylor's name, as well as the Biblical reference.

I skimmed through the next several yearbooks to see if I could match the other names on my list, but had no luck.

Okay, so what now? Cameron and Taylor had graduated last year. That meant they were probably eighteen or so. If they were planning on attending Paul's weekends away, they must either be still living in the city, or be traveling in and out. Maybe they were going to college locally. Maybe they were even living at home. I wondered how I could find out. At least I knew their last names now.

Maybe looking up and reading the actual biblical passages would help me in some way. I decided to find them on one of the library computers. But when I glanced around the room, all the computers were being used. I'd have to check on my own computer at home. Should I go now and do it? If I left now, I'd only miss part of my first afternoon class. There wasn't any real rush, except that I so desperately wanted to know what was going on and what it might have to do with Virginia.

Frozen with indecision, I was trying to make up my mind when something weird happened. Joe stepped into the library. Joe, Virginia's brother. He stood just inside the door, looking around. For a split second, I had the crazy, wonderful idea that maybe he was looking for me.

And then he saw me, and smiled, and my heart tumbled. But his eyes roamed around a little more, still searching, and of course I knew he wasn't looking for me. Why would he be? Still, it was a strange coincidence that he was here when his family and his sister were so much on my mind, so I gathered up my bag and walked toward him. He waited for me, holding the door open, and we both stepped out into the hallway together.

"Hey, Ivy," he said.

"Hi," I responded.

He smiled again.

"Joe, I'm sorry about your mom. How is she?" I asked.

"She's still in the hospital. She's doing okay," he said with difficulty, but meeting my eyes. "Thanks."

I liked that Joe wasn't embarrassed about being seen with a grade nine kid. I liked that he knew me, that he had held the door open for me, that he was standing here with me right now. I wanted to reach up and touch his hair. I wanted to lean into him, rest against him, feel his arms around me. The feelings swept over me. Everything would be all right if I could just hold his hand and sit with him for a while.

It wasn't possible, of course. It was never going to happen.

I knew that. And yet there it was. My longing created it, yearned for it, like an image of home or heaven, perfect and unobtainable.

The moment passed, and before the brief silence could turn into something awkward, I blurted out hurriedly, "Joe, can I ask you something?"

"Sure," he agreed easily. His eyes were scanning the hallway behind me, still looking for his girlfriend, I guess.

"Do you know these passages in the Bible?" I handed him the slip of paper. "Do you know what they're about?"

He glanced at it, then looked hard at me. "Why?" Now he was tense, his voice tight. "Why do you want to know?"

"Long story," I said. Suddenly I was uncomfortable. What did the references mean? Why did he seem disturbed by them? I had a moment of doubt. Maybe he was involved, too. I had thought I might confide in him, tell him the whole thing, my suspicions, but maybe he already knew what was going on with Paul. Maybe I had to be careful of saying too much to him. "Hey, forget it," I said. I reached out to take back the piece of paper, but he pulled his hand away, held it out of reach.

"No, wait a minute," Joe said slowly. "It's okay. I do know what these are. But why do you want to know? Where did you get these?"

I shrugged. "It's not important," I lied. "Look, can I have that back? I've got to get going." I felt queasy and scared. I just wanted to go.

I reached out again for the paper, but again he moved his arm away, held the paper high out of reach. "Hey, Ivy. You asked. Now let me tell you. Not everyone would be able to help you with this, but you've come to the right person." There was now a strange mocking tone to his voice. "I grew up memorizing the whole Bible, book, chapter, and verse. It became my special talent. It was a way for me to look like

I was participating in the whole church thing. It kind of let me fit in with the rest of my family, get by under the radar. And see how far it's got me? It's been incredibly useful." He grinned, joking. "It's made me into a real babe magnet." I smiled. "Anyway, that's what these are. Revelation and Ezekiel are the names of books in the Bible. The first numbers — twenty-two and three — are the chapters in the book, and the following numbers are the verses."

I nodded. I knew that. "But what are these particular verses about? Do you know?"

Abruptly, I stepped back out of the way of a tall grade eleven student who came bustling out of the library, head down, jamming papers into his knapsack.

And then Joe wasn't smiling anymore. "They're both pretty dark, actually. They're about the Apocalypse. Do you know what that is?"

"Sort of."

"Well, *apocalypse* actually means 'revelation.' There's this idea in Revelation that there's an ongoing fight between God and some evil force. Some people call it the Antichrist; some call it Satan, the angel that God has thrown out of heaven." He shrugged. "I can't quote directly from the book of Revelation anymore, but basically it's supposedly written by John, who was told by an angel of God what will happen on earth in the future. The book of Revelation goes on to describe how the earth will end after a period of horrible disasters and calamities, and how everyone will rise from the dead and be judged by God. There's a final battle, the battle of Armageddon, where the forces of evil are overcome by the powers of good. I *do* know that this verse of Revelation warns that 'the time is at hand.' Meaning the end of the world is going to be soon ..." Joe looked at me. "Ivy ..."

"And what's the Ezekiel one about?" I insisted. There

was more activity in the hallway now. People had finished their lunches, and some were heading back to their lockers. Someone down the hall broke into gales of loud laughing.

"I think those passages are the bit about the watchman. It's God telling the people that they should have a watchman who keeps an eye out for evil coming and then warns the people. If the people hear the warning and don't pay attention, whatever happens is their own fault, basically. But if they do listen to the warning, they'll be saved. And if the watchman doesn't sound the warning, and the people are slain or die, then their blood is on the hands of the watchman, before God. And then God says to Ezekiel, you're the watchman, buddy."

I swallowed hard. The word *watchman* spooked me. I had this sudden vision of Paul, dressed in black, with a sweeping cape, standing high in a tower, looking out over the darkened land with a trumpet in one hand and a sword in the other. He was the watchman. It was him! But not only that, he was also the guy planning the horrors that were coming. He was the guy brainwashing Cameron and Taylor and the others, arming them and setting them up.

Joe was still staring at me. "Ivy, what's this about? I want to know."

I hesitated. Joe was being really open with me, but could I trust him? If I told him, and he betrayed me, it could be dangerous for me. And Virginia.

"Ivy," he repeated.

There really wasn't anyone else I could turn to who would care, who might believe me, who might help me. I took a breath, and I took a leap of faith.

"You have to promise you won't tell anyone," I began. Joe shrugged noncommittally, but I kept going, the words coming in a rush. "It's complicated. It's about your brother, Paul, and ... Well, your brother ... I think he's planning something bad, something connected to this idea of the Apocalypse —"

"Wait, wait, wait, Ivy. That's ridiculous," Joe scoffed, interrupting me.

"Joe, just listen. You said you wanted to know —"

But maybe he really didn't. "I know Paul believes in some of this nonsense," he went on. "He calls himself 'the agent of God's plan.' But it doesn't mean *he's* planning anything dangerous. You've got it backward. *He's* the one who keeps proclaiming that bad things are coming, and that after that, all God's people will go to heaven." He forced a grin. "Not sure that includes me, though. Paul is kind of fed up with me because I won't attend his church or do everything he says anymore."

Locker doors were slamming shut. Two boys were walking down the hall, throwing a football back and forth. Joe turned and waved at one of them. "Don't drop it, Morris!" he called.

It felt like we'd been standing here forever. Was lunch period almost over? I knew I wouldn't be able to keep Joe's attention for much longer. "Joe, I'm not sure what you know and what you don't know, but I really think it's happening. Paul's planning something dangerous, and he's doing it secretly. So secretly that you might not have noticed. But Virginia is scared, your mother is scared — Joe, we have to stop him before —"

"Hang on there, Ivy!" Joe interrupted again. He was backing away, his smile fading. "Just slow down a minute. You're making some pretty wild accusations."

"Joe, please don't be blind," I pleaded. "You have to do something. You must have noticed that your whole family is … acting strangely. Your brother and sisters have managed to cocoon Gin, too, and she's telling me bizarre things, impossible things. How can you not see it? You're living there, too!" I hesitated. Should I tell him that she said she'd seen an angel? That she thought she was pregnant? Should I tell him about the papers I'd found at Turner Avenue? Should I reveal that I'd actually broken into the church house?

Joe was shaking his head. "Ivy, this is crazy! Where are you coming up with this stuff? My family is hyper-close. All of us still live at home, for God's sake, even Paul! How unusual is that! And Virginia has always believed in some things that might seem ... unbelievable ... to you and lots of other people. Paul is a control freak, and, yeah, he has this alternative church thing going on. But it doesn't mean there's anything wrong. You can't really —"

"Joe, do you know much about that other church? Do you know what they're up to?" My voice was rising, my tone desperate. "Well, I do. I think I do. Paul has a plan, and he's manipulated some teenagers, members of his church, into being part of it. He's sucked them in somehow. He's filling their heads with all kinds of crazy ideas, and he's been holding meetings, and I think he's even been training them to ..."

"Ivy, stop. I know Paul is forceful and really certain of what he believes ... When you talk to him, and he wants something from you ..." He shook his head again. "Even my girlfriend, Celia, tells me that he's pretty mesmerizing, has these arresting eyes, this pull ... It's as if people don't have a choice. They just feel ... compelled ... to agree with him. It almost seems impossible not to. It's almost easier to do it than not. And that doesn't seem like something God would want, not the God my dad taught me about. That God wants us to have to make difficult choices and be accountable for them."

Joe paused, ran his fingers through his hair. "But I'm the only one in the family that seems to feel that way, me and

Virginia, that is. I watch my mom and Anna Maria, Donna, and Teresa flutter around him, like moths around a candle. I think they just wanted to give in. He's family, and our dad is gone ... I don't know, but it's not for me, and so the best thing to do is stay away from him. And the more you stay away" — he shrugged — "the easier it gets. He can start to seem kinda repulsive in fact."

Joe's voice caught. He looked down.

"So, I don't go near that new church of his, and Virginia tries to stay away, too. Everyone says he's been like a father to her." He shook his head. "Not really. She's polite to him, and he tries to include her in what he's doing, but she just says no." He paused. "Virginia's remarkable, really," he said it almost as if he was just realizing this, "but I guess you probably know that about her, right? She has her own brand of faith, I guess," he said slowly, working it out. "It's not like mine — mine is pretty much by the book — and it's *not* like Paul's."

His attention was caught by something he saw over my shoulder, down the hallway, and his look softened. It was Celia. "Anyway, Ivy, all this is to say that I don't agree with Paul's views, but he means well, and he's living his life for God. He would never do anything that went against God, nothing violent, for sure." His eyes flickered away, toward his girlfriend, and then back to me. "So you may think you heard something or saw something, but you've misunderstood it. Misinterpreted it. Like these Bible verses, for example. They sound pretty ominous. But it depends where you heard them and for what purpose they're being used."

I couldn't stand it anymore. "Joe, I think he's teaching them to use weapons!" I blurted out. "I think Paul is going to persuade some of these guys to do something violent."

Joe's grin disappeared. His dark eyes narrowed. "Ivy ..."

I stopped abruptly. I'd gone too far, criticized his brother too much.

Joe shifted his knapsack on his shoulder, shrugged it into a different position, still without speaking.

"Joe ..." I wanted to take it all back. *Now.*

I stared at him, and it struck me for the first time that he and Paul shared the same high cheekbones, the same jawline.

What was he thinking?

"Ivy, did you actually see any weapons?"

I hesitated. "Well, no, I didn't actually *see* them, but —"

"So leave it alone then, Ivy. I'm sure nothing dangerous is happening, and the best advice I have for you is stay away. Stay away from him. Stay away from the house. Sure, hang out with Virginia, but don't believe everything she tells you either, about Paul or ... reality." He gave a short unhappy laugh, and then he looked at Celia again, coming behind me, and his face broke into a wide smile.

My time was up.

"Joe," I put my hand on his arm, "please don't mention this to anyone in your family." He glanced at me. Distracted, moving past me, he didn't answer.

"Joe," I said insistently.

"Okay," he replied nonchalantly, and then he was gone.

✝✝✝

"I'm back," he said, and she almost wept. She bowed her head so he would not see her eyes. Her knees trembling, she sank into a chair, wanting to go to him, to embrace him, but it seemed she was unable to stand.

He stood leaning against the window ledge, like before. His arms were folded. He looked like he had been there for ages, and like he might stay there always.

She had been trying to picture him in her mind, all the time he was gone. She had come up with an image, but it had been nothing like this. And yet he was the same now as he had been. She tried to imprint him on her eyes. She wanted to be able to remember him just as he was. But every time her mind began to gather these thoughts, they were overwhelmed by his presence. All she needed to know about him was right in front of her, was what she already knew.

Chapter Nineteen

At first, I thought maybe it was the crows. They came into my dream, cawing, squawking. Then gradually their noise faded, and I realized it was still early, only 10:00 p.m., and I'd fallen asleep at my desk. I looked out the window at the tall trees in my backyard. Were the crows there tonight? Were they sleeping, plotting, planning the future of the world?

Yawning, I stretched. Then, through the open window, I heard car doors slamming outside on the street. Curiosity drew me downstairs to look out the living-room windows. I saw a car pulled up in front of the Donatos' house. One person was at the trunk, opening it and unfolding a wheelchair. The other one — was it Teresa? — was opening the rear passenger door.

The front door of the Donato house opened, and two more figures came out, hurrying. Now they were helping, too, reaching into the backseat of the car, and out came Mrs. Donato, hands first, then arms stretched up, like they were lifting to heaven. Then her head and upper body emerged, and she was being guided, lifted, elbows bent now and being hoisted through the air and into the wheelchair. Now she was being propelled across the sidewalk and between the high hedges in front of her home.

I watched as she was carried up the stairs, one step at a time, and then inside she went, surrounded by helping hands, and the door closed behind her, and the porch light, moments later, went out. Evening's stillness fell again.

✛✛✛

"My mother is back," she told him, thanking him, dissolving with gratitude.

He nodded. "Yes."

*She waited, because now he had proved himself to her,
though he needn't have, proved his strength, proved what
he was capable of.*

"I'll do it," she said. "I would do anything."

*He nodded, "All right, then," and his anger was absent.
There was nothing between them but air.*

✝✝✝

In the morning, first thing, I phoned the Donatos' to speak
to Virginia. When I heard the male voice, something froze in
me. I couldn't speak. It wasn't Joe. I knew it had to be Paul.

"Hello? Hello?" he repeated, impatiently.

In my mind, I had made him into so many things, all of
them horrific, all of them beyond understanding. He was
capable of anything, of every violent act, of every evil.
His voice, mild and low in my ear, was alarming in its
humanness.

For a crazy moment, I considered asking him what was
going on, simply confronting him with my suspicions.
Then, instead, I managed to ask for Virginia.

There was a heartbeat of a pause.

I was certain he wouldn't recognize my voice. I had been
a child when we'd last spoken. But how many friends ever
called Virginia? Maybe he would know right away that it
was me, Ivy, the child he had frightened away from ever
setting foot in a church again. I hoped not. I felt irrationally
panicked, my courage shriveling inside me. Had Paul seen
me outside the Turner Avenue house? Had he noticed that
his papers had been disturbed? Had he checked for finger-
prints, found mine, chosen me now as a target to hurt?

"She's still asleep," said Paul.

I summoned my courage and managed to ask whether his mother was all right.

The doctors had felt she was well enough to be discharged, he told me. She would be visited by a nurse today and every day this week. In a week, she would return to see the hospital cardiologist. Her heart, for the moment, seemed fine.

I wanted to ask him to tell Virginia that I had called, but then I'd have to say my name, and I didn't want him to know who I was. So I just said thanks and hung up.

And then I did something that surprised me. I went and found my mother, and she wasn't drinking. She was reading a book, with a smile on her face, and I remembered that she had read to me every night when I was little. She had sat me on her lap and read aloud to me, had looked into my eyes to see if I was enjoying it, had happily agreed when I'd begged her to read the same favorite book over and over and over again.

I watched her for a moment, her face alight, her eyes scanning the words, and as she turned the page, I spoke, and she looked up, and her face softened when she saw me. I told her that Maria Donato had come home last night from the hospital and that her heart, for the moment, seemed fine.

"I'm so relieved," she said. And I think she meant it.

I was almost out the door when she spoke again. "Ivy, dear. You're a good girl." At least I think that's what she said, but I didn't stop. I pretended not to hear, and I carried on up to my room.

"*I*'m afraid," she confessed.

"I know," he said.

Three months ago, she had gone to the church. First, there had been a phone call for Anna Maria at home one evening. Virginia had answered. "She's not here," she told the caller.

"Please find her. It's urgent," the voice had insisted.

She had hesitated. "Just a minute, please."

Then she went out the back door, across the backyard, through the gate and into the yard of the property behind, and directly in the back door of that house, where she was now forbidden to enter because either they were protecting themselves or her, she couldn't know for certain. As she entered, putting her hand out so the screen didn't slam behind her, about to call out to Anna Maria, she heard Paul's raised voice.

It was a commanding tone.

It caught at her, forced her to halt, to listen. The power of it was irresistible.

Paul was crying out: "You are the chosen ones. Yes, it is you. And I am proud, and all the people will be proud. Not just in this country, not just in North America, but all the people, everywhere and forevermore. You are the Elite."

She was unable to step forward, unable to leave, and instead she let time stand still, the door against her palm, her body flexed, still entering. She didn't want to know or become a place where this knowledge resided, and yet something in his voice tapped into something eternal in her, warned her, sickened her. So, obeying this impulse, which might have been self-preservation or something more vast, she hovered, on the brink, and she heard him say, "You, young warriors, you will need to learn how to shoot rifles and how to throw grenades. The training will begin soon, in three two-day sessions. We have chosen targets. They are representatives. They are not bad or evil. They are simply sacrifices. They will die, but they will die for everyone to bring the End Days soon. They — and you — are God's instruments. It is what God wants."

And she heard that, and she knew she had heard enough, and she stepped forward, plunged over the edge, knowing that forward or back, either way dropped her over the edge. She had heard, and the knowledge was hers, and she had tipped into the ocean of responsibility. Paul had tried to show her the way to where she might agree with him, to where she might admire his crusade. He knew he was right. He was certain. He had no doubt. But she recoiled from the lie that God would welcome pain and violence to further his ends, the End. It was beyond thought. Her faith flooded through her veins, guiding her. Now the question was only would she fall forever, would she drown, or would she find a way to rise, in the nick of time, and recover from certain never-ending blackness?

Chapter Twenty

I had strange dreams that night. When I woke up on Saturday morning, staring at the ceiling from my bed, I remembered crows flying through my dreams. They were white, and they looked at me and laughed, a hoarse coughing sound. Then suddenly, I heard them again. How could that be? Maybe I wasn't awake, this waking only really a part of my dream. I felt dizzy, not knowing. I blinked, pressed my palms down against my bedsheets, alarmed at the idea that there was more than one place to be, and that it might not always be obvious which was which.

The moment stretched, spun and settled. Now I knew for certain that I was awake.

Or is it possible to be certain you are awake and be fooled, be in some other place?

I heard the crows again and knew that they were in my backyard, that if I got up, went to the window, leaned on the sill, I would see them vivid black against waving green. I knew that if I leaned farther out, and fell, headfirst, nightgown ballooning, there would be no switching of scene, no dream rescue, no opening my arms, shifting my weight, lifting my shoulders and flying. Undreamlike, I would plummet, dense bones, featherless and sheer weight. It wasn't far, but underneath was pavement where I might splatter; my head cracking open egglike, or, depending on the angle, I might get hooked in the branches of one of the small trees beneath and sprawl, dangle, brought up short and broken.

All that weekend, I did my homework and my studying. I thought about Virginia endlessly. I puzzled over what I'd found in the church house. I babysat at the Hendricks on Saturday night. I ran.

By Sunday night, I couldn't stand it anymore. I knew I

had to do something. I had to keep trying to put the pieces together.

I thought I might be able to find out something more about Cameron or Taylor by looking them up on Facebook. There was no way I wanted to risk trying to contact them directly online — I wouldn't be able to do it anonymously, and I sure didn't want them knowing who I was — but maybe I could access their profiles. But when I typed in their names and found them, all I could view was their photos.

The only other thing I could think of was to try to talk to one of the boys, maybe indirectly somehow. Maybe I was completely wrong about them. Maybe I was completely wrong about everything. But I had to find out.

On Monday morning, I went into the school office. I smiled at the secretary and lied through my teeth. "Hi, Ms. Singh. I'm trying to get in touch with Cameron Handler and Taylor Packham. They're graduates from last year. Maybe you remember them?"

"Yes, I do," she said. She began to frown.

"Well, I'm wondering if you'd have their current phone numbers and addresses?"

"I'd have their contact information as of last year, when they were students here. But I can't release that information to just anyone. Why do you need to get in touch with them?" Ms. Singh asked, tapping her pencil.

I swallowed. I tried to look forlorn instead of just plain scared. "A friend of our family — a friend of my father's, actually — used to teach them in elementary school. He's very ill, and there are a few of his old students that he'd like to get in touch with ... before it's too late."

She was looking skeptical. Maybe I'd gone a little too far.

"And Cameron and Taylor are two of these students?" she said disbelievingly.

I tried to guess what was causing her response. "Well, he didn't think they were terrific students ..." I paused, waiting for her reaction. She nodded. Yes, I was on the right track. "But he really worked hard with them and thought they had great potential. He just wanted to find out what had happened to them, really."

Ms. Singh was shaking her head, now. "Well, I'm afraid your father's friend would be very disappointed. Cameron didn't graduate. He has a few grade twelve courses still left to do in order to complete his high school degree. That in and of itself isn't such a terrible thing. It's just that his attitude is ..." She caught herself. I guess she wasn't supposed to be telling me all this.

"And Taylor?" I asked.

"He did graduate," she said. "But ..."

Another student came into the office. When she spoke to me again, it was more formally. "I can provide your father's friend with their phone numbers if he wishes to call himself for them."

"But he's too sick ..." I began to protest.

"Then I suggest you get your father to call or send a note," she said, firmly.

I felt like I was turning into a criminal. The next day, I came to school with a fake note from my father, asking for the information. I'd forged his signature.

The secretary didn't inspect it very closely. She went into the back room and looked through some files. I soon had the addresses and phone numbers of both the boys. I stuck the paper in the back pocket of my jeans. It felt like it was burning a hole in them. What was I going to do with this information? I had lied to get it. Now what was I going to do with it? Just knock on their doors and confront them? Ask them what was going on? What horrible violent act they were planning?

At the end of the day, after the cross-country practice, I hurried home and dropped my books on the front porch. I didn't even go into my house. Joe had suggested one thing — that I "stay away," and it was probably good advice — but I couldn't. I saw Virginia sitting on her front porch, alone, and I walked over.

It was like the very first time. She was sitting in the chair, still, serene. Instead of a summer dress, she was wearing a tunic and tights, but her body was the same, balanced, poised as if on the edge of falling or flying.

I didn't call out as I came up the front walk. I was hoping I could spend a few minutes there alone with her before anyone inside the house realized I was there.

When Virginia saw me, she smiled.

"How are you?" I asked, leaning against the porch railing. "I called the other day, on the weekend. I thought I saw your mother coming home from the hospital. That's really great."

"Yes, I'm so happy," she replied. "I'm so happy she's home." The words sounded sincere, but her voice trembled, as if her relief at having her mother home was tempered by some other kind of emotion. I'm sure it was. Fear, anxiety, worry about her own situation ... Plus, what would it be like to live in a house with Teresa, with Anna Maria ... with Paul? I shuddered.

I sat down on the top step and stretched out my legs. I leaned my head against the porch pillar. I was tired from cross-country practice. Maybe I could just sit here with Virginia for a while without talking about angels or babies or secret churches ... My classes had been okay; my run had been good; the day had gone well so far. Gin's mother was home from the hospital. It should have felt good to sit in the sun with Virginia for a minute and just enjoy together some happiness from these good things, real things.

I would try to let it feel good. We sat in silence, and I did try.

But whatever feelings of contentment I'd brought with me were no match for what hovered in the air around us. Virginia looked pale and weary, as if she hadn't slept well for a few days. Her eyes kept resting on me and then shifting away nervously. The air was full of angel wings and threats of destruction. They swirled around Virginia, and they were not imaginary. They had become as real as the muscles in my legs, the chair, the sun. The angel existed in her mind; a scene of violence existed in mine. And so we had made these things real, she and I. We had helped to give birth to them, to create them. If nowhere else, they existed in us, held by our minds, cradled there and shared between us.

I took a deep breath. "I thought we should talk some more. About your decision."

"Oh, Ivy." Gin shook her head. "You know I've already made my decision."

"Yes, but —"

"And *you* have news," she said, expectantly.

I didn't say anything right away. I wasn't sure what she was talking about. My upcoming race? The trespassing into the Turner Avenue property? *Had* she seen me that night? I frowned.

And just then the front door opened, and Joe came out. That girl was with him, Celia, his girlfriend.

"Hi, Ivy," Joe said casually.

I moved to the side, pulling in my legs, turning my face away. "Hi."

He and Celia walked down the steps and out toward the sidewalk. I didn't watch them. I looked up at Virginia.

"So tell me about your news. You know, the wedding,"

Virginia said, and then I remembered Katie and Russ and felt relief.

"Right," I agreed, stretching out my legs again. "Katie and Russ."

"So when are they getting married? When's the wedding?" Gin's voice was happy and excited, the way people are supposed to sound when they hear about people getting married. My heart swelled a little. She made it seem like such an uncomplicated, anticipated event.

"It's this Saturday. I haven't even picked out what I'm going to wear." I realized this as I said it. I felt a tiny rush of excitement. My sister was getting married!

"Wear where?" Joe said the two words. My head turning to his voice, I saw him smile, and behind him, moving away down the sidewalk, leaving, alone, was the girl.

"Ivy's sister, Katie, is getting married," Gin told him.

"Wow, imagine that." He seemed genuinely pleased. He casually folded his arms and placed one foot on the bottom step. "Go, Katie!"

"This Saturday," I added. I heard pride in my voice, like this was an achievement, like she had accomplished something monumental.

"That's wonderful," said Gin softly.

"Yeah," I agreed, thinking that maybe it could be so, maybe it could be wonderful, after all.

I moved my legs so that I wouldn't block Joe from going back into the house, but he didn't move. He just stood with the sunlight pouring pleasantly down on his head, the warmth welcomed, not overpowering, pouring down on Gin, too, and on me.

"Amazing," Joe said, as if he couldn't imagine it, as if it was a leap of faith that required courage and love and conviction, things that you could be proud of, things that you could dream of, that you could only hope to have yourself one day.

"It's just a small wedding," I told them.

"Yes," Gin nodded. "Mama told me. Katie invited her. Friend of the bride's mother, she said."

I nodded back as if I knew, but I hadn't heard. I was astonished. Katie had done this for Mom. In spite of everything. Katie had found someone who would want to celebrate this with our mother, someone with the decency to agree to come, someone who Mom hadn't shamed or humiliated or alienated, someone with discretion, someone who had always been at the right distance, who hadn't allowed herself to be drawn in or pushed away, a faithful neighbor.

I marveled at my sister's ability to do this for Mom after what Mom had done to her.

"Is your mother coming?" I asked finally. "Is she able to come so soon after being in the hospital?"

"Yes," Gin said. "She says she wouldn't miss it. She was so pleased to be asked." Then she asked in a teasing voice, "And who's your date?"

"Oh, I'm not taking a date." I was painfully aware of Joe standing, listening. "You know. A family wedding. It wouldn't work to take anyone." I was mumbling, trying to be obscure. But I think she knew what I meant.

"I'll go." Joe said it like a solution. Like there was a problem, and he was there to solve it.

I blushed. "Hey, I don't really need anyone ..."

"No, really. I'd like to go."

A heartbeat of time. The surprise of his words stretched the moment, made it swell. Two heartbeats, three ... He held me with his mild gaze until I pulled my eyes away.

Virginia was smiling gently, almost as if she saw and understood, had herself felt disbelief turn to hope.

Then, "It'll let me keep an eye on Mama at the same

time," Joe added. And he made it sound as if this were not the real reason for going, but suddenly, Celia's form now rounding the end of the block, I knew it was. Joy bled away.

"So what do you say?" Joe was asking again.

"Sure," I said as casually as I could, masking my disappointment. "Why not?"

Virginia had got up. "See you later, Ivy," she said. "Congratulations again," and she slipped away from me. We hadn't talked again about her decision after all, and it felt like she was escaping. As if I was now one more person to avoid.

✟✟✟

She had seen them from her bedroom window, weeks ago, boxes carried in darkness, heaved out of the yawning doors of a vehicle, a blue van, and into the church house behind, through its back door. She heard them, hushed voices, excited, urgent. She had seen an arm reach inside, lift a glinting barrel in the moonlight, then a shadowed hand stroke it, replace it, God's vengeance.

Chapter Twenty-one

I felt sick. I wanted to forget about the Donatos, all of them, ignore them all and focus on my own sister's wedding for a few days, but it was like I was on an out-of-control ride in an amusement park. It had trapped me, caught me, locked me in, and Virginia was in one car, and Paul was in another, and Joe was there, too, and Cameron and Taylor, and who knew how many other people. It was making me churn and fret, making me nauseous and dizzy, and it was going to keep going, up and down, up and down, faster and faster, and it wouldn't stop until it crashed.

I knew that when I tried to do my homework tonight, when I tried to get to sleep, when I tried to concentrate in class tomorrow, it would be spinning me round, scrambling my thoughts, turning them black and tangled. I couldn't get off. None of us could. And I couldn't just wait until it hit a wall or derailed and all the cars, and all the riders in them, sailed through the air, tumbling, falling. I had to find a way to shut it off.

So, before I could talk myself out of it, before Joe followed Virginia inside, I forced myself to speak to him. I tried to choose my words carefully. "Remember our conversation at school? About those biblical references?"

"Yeah?"

I glanced anxiously at the front door of his house. "Joe, can we talk for just a minute? Or maybe you could just walk me home?"

Joe shrugged. "Okay, if you want."

We walked together to the sidewalk and headed toward my house. Tall maple and oak trees shaded the street. The leaves on some of the older trees were beginning to display some early orange and yellow splashes of color.

"Joe, I know I told you a lot already, and I know you warned me to stay out of it and to leave you out of it, too. But I haven't told you everything, and I think I should. I promised her I wouldn't tell anyone, but ... I need to. I need to tell you more about Virginia."

Joe's head whipped around. "What about Virginia?"

"Joe." I stopped. I looked down at my hands. "I told you that Gin's been talking a little crazy. Well, she's sort of imagining things."

I paused, and in that moment before telling, I heard Virginia's words in my mind: "You can't tell. If you break this promise, it would be like betraying something monumental, something beyond both of us. I think something bad would happen."

We had been standing in sunshine, but a cloud must have passed in front of the sun because suddenly a shadow reached out to us, engulfed us, and I shivered.

"What do you mean?" Joe asked. "What kind of things?"

It seemed a cruel choice. I had to tell in order to help Virginia, and it would be a betrayal of sorts, of her trust in me and the promise I had made to her, but I couldn't believe that it meant I would be betraying the world, that I would be denying us all the birth of God's child. I couldn't believe it because I knew this could not happen; she was not carrying God's child. It was impossible.

And what angel would raise his sword against me, against us? What angel would punish caring and friendship?

I was more afraid of Paul Donato. If I did *not* tell, something bad would happen. If I did *nothing*, I would be betraying something precious, my friendship with Virginia. By betraying her secret, I hoped to save her.

And yet, as I spoke the words, I felt both a huge sense of

relief — it was so good to finally share this with someone else — and a sense of dread. "Joe, Virginia actually thinks she's pregnant."

"What? Pregnant?!" Shock, anger, fear, disbelief ... I saw them all on his face, heard them in his voice. "No, she can't be. You're joking ...".

"It's okay," I reassured him. "She isn't pregnant. She *thinks* she is, but she *isn't*. Or, at least, not yet. I don't think. But she *says* she will be soon."

"What? What are you talking about? Why would she ... ?" he stammered.

"Joe." I cleared my throat. "Virginia says ... she says she's going to become pregnant with God's child. That an angel told her so."

Joe's eyes widened. "You're kidding. You've got to be kidding."

I shook my head. "No, I wish I were, but I'm not. She really believes it."

"Oh my God ..." he mumbled, staring at me. "That is ... This is wild ..."

"Yeah, it is," I agreed. "So that's why. That's why you've got to do something. You've got to help her. I don't know what's driven her to this, but I really think it must have something to do with your brother and his church, the things that he's up to."

Joe was still staring at me. "Ivy, would you give up on this stuff with Paul and his church? The whole bunch of them are just completely over the top with this religious stuff. I know that." He scowled, balling his hands into fists. His eyes were deep blue, blue enough to swim in or fly through. "But I just don't believe that there's anything actually dangerous going on. And this ... this stuff with Virginia doesn't point to that at all."

"No? Well, there's more." I hesitated, but then went on.

"I think that Paul is running a training camp. I told you that I think he's teaching some young guys in his youth group how to use weapons. Well, I think he might be planning some kind of group attack. And Joe," I insisted, "even if you don't believe there are weapons involved, that Paul is planning anything really sinister, you've *got* to see that whatever he *is* doing is hurting Virginia. It's upsetting her enough that she's hallucinating," I emphasized. "I know the two things are connected somehow. Joe, your sister needs help. I can't do it alone. She needs your help, too."

Joe didn't speak for a moment. He looked away, running his fingers through his hair, and while he did, I stared at him. And I couldn't believe it, but even though he was way out of my league, a senior, had a gorgeous girlfriend, even though he was reluctant to step in and help his own sister, as I stared at him, my heart pounded, and part of me knew it was heaven to stand next to him out on the street. I memorized the line of his jaw, the way his lips swelled and then subsided at the edges, the way his eyes tightened as he considered what I'd said.

Then Joe looked back at me. He wasn't smiling. He had a reflective look on his face, calm and intense. He searched my eyes. And then he said, "Ivy, maybe an angel *did* come to her. Maybe she *is* carrying God's child. If there's anyone on earth an angel might choose, it would be Virginia. She's … special."

We stood on the street, halfway between my house and his, and a light breeze blew. The air felt delicious against my bare skin, like the brush of thousands of feather tips. I heard what he said, and the thought settled on me gently, and it seemed almost plausible. For a moment, it wasn't a crashing contradiction of reality and belief, a sign of a mind under stress and crumbling, but an easing into something new and better, beyond our dreams but not impossible.

A look of pain crossed Joe's face. "I love my sister, Ivy, and I want to help her. I do. But how? For years, I've lived there and ignored it all, all the secrecy, the watching, the planning. I don't *know* anything, and I don't *suspect* anything, and I leave them alone, and they leave me alone, and if I didn't, I don't know what would happen, whether they'd even let me stay. I don't know *what* they'd do, but in one more year, I'm out of there." He took a deep breath. "I've been biding my time until I'm done high school, and I'm out." He bit his lip. Then he shook his head. "Virginia ... she seemed to be doing all right, better than me, actually. She seemed to be able to skim along the surface of it all, sort of part of it but above it all, protected somehow." He paused. "I always thought she'd be okay, that maybe when I left, I could take her with me, if it wasn't too late. But now what? I don't see what I can do to help her."

"*Joe*," I wailed. I wanted to shake him. "You can't bail out on Virginia just because you don't know what to do. She needs help. She needs to talk to someone, a counselor, a professional of some kind, a psychiatrist."

A neighbor walked past, smiling at us. I paused until she was just out of earshot, then I roared ahead. "*I* can't persuade Virginia to do anything. She and I hardly know each other anymore. She's barely even confided in me. I think she only chose me because she doesn't have any other friends! And she didn't tell me because she wants my advice or my help. The only reason she's telling me what's happening is because she wants a witness to this ... 'miracle.' She wants someone to know so it can be documented and celebrated later, so people will know it happened, that it was real. Or at least that's what she's telling herself."

I was sweating and breathing hard. I turned and began walking again, toward my house, and Joe walked beside me.

"Joe, you're her brother. You're closer to her than anyone. You have to talk to her and get her some help!" I braced myself and went on. "And that's not all. First, before that even, we have to do something to stop Paul, or at least find out what he's up to."

Joe started to speak, but I went on, "I know you don't believe it, and I don't have much proof. But something is being set in motion, and we have to find out what it is and stop it before it's too late." I knew I had his attention now. I had to keep going. I had to say the one thing that might tip the balance.

We had reached my house. I stopped and looked directly into his eyes. "Joe, if you really thought I was nuts, if you really thought this was crazy, you'd go to Paul. You'd simply go to Paul and ask him about his group, about his plans, about the youth meetings." I paused, trying not to shake. "Why don't you do that? Ask him."

I held his gaze without wavering.

"You don't want to ask him because deep down, in some part of yourself, you know that he's capable of doing something bad. You know there's something about him that can convince those he chooses to do what he wants. You know you're afraid of him."

He stared at me without speaking. I couldn't interpret his look. I didn't know what he thought of me, or what he might decide.

Finally he spoke.

"Okay, I'll help. So what do you suggest we do?"

✝✝✝

She wanted to tell someone, but she was afraid. They were watching her.

Who could help her? Her mother? Before her mother's attack, they had been shepherding her mother back and forth, back and forth, to and from the church, and did her mother know about the guns? That the words had become solid steel that you could hold in your hands and aim and with which you could change other words and other lives forever?

She couldn't ask her what to do because Mama wasn't well, not completely. She had been in the hospital, but there was more. Even before that, Mama had been getting more vague. Now her mind was able to transform what she saw. Her mother sometimes called her by the name of the baby that hadn't lived, Angela, and at first, she had minded a lot. It had alarmed her to think her mother was looking at her and seeing someone else, someone who had never become a girl, a young woman, and she felt her own self erased in those moments. But then she had become more comfortable with it, believing that her mother had found a way to accept losing the baby by imagining a future for her, as if she stood in the flesh and walked the Earth after all. Sometimes Mama would look at Paul, and it seemed she would see her husband, and she would occasionally call Paul by Papa's name, Gus. Could one person become two? It amazed her to think that this impossibility existed.

And so Mama hadn't been able to help her in a long time, and she certainly couldn't talk to her now. She certainly couldn't talk to her about the church because Mama didn't approve of it. As Paul's ideas changed and became more radical, Mama was distressed, and yet Paul was still Mama's son. She watched to see if Mama's heart would break, but her mother looked at her son and more than anything wanted to see what was good and pure, and she knew that Mama had done something almost miraculous.

She had transformed what frightened her, what she could not accept, into something, someone, she could.

So it was possible to make Paul's vision all right. She saw that.

But she *couldn't do it. She couldn't make it all right for herself, even though she was Paul's sister, was family. She didn't know what complicated twists and turns could possibly be making this pure in God's eyes. It frightened her to think about it too closely, and so she had stopped.*

And she didn't know anymore what her place was, where she fit into the connecting structure that had once, a long time ago, been her beautiful family. Paul had groomed and stroked and shaped it into something quite different, something brittle and meticulous, and would she be the one to break it by telling what she knew, what she had seen? How could she?

But how could she not?

Chapter Twenty-two

It was Wednesday evening. I should have been shopping for a dress to wear to Katie's wedding. Instead, Joe and I were lurking outside Cameron Handler's house. We had strolled past twice, casually, hoping to catch sight of Cameron coming or going. My lame plan was just that: to catch sight of Cameron and try to learn something about him, maybe convince ourselves that he wasn't the kind of person to do something crazy.

His house was in a neighborhood adjacent to ours but a lot more well off. The detached house was three stories tall, with a renovation that made it stretch wide and long. It had big windows with wooden shutters. There were two fancy cars in the driveway and a basketball hoop on one of those portable poles that you can wheel onto the street. The lawn was neatly groomed. The Handlers were doing okay.

"Ivy, this could be a big waste of time," Joe complained.

"Yeah, I know."

I think Joe felt blackmailed into coming with me, but I didn't care. It felt better to have someone with me than to be doing this alone. And it felt better to be doing something than nothing.

An hour later, we hadn't seen any sign of activity in the house. We had walked up and down the street several times, had lingered on a corner a few blocks away so as not to be too obvious in our spying and were getting restless.

"Okay, so this isn't working out too well," Joe said.

"Well, I don't know. We might have to come back a few times," I said lamely. "This was just a shot in the dark."

Joe lifted his eyebrows. "Ivy, don't be nuts. We aren't professionals. We can't spend our lives on stakeouts, hoping to see … we don't know what."

I was bored, exasperated and nervous. I shifted from one foot to the other. I also felt scared, like we might be close to something explosive. "So what's *your* great idea?"

"Let's go to the door."

"I don't think anyone's home. And if there is, what do we say if someone answers?"

Joe thought for a moment.

"Okay. I've got it," he said. He began walking toward the house.

"Hey!" I cried, scrambling to catch up. "Want to let me in on this?"

He just smiled cryptically. "Come on."

We walked up the wide front steps, decorated with flowerpots, to the Handlers' front door. Joe knocked.

We waited. He knocked again. We waited some more.

"Okay," I said, relieved. "No one's home. Let's go."

"Okay, so now we can poke around a bit, look into some windows. Let's go into the backyard and see if we can look in the back door."

It had been my idea to come here, but now I was the one with cold feet. Just standing on the porch was making me squirm.

"Joe, I don't know if that's —"

Abruptly the front door opened. A man stood there, balancing a newspaper and a wine glass in one large hand, holding the doorknob with the other. He was heavyset with broad shoulders. The first few buttons of his dress shirt were undone, his tie loosened. "Yes?"

"Hello, sir," said Joe, cheerfully. "Is Cameron here?"

I put a big innocent smile on my face, determined to play along, trying not to look panicked.

He answered abruptly. "No."

I sensed Joe relaxing slightly. He was relieved, and so was I. But the man seemed very uptight. "Why? Who are you?" I kept my friendly smile plastered on my face. "I'm Cameron's father," he offered.

"I'm a friend of his from high school," said Joe. "Well, not a friend exactly. I'm a year behind him ... I knew Cameron at high school. Last spring he mentioned something about a weekend program for youth. It might be too late for this fall, but I thought I'd look into it. I don't know his cell number, but a buddy told me where he lived. I thought I'd just stop by and see if he was here." He gestured at me. "We live nearby. You wouldn't happen to know any details about the program, would you?"

I held my breath. Impressively, Joe had managed to give out almost no information while asking for plenty.

Mr. Handler hesitated. "Yes, he's been on that course this fall. The leadership course?"

"Yes, that's it." Joe nodded.

"Well, Cameron's actually done two of the three weekends already..."

"Okay, I see," Joe said. "So it's too late for me to do this session. But if you could give me any information, that would be helpful. You know, where it is, who to get in touch with." Joe waited. I continued smiling.

"I'll go and look. I think he wrote it down somewhere." Joe nodded. "We keep a calendar in the kitchen."

He turned around and went back into the house. He didn't ask us to step in.

I whispered, "Joe, what if Cameron —?!"

Joe cut a glance at me, putting his finger to his lips, silencing me.

My heart was pounding. What if Cameron came home right now, while we were standing here? I wanted to ask. How would we explain our visit?

Mr. Handler was gone a really long time.

I kept glancing down the street, dreading that I might see

a blond guy heading our way. But maybe he had a car? Or maybe he'd show up on a bike?

"Joe ..." I began again. This time he put his hand on my arm and squeezed. Mr. Handler was coming toward the front door, a piece of paper in hand.

"So you know Cameron how?" he asked. He leaned on the door frame, looking from Joe to me, curiously.

"Like I said, from high school last year. I actually don't really know him well at all. We were both on the football team, but I'm not much of a star, so he probably wouldn't even remember my face. I remembered him talking in the locker room one time after practice about how he was getting involved with this youth group, and they had these weekends away, doing some kind of training, leadership training ..." Joe faltered a bit. Hesitated. Then recovered. "That was a while back. I remembered what he'd said, and then someone else, a buddy of his, mentioned him and the course, and well, my dad has been after me to do some more extra-curricular things, to bump up my résumé a bit — I'll be graduating this spring — and I remembered what Cameron had described. It sounded cool."

Joe was amazing. What he said even sounded plausible. But my mouth was dry. I wanted to grab the paper and run. Mr. Handler raised his eyebrows. "Yeah, the youth group," he nodded. "He started up with them some time ago. I don't know much about it. Cameron plays his cards pretty close to his chest. There's some religious aspect to it, isn't there?" he asked casually. "Is it this youth group that's putting on the leadership weekends?"

I wanted to get out of here. I didn't want us to be having an actual conversation with Cameron's father. The more Joe said, the more chance he'd give us away. And the longer we stood there, the more chance there was Cameron would come home and find us here.

"I'm not sure," Joe shrugged. "Maybe. But he didn't mention anything about religion. I don't remember anything about that."

"It's not something I would have thought Cameron would be interested in," his father remarked. He looked at Joe carefully.

I had told Joe what the school secretary had said to me about Cameron. Other than that and what was in the yearbook, we knew nothing about him or what kind of a guy he was.

"Yeah, me neither." Joe shrugged again. "He made the course sound kind of practical, a bit tough, though. Maybe some outdoor training. Ropes courses. Some wilderness survival skills, things like that."

Mr. Handler nodded. Joe was good at this. "Yeah. That's what Cameron told me. I just wondered if it might be connected to that religious group he's been involved with. It makes me nervous. He's not a sweetness and light kind of guy. Just the opposite in fact. So I'm not sure what he's doing hanging out with Bible-thumpers, exactly. I guess it can't be a bad thing. I keep waiting for them to have a good influence on him." He laughed bitterly. "But I don't know. I sure haven't seen it yet. If anything ..." He frowned, stopped himself. "So you don't know my son well?"

Joe shook his head. "No, sir. Not well at all." He held out his hand. "So, is that it, the information about the course?"

Mr. Handler didn't move. He looked at Joe a little more closely. "And what's your name again, young man?"

Joe shook his head again. "Cameron wouldn't remember my name, sir. Really."

"Well, just in case," Mr. Handler said. "You know," he looked at his watch, "if you can hang on a few minutes, he should be arriving home. In fact, he should have been home half an hour ago. He borrowed my car." He frowned.

I could hardly breathe.

I looked at my watch. "Ohmigosh, thanks for mentioning the time." I pretended to look horrified. "Look how late it is! We really have to go," I said to Mr. Handler. I turned to Joe. "My mom will kill me if I'm not home soon. I told her I'd be back about twenty minutes ago," I started to edge away slowly. "And I didn't bring my cell phone."

Joe grimaced. "Me either. Okay, we better leave." He looked at Mr. Handler. "Sir, could I have that information please? It'd be really helpful."

I shifted from foot to foot, miming impatience, and looking at my watch again.

Mr. Handler didn't budge. "So, your name?" he said to Joe. "So I can tell him you came by?"

Joe looked sheepish. "Tell him 'Scooter.' That's my team nickname. He might remember me by that."

"Okay. Scooter." Cameron's father nodded. He waved the paper. "I only copied down what's on the calendar, and there's not much there. My son's pretty independent now. Told me just enough so I'd pay for it." He let out a short laugh. "He comes and goes now. Didn't get all his high school credits. Says he wants to take a year off, and then he'll see." He shook the paper. "If it's what he says it is, maybe a workshop like this might help him get a job." He handed Joe the paper.

We thanked Cameron's father and tried to leave. I fought the urge to keep looking down the street to see if Cameron was coming. It seemed the more we wanted to go, the more reluctant Mr. Handler was to let us go.

"The leadership camp is on a small acreage close to Harrington, off a sideroad called Samter Sideroad. It's all on the paper," he said. "So, do you really think you might go this weekend?"

"It's *this* weekend? Oh, I don't know, sir. I doubt it. I probably wouldn't be able to register anymore. So thanks again ..."

The last weekend was *this* weekend? My heart sank. It was too soon. And the wedding ...

"Yeah, I guess you're right." He refused to say good-bye. "Hey, have you ever met any members of this youth group? One of Cameron's friends, Taylor, seems to be involved, but he's not exactly anyone's example of a role model." He let out another short, barking laugh. "Kind of a hoodlum, if you ask me. Tattoos on his hands. Wears a big silver cross and black army boots. He's only been here once or twice. Not a relationship I'm encouraging. Not that I really have that much influence on Cam anymore."

"Sorry, sir, but we really need to go." Joe and I stepped off the front stoop. We began sidling down the front walkway.

I shot a look over my shoulder. A small blue Honda was coming down the street. I tugged on Joe's sleeve.

"Cam's changed since all this started," Mr. Handler was saying in a low voice. "He says there's no point to finishing his courses. Stays out late, sleeps in late. I don't know if it's really something you should get involved in, son. You should run it by your parents first."

This was exactly the kind of information we needed, but it was coming too late. The blue Honda was slowing down as it came closer. My heart jumped into my throat. It had to be Cameron.

"You're probably right. Thanks for the advice. So, we really have to hurry now. Thanks again!" Joe called. We had reached the sidewalk. I saw Mr. Handler look toward the blue car. If he smiled, if he waved, we'd run.

"Turn right, not left," Joe whispered as we reached the sidewalk. This was the direction opposite to our street.

"Let's go, let's go, let's go," I muttered under my breath to Joe, in a panic.

We were going to be caught by Cameron. His dad would say, hey, here are some kids asking about your youth camp, and Cameron's face would turn red and nasty, and he'd stalk up to us on lumberjack legs, and he'd hit Joe or threaten us, or he'd call Paul, or he'd ...

I tried not to run.

As the blue car went past us, I exhaled. It continued on and pulled into a driveway close by. It was a neighbor of Mr. Handler's, not Cameron.

I didn't feel safe until we were several blocks away. We turned and headed in the real direction of home. My pulse rate had more or less returned to normal.

"Scooter?" I said to Joe.

"Yeah. One kid on the football team last year was actually called that. But then he moved away after a few months. Didn't finish out the season, even. I thought Cameron might remember the name but not recall the whole story about the guy."

"Smart."

We walked in silence for another block. I tried to evaluate whether the plan had been successful, whether what we had learned had been worth the risk that Cameron might figure out something was up and warn Paul. It might even precipitate events.

"Joe, you did a great job. A really great job. I could never have come up with all those ... scenarios. It was perfect ... But what if Mr. Handler tells Cameron someone came by asking about the leadership camp? Won't he be suspicious? The weekends are probably secret. He probably hasn't talked to anyone about them, other than Taylor. Won't he know something's up?" My voice shook.

Joe looked at me. "Ivy, it went okay. We found out when the last youth meeting is, and where. We took a risk, but I think it was worth it. I think we did okay."

"Yeah." I tried to believe it.

We walked on quickly. It was twilight, and as we walked, the streetlights came on.

It wasn't until we were almost home that we dared to stop and look at what was on the paper. Mr. Handler's handwriting was difficult to read but we could make out:

Leadership training program (meals and transportation provided) — $450

August 28–30, September 11–13, September 25–27

Hardwood area — 5 km from village of Harrington — north on Samter Sideroad — 15 km to unmarked dirt road

We continued on up our street without speaking and stopped in front of Joe's house.

"That's about an hour away," he said. "The Hardwood area. It seems familiar for some reason ..."

I didn't know what to say. I felt exhausted. I wanted to go home and lie down and sleep for a week. I also wanted to stand there forever with Joe.

We lingered in the evening air. There were sounds of laughter from a backyard. A dog barked.

Joe looked down at the piece of paper in his hand and then handed it to me. "Ivy, the third weekend in this series is this one. The weekend coming up."

"I know."

He stood motionless, his head bowed. I looked at his hair, suddenly felt an incredible urge to reach out and touch it, run my fingers through it, let them slide down and trace his cheekbone, the angle of his jaw.

"Ivy, I still don't believe Paul is planning anything dangerous. I just don't believe it."

I felt overwhelmed with fatigue. I didn't want to keep arguing, not tonight. I didn't want to try to persuade him, go back again over all my worries, the evidence, the signs.

"But that was weird," he went on. "Listening to Mr. Handler talk about the youth group and Cameron. He seemed so ... uneasy about it, suspicious. Just like you. And why would Cameron be trying to keep it all secret from his own father? Because he's embarrassed to be at a religious youth camp?" Finally, Joe lifted his face and looked into mine. "Or because there's more to it than that?"

Relief slid through me. A weight lifted. Joe didn't think I was crazy. Joe was going to help. Maybe this would get a little easier. Suddenly I didn't feel so tired. Suddenly it didn't seem impossible to keep trying, to try to fix everything.

"This weekend," he repeated, still looking at me. "This Saturday is your sister's wedding."

"I know, I know," I agreed. "But Joe, we *have* to go there. We have to go to the site and look. See for ourselves what's going on. Do you think that's possible? Could you get a car somehow? Could we go?"

"And the wedding? You'd risk being late for your sister's wedding? Risk maybe missing it?"

"We'd have to time it right. Go really early and be back on time. We could do it." I held his gaze. "But yes, I'd risk it. We have to. This is important, Joe." My hands were fists, clenched with emotion.

Then the Donatos' porch light flickered on. I was instantly uneasy. There were probably eyes observing us.

"I better go," I said, anxiously.

For a moment, Joe didn't answer. Had I finally convinced him of how dangerous the situation might be? Of how desperately Virginia needed us to do something?

Joe had noticed the porch light too. "Okay, I'll try to

figure it out," he said. "I'd better go in now. Talk to you soon."

As I turned away, to walk home, I saw the closed living-room curtains twitch. Someone had definitely been watching.

⁜

Maybe she could tell Joe about the guns. Maybe she could tell Ivy that she had seen guns. That Paul had guns in the boxes in the basement of the church.

Maybe she could.

But would they believe her?

And would it do any good?

She placed her hands on her belly and paced.

Chapter Twenty-three

I was a bundle of nerves on Thursday. I didn't see Virginia at school. I wondered if she was at home sick, but I didn't want to call or drop by. It seemed better just to stay away for now.

After school, I jumped on the bus and went shopping for a dress to wear to Katie's wedding but found nothing.

When I came home, empty-handed and feeling slightly panicky, I made dinner. Dad told me that Mom wouldn't be eating with us. She was upstairs in her room, unavailable. I would not think of her. It didn't help.

And so I set the table with forks and knives and tossed the salad, and I was moving away to call my father for dinner, but my eyes lingered. Suddenly the emptiness of the table, the two solitary place mats with fork and knife, alarmed me. It wasn't enough. It wasn't evidence of a family, of the huge space that the four of us took up with our laughing, our splashing through the waves together at the beach in Jamaica four winters ago, my mother's bronze curls cascading down her back when she pulled the clips from her hair the night we waltzed into dinner arm in arm, my father's white legs scissoring through the air as he dove off the diving board to my mother's squealing applause, my body, and Katie's, flung out between them on the king-sized bed as we ate microwave popcorn in our hotel room and watched a side-splitting movie that I had hoped would never end.

I could not agree to this, to just the two of us, as if she did not exist, as if she was ill or indisposed or wanted to be here but couldn't be. What was wrong with her? What was so bad about this life that she didn't want to live it with us? Why couldn't she find it within herself to confront it, to stare it down? Weren't we worth it?

So I moved the place mats outdoors to the patio table and served our dinner outside because it was still September and warm, and we could enjoy the warmth in the air and the flowers in the garden, and it would not feel like anyone was missing. It would not. And it didn't.

After dinner, I told my dad I had to go back to the mall. I was without my mother's help again, but at least my dad offered to take me this time. He roamed the aisles of a bookstore while I looked in a few stores. When I finally found a dress I liked, I tried it on, then took it to the front cash. Before actually paying for it, I dragged Dad in to look at it.

"Oh, *I* don't know," he said.

I held it up against me, and he must have seen me wanting it to look pretty, wanting it to be the one, because then he said, "Oh, yes, Ivy. There. Now I see. It will look beautiful on you. Just beautiful."

And I believed him, and we bought it.

On Friday, I finally saw Joe. He found me at my locker at lunchtime. While Celia waited across the hall, looking at her nails, he hurried over and told me Paul had gone out of town this morning and would be away all weekend. I opened my mouth, but he said it first. "He's probably going to the leadership camp." He looked me right in the eye and said, "We'll have to be *really* careful we don't run into him. I don't know how we'd explain showing up there." Then he told me he'd pick me up the next morning at 6:30 on a corner several blocks away from our street. He rushed away before I had a chance to ask any questions.

I could hardly sleep that night. I called Katie to ask what time she needed Dad and me to help the next day. Luckily, she said the afternoon was good. I explained to Dad that I had to go out early Saturday morning for an extended training session with the cross-country team. I told him I'd tried to get out of it because of the wedding but the coach had said it was compulsory and promised it would be done by noon. I arranged to hook up with Dad at 1:00 p.m. Then I spent ages surfing the Net on my computer, trying to bore myself to sleep. I even looked up crows again. I found another prophecy poem.

> *One crow for sorrow*
> *Two crows for joy*
> *Three crows for a girl*
> *Four crows for a boy*
> *Five crows for silver*
> *Six crows for gold*
> *Seven crows for a secret never told*
> *Eight for heaven, nine for hell*
> *And ten for the devil's own sel'.*

When I finally lay down, I practiced saying it over and over, memorizing it. I was awake every hour, jolted out of dreams by nothing but tension. At 5:30, I got up, had a light breakfast and was sitting on the corner, stretching, by 6:10.

At 6:25, Joe pulled up in his father's old Ford. Dressed in my running pants and jacket, I went over to the car.

Virginia was sitting in the passenger seat.

"Gin!" I said, shocked. "Hi!"

Joe shot me a warning glance. "Yeah, who would have thought I could get her up and out so early, eh, Ivy? She's the queen of sleeping in."

I forced a laugh and climbed into the backseat.

"It's nice of you to come," Virginia said hesitantly.

"No problem," I replied awkwardly, uncertain what she'd been told about our journey.

"I haven't been bird-watching in so long. Not since Papa died. It's something he and I used to do together when I was little."

"Yeah, Joe told me when he asked me to come along," I lied.

I leaned back and buckled up. So Virginia didn't know what we were really doing this morning. It might be difficult to find a way to sneak around the site without her asking questions, but the bird-watching did give us a good alibi for lurking in the woods. Joe was pretty smart. I wondered what clever tactics he had used to spring Virginia out of the castle without the sisters blocking his attempt.

I found out after about twenty minutes. We were driving north out of the city and then west. Virginia hadn't spoken in a while when she turned to her brother and said nervously, "Do you think Teresa will worry when she gets up and realizes we're not home? She might be angry."

"I left a note on the kitchen table explaining that we thought of this late last night — the bird-watching — after they were all asleep, and that we didn't want to disturb them. I said we'd get up really early so we could take our time, enjoy being out in the woods and then get back home again by noon, so I'll have time to get all polished up for Katie's wedding." He spoke easily, reassuringly.

Virginia nodded, considering his words. "They won't like it, though." Her voice was flat.

So was Joe's when he replied, "No, they won't."

They didn't speak again for a while, although once Virginia turned to Joe and looked like she wanted to tell him something, but he was looking off to the west, caught up in some deep thoughts of his own. She settled back into her seat, and we drove on in silence.

I sat there, almost in agony. This whole trip seemed surreal. We were going to spy on Virginia's brother because we — I, at least — believed he might be planning to hurt or even kill innocent people. Although I was trying hard to convince Joe that it was true, I still was having difficulty really believing it myself. I stared out the window. It almost wasn't possible. Almost.

But then look at life itself. Life itself almost wasn't possible.

I leaned my head against the door frame. Looking at the clouds scudding across the blue sky — it was going to be a beautiful day for Katie's wedding — I tried to imagine Earth millions, billions of years ago. A lifeless planet. It was hard to picture. It would have been rock, gases. And then everything changed. Maybe it happened overnight; maybe it took millions of years. But for certain, from no life at all came life.

How did it happen? Were there a bunch of inert cells that, left alone, would have remained just like all the other billion-plus cells on the planet — simple, normal and lifeless, but then something happened to them, to those particular ones, for some reason or for no reason, and then, zap, eventually they become alive, or become part of the process that leads to life?

I stared out the window as we drove past field after field. Or maybe those cells weren't actually just like all the others. Maybe those ones were particularly prone to being activated. Maybe there was something in them right from the start, just waiting to be called forth.

I closed my eyes for a moment as my mind drifted. What actually *did* the calling forth? I wondered. Was it circumstance, coincidence, the coming together of the conditions surrounding those cells that sparked whatever potential lay within them? Or was it more than that? Were they chosen deliberately by something grander than luck or fate? Something with purpose? Something with passion and intention and sweeping drive that made it impossible for anything other than this to happen, no matter how wide open and full of possibility the empty horizon seemed?

I opened my eyes again. Paul believed that God had

chosen him to act. He was certain, *certain*, that what he believed, what he knew, was true. Was it really possible that it was God, or some kind of divine power, that had ignited this fire in Paul, that had filled him with such frightening, compelling conviction, that there wasn't any room left for the tiniest bit of doubt? The idea scared me.

So did our plan for this morning.

I tried to focus on what I could see out the window, but my thoughts had taken off, were swirling dizzily, out of control. What would happen if we ran into Paul? What if Paul was angry, really angry? Mrs. Donato had warned that someone could get hurt. Would we get hurt? Would I make it to Katie's wedding?

Joe's eyes caught mine in the rearview mirror. "Okay there, Ivy?" Did I look as crazy as I was feeling?

"Yeah. I'm fine," I replied, another lie.

I asked Joe to turn some music on, and it helped. And when Joe and Virginia began chatting, I concentrated on emptying my mind and listening to them.

Joe had a nice rapport with Virginia. He joked with her, trying to keep the mood light, and he didn't seem to mind that she didn't seem able to reciprocate, that she would answer with earnestness.

After a time, it struck me. I'd always believed she was a little out of it, a step behind everything, and it had driven me kind of nuts. But listening now, as she and her brother talked, I noticed that he seemed to like the measuredness of her ways. Joe would ask a question and then patiently wait during her pause before answering, as, I guess, she considered both what he'd said and how she'd respond. The silent parts didn't mean nothing was happening. They were just the time needed for his words to whorl their way into her consciousness. It reminded me of listening to a newscaster on television talk to a reporter in a remote location. It was like their conversation had a time delay in one direction. And it was as if Joe didn't mind the need to be so patient because his sister was so very far away, and her responses let him peek into her country and enjoy her part of the world.

We'd been driving for about an hour when we entered the town of Harrington. Joe asked me to jump out and ask a local how to find Samter Sideroad. Then we headed north along a minor highway. Mr. Handler's directions told us to drive for five kilometers. We found Samter Sideroad pretty easily. We turned and now needed to go fifteen kilometers until we reached the dirt road.

But at the fifteen-kilometer mark, there was nothing.

"I guess I'll just keep going," Joe suggested, with a shrug.

I tried not to worry as we drove on. After two kilometers or so, the fields ended abruptly and forest began. Still no dirt sideroad, but now Virginia said softly, "This looks kind of familiar." And as Joe looked puzzled, she turned to him and said, "Are you taking me to the place where Papa and I always used to come bird-watching?"

Joe shot me a look in the rearview mirror. A look of disbelief. Because for a moment, it seemed an unbelievable coincidence.

But then suddenly it made total sense. It made sense that Paul, trying to think of an out-of-the-way private place for his training camp, would choose a spot he knew, this place, somewhere that Mr. Donato must have brought him to when he was young.

Joe had figured it out as well, and he was looking in the mirror at me to see if I had, and he said to his sister, "That's right. You guessed it!"

Gin pressed her hands together. "It's so nice there," she said in a thin voice. "Papa liked it a lot." She pointed. "There it is. The road in."

And we came to an unmarked dirt road.

Joe slowed down as we reached it. There were no other cars in sight. No people, no houses, no animals.

A sudden wave of fear swept over me. What would happen if we went down there? No one even really knew where we'd gone. What if we never came out of here again? My parents might never know what had happened to me. I had been stupid not to leave some kind of emergency note hidden in my desk, in case they did a frantic search later tonight, hours after I should have been back, after the wedding was over, had been wrecked because I hadn't shown up and everyone was so worried. Should I send them a quick text message on my phone ...?

Maybe Joe was feeling hesitant, too, because he stopped the car for a moment, with the indicator on. Stopped right in the middle of the road, and he looked left, down the dirt road, and we just waited there.

But then Virginia said, "It's okay, Joe. That's it. Really. That's the way in." And so he slowly drove forward along the rutted and potholed road. I moved over to sit in the middle of the backseat and leaned forward, peering nervously out the front window. There wasn't much to look at except trees on either side, and it was difficult to see ahead because of the winding road.

Then we came around one bend, and now suddenly there was a clearing up ahead.

"Joe," I said. I clutched the back of the seat, swallowed hard.

"Yeah."

He slowed the car. "I think we'll park here, back here where it's forested, Gin. I'll just turn the car around now, before we get out. It'll make it easier when we need to leave." He did an awkward U-turn on the narrow road.

"There's a small camp there," Virginia said softly. "A main building, some cabins, an open area over that way."

She pointed. "It's about a twenty-minute walk. There used to be a path ..."

Virginia's voice was shaky. Her face was pale. I was nervous, but she seemed a little overwhelmed.

Joe parked the car. We all got out.

Joe held a pair of binoculars in his hand. "We'll share," he told me. He handed Virginia her own pair. And then he looked at her closely. "Gin," he said gently.

She was crying. There were tears on her cheeks, in her eyes, one was caught on her lips.

"Oh, Gin," he said.

And he gathered her in his arms.

After a time he said, "Gin, I shouldn't have brought you here." But she shook her head. "No, it's all right. It's just ... Papa ... I miss him."

I stood there uncomfortably, and despite Virginia's obvious distress, I couldn't help but think that at any moment someone would walk up the road and see us, or see the car, and this was a wrinkle in the plan that we hadn't expected, and that we should really get going, get in and get out of there.

Then, incredibly, everything kind of fell into place because Virginia said, "Do you mind if I just sit here in the car? Alone for a while? Do you mind?"

Joe protested a bit, but she was determined. She really seemed to want to just sit and grieve by herself. "You two go ahead. Here, take my binoculars. I'll be fine here. The air is nice, and the trees."

"Gin," I told her. "Give me your cell number and leave your phone on. We'll check in with you every once in a while."

Her face looked blank. Joe shook his head. "We don't have cell phones," he told me apologetically.

He turned back to Virginia. "We'll be two hours, max. Okay? Two hours. We'll look at some birds, and then we'll be back." She said okay. He told her firmly, "If you see anyone coming this way, anyone at all, put the windows up and lock all the doors. Lock yourself in the car and don't get out. Here, I'll leave the key with you."

He didn't explain why, but she agreed, and then he and I hurried away.

"I hope she'll be all right there," Joe said as he led the way north into the woods.

✛✛✛

She hadn't wanted to go with them. She knew immediately it was too risky. It wasn't part of Gabriel's plan. She had to be careful, had to protect herself because she was meant to bear a child. Gabriel had told her so. He expected this of her, and she had agreed. She was indispensable.

But it had happened so quickly. Joe told her about the bird-watching idea late in the evening, and then he came in early, his finger to his lips, cautioning her, "Shhhh ...," because they didn't want to wake anyone. She quickly got dressed, and then Joe grabbed some muffins and said, "Okay, Gin, let's go."
He looked so nervous, almost frightened. She didn't want to let him down, so she would just go along.

As they drove, she wondered again, should she tell them?

She even turned to Joe, opened her mouth to say it. Then a thought came to her, settled around her shoulders like a shroud: Gabriel would be angry. He hadn't asked her to tell. Gabriel had said that she would have a baby. This was the way to stop them. The baby. If all she needed to do was tell, Gabriel would have asked her to do this. And she knew she would have found the courage to do it.

It had been risky even telling Ivy. Even that might have angered Gabriel, but perhaps he had chosen to overlook it, seen that Ivy would indeed be a witness and so make this story live forever. She had thought of telling Mama but hadn't.

No, it was clear to her that Gabriel knew Paul could not be stopped by words, but only by an act of faith, only by the birth of her baby, God's baby.

Driving toward this encounter, she wished she could tell Joe and Ivy that there was no point at all in trying, that they could find out everything, the whole thing, all the details of the plan, and it wouldn't be enough. They actually imagined there was some earthly way he could be stopped, but there wasn't.

Chapter Twenty-four

We headed into the woods, traveling in the direction Virginia had indicated. From her description, the campsite was simple. Our plan was just to try to see as much as possible without getting caught.

I followed Joe, and at first it was rough going. This was a natural forest, and we had to struggle through lots of undergrowth. But soon we came across the path that Virginia had mentioned. Terrified of running into Paul and his group, Joe and I agreed to travel along it, but cautiously, standing still and listening every five minutes or so. We had no idea what the group might be doing at 8:30 in the morning. Breakfast, we hoped, and not a nature hike in the woods.

About half an hour after leaving the car, we could see the clearing through the trees ahead, but we weren't yet close enough to catch sight of any buildings or people.

"Let's get off the path now," Joe said, in a low, urgent voice.

I followed him into the brush, and we traveled away from the path, keeping the clearing over our right shoulders, for several hundred meters. Then, feeling a little more safe from being spotted, we paused to catch our breath. While Joe scanned around carefully for any signs of movement, I bent down to retie my shoes. My hands were trembling.

"Okay, let's move up to the edge of the clearing," Joe suggested. "We'll just stay there and see what we can see."

I nodded. We crept forward. Approaching the tree line, we dropped to a crouch and stopped. Through the trees, we could see the layout. One larger building, wooden, was on the other side of the clearing, the north side, and three smaller cabins in a row were near the eastern edge. The clearing itself was small, about the size of a football field.

Joe gestured for me to go down on my hands and knees, and we crawled forward even farther. Using the undergrowth as cover, we inched from a heap of brush to some large rocks to some small scraggly pine trees.

Now we had a better view of the eastern edge of the clearing. We could see a road, maybe the continuation of the road that we'd driven in on, running alongside the clearing and then on northward. Just where the road turned were a blue van and a small black car. They'd been driven onto the field a little ways and were parked on the grass. I imagined there'd be a few large Keep Out signs nearby.

Suddenly Joe hissed, "Ivy!" Someone had come out of the main building.

Instantly, we flattened ourselves. My face was pressed into a pile of damp leaves. Roots stabbed into my stomach. My heart was pounding, and there was a rushing in my ears. Had anyone seen us?

As my breathing slowed, and the noise in my ears subsided, I heard Joe's low voice. "Ivy. It's all right."

But it wasn't all right. Not by a long shot. Lying there, face down, uncomfortable, I had started to tremble. There was something here, something on the move, something bad, scary, unstoppable. It was slouching toward its destination. I had felt this way before. I must have been in its path before. And suddenly I remembered. Me, after going to church with the Donatos. Paul with his eyes on me, asking if I wanted to know God, his God, wanting to sweep me into his fold, sweep me along with him and never let me go. I felt it all again, but now it was so much stronger. It was making me shake, and I began to sweat.

I heard a shout from the clearing. I lifted my head, forced myself to look, and there he was, 100 meters from me, standing in the middle of the clearing facing the cabins, but I had already known it was him because that was why we were here.

It was Paul.

Do you want to get to know God?

His power was immense, insinuating, and yet, dreading him, still I felt something in me reaching out to him. I wanted to go to him, listen to him, sit at his feet. What did this mean about me, about him and his almost irresistible power, about what was going on? I had never felt so certain that Paul had to be stopped, soon, forever, before the power continued to grow any stronger. Something was very wrong. Something worse than bad was happening here.

Paul was dressed entirely in black. He was standing erect, watching the cabins, waiting, and then we saw a group of young men come hurrying out. The screen doors banged closed behind them. They rushed to form a line in front of Paul. They arranged themselves, standing shoulder to shoulder, wearing combat fatigues. Did they have any weapons? None that I could see. I counted the guys: there were eight.

Eight is for grief.

Eight is for heaven.

But these weren't crows; these were boys, young men. They weren't just signs pointing toward the future; they *were* the future, could actually create the future.

I shuddered. The ominous words I'd read in Paul's church, seen in his handwritten notes, suddenly came back to me: *It will take 8 brave souls. Courage. Which of you will serve?*

I could almost hear Paul saying the lines. They rang in my ears, and these too: *Violence is not outside God's plan.*

Joe had lifted the binoculars to his eyes and was peering intently at the group.

We have obtained the means. Now, the method —
Training must begin. Who will commit ...?

I also peered through my binoculars, examining the young men closely, trying to match the faces with the two I'd seen in the yearbook.

Then I saw him: Cameron. It had to be him. He was the exact image of a younger Mr. Handler, but with a buzz-cut. He was heavyset with broad shoulders, big hands and a slight paunch. He was focused intently on Paul.

Paul barked out words at the young men. Immediately, Cameron adjusted his position so that he was an arm's length from the guy on his right. Everyone else did too.

I lowered the glasses. There was silence for a moment. Paul and the eight young men stood motionless, waiting.

Then Paul began speaking again, softly.

We strained to hear but couldn't make out a word. Maybe he was giving them instructions about the mission he wanted them to carry out. But we couldn't move any closer to listen.

Paul's tone remained frustratingly low. He talked for quite a while. None of the young men fidgeted or even shifted position. Joe glanced at his watch.

Then, as Paul continued, his words became louder, more intense. We heard him shout: "The time is at hand! Are you ready?" And they all shouted back, "Yes!" And again, "The time is at hand! Are you ready?" "Yes!"

Carrying on, his voice dropped, slipping and sliding, and then it rose again, but not to this same fever pitch. Now it dropped again, and it was undulating, insinuating, like a snake weaving its way through their minds and their motives.

He stopped speaking. Paul, tall and commanding, suddenly held out his arms, lifting them gracefully — as a raptor might lift its wings when climbing to a great height before plunging. His arms were out, palms up, as if he was asking for God's blessing, and then the palms were turning toward the young men, as if he might gather them in and embrace them all, as if he could, as if his size was malleable, his capacity infinite.

As one, the boys swayed forward, almost imperceptibly, drawn into his irresistible aura.

And as they leaned toward him, Paul leaned away, teasingly, as if saying, Not yet. Not until it is done.

Abruptly, he finished. He walked off to the side, and at once the boys turned so they were one behind the other and began marching. It looked like it was part of a regular ritual. Paul watched them carefully as they moved in single file up the field and then back, knees high, eyes forward. They were showing off, giving it their all. Maybe the assignments hadn't been divided up yet. Maybe each one of them wanted to be picked for the central role. As they marched, they chanted in a military-sounding call and echo, *"Jesus is God's gift to you ... And you must decide what you want to do ... Jesus is God's gift to you ... And we know what we're going to do ..."* And then they switched to: *"We will give praise from the heart ... Lead us all to do our part."*

Joe was looking more and more uncomfortable. "This is *so* bizarre ..."

He glanced anxiously at his watch, and I knew we were both worried about how long we were taking, about Virginia, sitting alone in the car on the side of the road.

Now the young men followed Paul in five minutes of simple stretching exercises.

Where were the weapons? Were they in the cabins? Not likely. In the main building maybe? In a hidden shed in the woods?

Were these guys about to go and get their arsenal of weapons, reappear for some training with a rifle over their shoulders? If I took a photo or two with my cell phone, we'd actually have proof.

"They're heading out for a run," Joe whispered.

Paul was in the lead. The eight boys fell in behind him and did a slow jog around the clearing. As they approached where we were hiding, we tried to make ourselves invisible, flattening our bodies to the ground among the weeds and grasses. I closed my eyes and took deep breaths as they pounded past only meters away.

The second time they circled, I actually got up the nerve to click a few photos. They were running up the western edge of the field when suddenly Paul turned off and disappeared into the woods. One by one, the others did the same, turning and filing into the woods after him. Joe whipped up his binoculars and stared at the spot.

"There's a path there, too. I hadn't noticed it before. Some kind of a jogging trail, I guess."

They were gone.

Joe and I looked at each other, uncertainly. "Okay," Joe said quickly. "Now what?"

My mind raced.

"I can't believe it! No weapons! They didn't pull out the weapons!"

"Ivy, there may not be any —"

"*There are.* I know there are." My pulse quickened. "Let's search the main building." I began to scramble up to my knees, brushing vegetation off my legs. "Maybe we can find something important there."

Joe grabbed my shoulder. "Okay, but wait a minute, wait a minute! Stay down, Ivy. There might be someone in that building, and we don't know how long they're going to be away on their run. They might be back in five minutes! We have to be careful."

"Right, okay. So what do you think we should do?" I asked bluntly. I felt flushed, excited.

"How about this?" Joe was rapidly scanning the area.

"We'll move closer to the main building, but we'll keep to the woods and try to stay concealed as we go. When we're sure no one's around, we'll try to go in."

"Okay, fine," I agreed quickly. "Let's go."

We immediately were on the move, making our way around the perimeter, trying to hurry, trying to stay at least partially concealed by the trees and underbrush. We had to step carefully, pushing branches out of the way, dodging piles of decaying vegetation.

Soon we were directly behind the main building. I halted. Joe stood close behind me. For a moment, I could feel his breath on my neck. Despite my nervousness, my sense of time running out, I was momentarily overwhelmed by his proximity. He was inches away. His shoulder brushed up against my back.

"Looks good. No sign of anyone through the windows," he whispered in my ear.

"Yeah," I agreed.

"So, you stay here for a minute. Get down among these trees." Joe pulled me back and positioned me among some scraggly pine trees. We both squatted there, eyeing the building and the door on its eastern side. "I'll go to the door. Knock. If someone's in there, I'll just ... I'll say I'm Joe Donato, and I'm looking for Paul. I'll make something up, some reason for being here."

"Okay. So just *go* now," I urged him. "We have to hurry."

And then the door opened and two people stepped out.

We froze, squatting behind the trees. Ice ran through my veins.

It was a man and a young woman. Instantly, I recognized them. They were two of the visitors I had seen on the Donatos' porch many times this summer. I glanced at Joe. From the look on his face, I could tell he knew them. Each was carrying a briefcase. They were dressed formally, in suit jackets, the man in pants and the woman in a skirt and low-heeled pumps. They looked prim and proper, like they might be about to go door to door, selling encyclopedias or preaching salvation, not holed up in a lodge in the woods conspiring to bring about the End Days through violent means.

Had they seen us? It seemed not. The woman was preoccupied with trying to lock the door. She was fumbling with a set of keys. The man looked at his watch. "We're going to be late. Paul won't like that."

The woman set down her briefcase to use both hands for the keys. "It's just one final look-around. There's no rush on the other end," she said, jiggling the key in the lock ineffectively.

"Janie. It's important."

The woman yanked the key out of the lock, opened the door and pulled it closed, hard, inserted the key back in the lock and tried again.

"I know it's important." She sounded tense. She was trying another key. "Everything is important now, Frank. Every last detail. It could be the difference between success and failure. I just meant that we don't need to rush. In fact, we shouldn't rush. Rushing can make you overlook things." She opened the door again and once more slammed it closed. She fumbled with another key.

"Let me try," the man offered impatiently. "That lock is finicky."

She glared at him and kept trying. The man looked at his watch again, a frown furrowing his brow. He glanced toward the trail along which Paul and the young men had run into the woods. "Okay, well let's just leave it then," he said abruptly. "There's no one around, and there's no one else expected. Paul and the others will be back soon" — he looked at his watch again — "in about twenty minutes. The place is certainly safe until then."

The woman jiggled yet another key in the lock.

"Come on, Janie," the man said firmly. He tapped his watch. "Come on. It'll be fine. Let's go."

"Okay, okay," she agreed, irritated.

Finally. They hurried away toward the edge of the clearing where the van and the car were parked. The woman's heels sank into the grass as she walked, her skirt forcing her to take short steps.

As soon as they were out of hearing, I grabbed Joe's arm. "Oh my God, that was close. One more second and they'd have met you, coming up to the door ..."

"Yeah. But Ivy, listen. What if they drive in the direction of our car? What if they find it and Virginia? They've been to our house plenty of times. They'll recognize Virginia, ask her what she's doing here."

And then what would happen? I imagined them pounding on the window of the car, dragging Virginia out of it and into their car, hauling her back here and Paul confronting her accusingly. But at least she didn't know our real reason for being here. She wouldn't tell because she had nothing to hide. She really did think we were here bird-watching ... didn't she?

Joe's blue eyes bored into mine. "We should go. We should head back to the car *now*. In case they go that way. In case they find the car, and her. That way we'll be there to help her." He started to move.

I grabbed his arm. "Joe, wait!" I hissed. "There's a fifty-fifty chance they'll go in the other direction. If we leave now, we'll never know what's in this building. There must be something important in there or they wouldn't have worried so much about leaving the door unlocked. Plus, we'll never get to your car before those two do anyway. It's already too late."

Joe shook his head, "We can't risk leaving her all alone with them. We don't know what they'll do." He began to get up again. "I think we should go. She's my sister."

"Joe, they might scare her, but I don't think they'll hurt her." The words sounded harsh, even to my own ears. I was the one who'd been telling him he had a responsibility to help his sister, and now I was trying to convince him that she wasn't actually the highest priority, that there was more at stake. "Joe, wait a minute. Just wait. Let's see which way they drive. If they head toward your car, we'll take off. We'll run straight across the field, out in the open, and down the road, because" — I spread my arms — "there's no one here to see us right now, and we'll get there quickly, in time to help her. Joe, let's just wait. We don't want to lose this chance."

The pair were nearing their vehicle.

Joe remained crouching, uncertain.

I raised my binoculars and trained them on the two, and then Joe did the same. We watched, tense, holding our breath, as they got in the car and headed out, then we expelled it with relief when we saw the car turn and go north. "That was a close one," Joe said. "If anything had happened to Virginia ..."

He let the thought trail away.

Then he looked at me, his lips pressed together. "Okay, let's get this over with." He glanced toward the main building. "They said Paul would be gone for twenty minutes. So we don't have much time now. Only about fifteen minutes or so."

"Right."

Joe stood up. I began to get to my feet, too, but he put a hand on my shoulder. "Wait. I know they said no one else was in there, but I'll just make sure. Then we'll both go in."

Joe scanned the field once more, then sprinted out into the clearing and toward the main building. I watched, my arms folded tightly across my chest, while he knocked on the door once, then twice. No response. He whipped open the door and poked his head in.

What if someone *was* there? What if someone grabbed him, hit him, punched him, shot him?

I felt nauseous. It would be unbearable.

But now Joe was turning, waving to me. It was all clear.

I ran to join him, followed him inside.

It took my eyes a moment to adjust to the dark interior. There was a large plain room with a kitchen on one side and a hallway down the other. In this main room, obviously a dining area, there were large curtained windows facing north. Five or six long wooden tables and benches filled most of the room. There was nothing suspicious looking here. No place to hide anything.

Cupboard doors were banging. Drawers being opened and closed. Joe rushed out of the narrow kitchen. "Nothing there," he said briskly. "Just normal kitchen stuff." He glanced at his watch.

We kept moving, hurrying now to investigate the hallway that ran along the other side of the main hall. There were two rooms, and then at the end of the hallway, through an open door, was a large bathroom. Nothing interesting there.

We went into the room nearest the bathroom. It seemed to be a common room, maybe a place for meeting or for relaxing. In it were five or six comfortable old chairs, two sofas, a beat-up coffee table and four floor lamps. Against one wall was a shelf of books. There were a radio and a portable CD player on one of the shelves, and some CDs. On a wall was a picture of a gladiator wearing body armor and brandishing a sword, hair flowing. It seemed out of place somehow. I did a double-take. It *was* a gladiator, I guess, but the guy was wearing a crown of thorns, which I know means he was supposed to be Jesus. I'd seen it in other depictions of him. He didn't look angry. Just calm and totally fed up. Weapon in hand, powerful, and ready to wreak havoc. It gave me a chill.

I hurried past to the window that faced west and quickly checked for signs of any activity outside. "All clear," I reported, my voice shaking.

But Joe had found something. "Look!" he said. "Have a look at these!" He was behind one of the sofas. He had found two cardboard boxes on the floor, both sealed with packing tape. No labels on the exterior. Joe pushed at one, then lifted it. "It's heavy." He hefted it, shook it. "We should open it."

"Okay," I instantly agreed. We didn't have time to consider anything too carefully. But right now nothing seemed too risky. We hadn't gone to protect Virginia. Suddenly, nothing seemed too dangerous to stand in the way of finding out what was really going on here.

Yes to risk, because it is for God.

More of Paul's words. I was beginning to understand how one might accept crossing the line into uncertain territory if the ordinary rules seemed changed, if the cost of doing nothing seemed too high.

Joe pulled a Swiss army knife from his back pocket, unfolded the blade and delicately sliced down the tape along all three edges of one of the top flaps. He lifted the flap.

No guns. No grenades. No bombs.

Magazines and books.

Joe dug down, trying not to disturb the packing too much. More books.

Quickly, he turned to the second box, opening it efficiently and rapidly. Also magazines and books with titles such as *The Second Coming*, *Interpreting the Bible*, *How I See It: The Road to Faith*.

"Okay, then," Joe said with relief, sitting back on his heels. He began trying to stick back down the flaps as best he could.

"Joe! Forget that!" I snapped. It seemed the least of our problems. "We have to keep looking. Just because these boxes don't contain any weapons doesn't mean they aren't here!" I stood up. "If we can't find them, it only means they're hidden somewhere else, and maybe we won't have time to discover them, and then we won't be able to prove anything. We won't be able to stop them!"

"You're right," he conceded quickly. Joe stood up, replaced the knife in his pocket. "Let's go then. Let's try the other room."

But we couldn't get in the other room.

I shook the door handle. "It's locked!" I stared at Joe. "They're probably in here, the weapons, whatever they are, and that's why the door is locked. Joe, we have to get in. We have to get in here and see!"

"How? We can't knock the door down," Joe protested.

"No, but can't you … can't you use your knife, somehow? Use it to take the door handle right off?" I suggested frantically. "Would that get us in?"

He glanced at his watch. "Not enough time. We've only got about five or six minutes until Paul and the others are back."

"But —"

"Listen, let's try to look in from the outside. Maybe there's a window to this room," Joe suggested. "But let's do it fast." He grabbed my hand and pulled me after him. We hurried outdoors and around the side of the building. We found the window.

Joe pushed at the glass, but the window was closed tight. We peered in, holding our hands against the glass to try to reduce the reflection from the morning sun. It was an office with little in it: a low bookcase holding a few books and some documents, a chair and a trestle desk without any drawers. There were no weapons in sight. No closet, no filing cabinet, no place for weapons to be concealed. But on the desktop were neat stacks of file folders and papers and ... a laptop computer with the screen up and the power light on.

"Joe." I gripped his arm. "We have to get in there. We have to look at that computer. It's probably loaded with all the plans. Everything. Whatever it is that's going to happen. Joe, we have to look at it."

Joe glanced over his shoulder toward the trail, then back at me. "Ivy, the door was locked ..."

"I'm going in," I told him. I had done it before. I had gone into Paul's church through the basement window. I could go in through this window, too. I had to.

"Ivy," he began to protest.

I was pushing at the glass pane, pressing against it with my fingertips, trying to encourage it to slide. Had Paul locked the windows? Or had he made a tiny, tiny mistake and, on one hot, sunny day, opened them, let the breeze cool him while he talked to God and promised to precipitate the End Days, and then closed them at day's end and simply forgotten to lock them when one of the boys came to him, wanting to discuss the targets, or how many times to shoot, or practice the techniques of detonation or ...?

"Joe." The pane had moved. I pressed and pushed a little more, and again it shifted slightly. One more time, and now it slid open.

The opening wasn't big, but I knew I could fit through.

"Joe," I said again.

"Ivy ..." His eyes were doubtful. "What if they come back while you're in there? What if ..." For the first time, I saw fear in his eyes as well, fear for my safety.

"It'll be fine. Come on. Let's do it," I told him. "The sooner I'm in, the sooner I'm out." I was beyond fear about what might happen to us. I was consumed by the horror of what they might do to others. I was on autopilot. I wasn't going to argue.

It must have showed, because Joe didn't even try to continue talking me out of it. He simply bent down and formed a stirrup with his hands, and I stepped in and he hoisted me up. In one smooth movement, as if we'd practiced over and over for this exact situation, I was through the window. I pulled my legs in, and for a moment I balanced on the ledge, almost falling except Joe was steadying me from behind. I remembered when he had caught me as I flew through the air off his porch, and then I was dropping to the floor and landing on my feet.

I hurried across the room, straight to the computer, my heart pounding. I yanked out the chair and sat down at the desk. When I touched the computer keypad, the screen lit up. I inhaled sharply. On it was a hand-drawn map and markings. Xs and arrows. Squares that looked like buildings on a street. There were numbers, but there were no labels, no words to identify anything. Was this it? Was this where it was going to happen?

"Joe, there's a map on here! A map of a building site," I called. My heart was racing. What if this building was a school or a mall, or an airport? I stared at it, desperate to recognize it. I couldn't. And yet ... maybe someone could identify it, someone who knew our city. Or maybe it could be plugged into a fancy computer system and matched up with an existing map?

I looked around for a flash drive. Well done, Paul. He

didn't have very many supplies on hand here, but I spotted several flash drives, still in their package.

"Okay, Ivy, wrap it up!" Joe's voice was adamant. "You've got about one more minute."

I grabbed one of the flash drives and stuck it in the back of the laptop. I saved the map to the drive. Then I went into the main menu and began randomly saving other files. Their names were useless and didn't give me any clue as to what information they contained. I had a dreadful feeling that the ones I was randomly saving were Paul's sermons, or his attempts at poetry, or egomaniacal descriptions of how great he was, how perfect, how much better than anyone else on earth, and that I would run out of time to make copies of ones that might actually have real evidence of his planning or details about what he was up to.

And then Joe hissed, "Ivy, I hear them. You have to come NOW!"

Adrenaline surged through my veins. I quickly exited the flash drive, yanked it out of the computer and shoved it in my pocket. Leaving the screen as it was, with the map showing, I replaced the chair under the desk as I'd found it and then ran to the window. Whispering loudly, "Joe. I'm coming," I hoisted myself back up to the ledge and launched myself out the window.

He caught me, this time for real, as I was reaching for him, arms out, counting on him being there.

And then almost as my feet touched the ground, he was pulling me along after him, fast, back toward the forest. We dove for cover, and for a few moments just lay in the underbrush, panting, hoping we hadn't been seen.

Joe whispered, "I couldn't see them, but I heard them. They were singing a song, some kind of hymn. But you got out quick. I don't think they saw us."

The building was between us and them, so we couldn't

tell for certain, but as soon we got our breath, Joe said, "Let's get out of here," and we began scuttling back through the trees, away from the edge of the clearing and away from Paul.

✛✛✛

As they drove through the morning light and drew near, she realized that they were taking her to the place where she and Papa used to go bird-watching. It was astonishing because it brought back memories that gripped her so tightly she could hardly breathe. She did not know she could miss anyone else so much.

When they arrived, she wept, and Joe held her.

After Joe and Ivy hurried away, she sat in the car for a time. Then she got out and walked down the road in the direction they'd gone, and she found him. Paul was there, in the field. And she walked across the field toward him, and she could hear the birds in the woods.

Chapter Twenty-five

We hadn't gone far, but Joe was moving quickly, and I was nervous I would lose him and lose my way. I was going as fast as I could, trying to stay low, dodging branches, bushes, roots. I was just telling myself that Joe would turn back any second now, see me struggling to keep up, and wait for me, when suddenly ...

I froze in my tracks.

No, it couldn't be.

I had a terrible, sinking feeling.

I shoved the binoculars under one arm and with both hands frantically patted the front pockets of my track pants, then the back pockets, then stuck my hands in the front pockets and then the back ones, pulled all four of them inside out.

I didn't have the flash drive.

I'd lost the flash drive! How could I be so stupid?

No, no, I hadn't lost it. Calm down. Just think for a moment.

My mind raced, retracing my movements. I'd put it in my pocket before diving out the window. Had it fallen out? Was it back near the building?

How could I be so careless!?

I looked ahead toward Joe. He was moving low and fast. I didn't dare call out to him in case someone heard. And now he was out of sight, gone, and there was no time to lose. I couldn't go on without the flash drive. I had to go back.

I turned, hesitated. What if Paul and the others saw me this time?

There wasn't time to think it through, to make up excuses

not to go back and get it. I had to hurry. I turned and headed back.

I was sweating from exertion, and also now from fear. I kept my head and shoulders down, crouching, and soon I was close enough to the edge of the forest to see the boys, so it was possible they might be able to see me as well. They were together in the middle of the field doing a series of exercises. Push-ups, sit-ups. I couldn't see Paul.

The binoculars were dangling around my neck, getting in the way, so I snatched them off. With my other hand, I pushed away low-lying branches as I hunkered forward, moving around the edge of the clearing until I'd put the building between me and Paul's boys.

The sweat was trickling into my eyes, making them sting, making everything blurry. I swiped at my eyes with the back of my hand. I would not panic. I would not cry.

If I moved now, if I ran, I could get to the building, grab the flash drive, and run back, and maybe no one would see me. If Joe had been here, he could have played lookout for me again, but I didn't know if he'd even realized I was gone.

Would Joe come to find me? Would he be scared something bad had happened to me?

There was no time to wait. I steadied my breathing. You've got to do this, I told myself. It's easy because there's no choice. You need the flash drive.

But where was Paul? I didn't want him to find me. I didn't want to get caught here.

I took one more look around and then ran forward to the side of the building. Crouching, I began searching frantically under the window.

Where was it? Where was the drive? It was metallic, small, the size of a stick of gum, but it should jump right out at me.

I felt incredibly vulnerable out in the open like this. I was dangerously close to Paul's boys. They might spot me at any second. Paul might spot me.

They might see some dumb girl poking around their campsite — "What are you doing here?" — and what could I possibly say? How could I possibly explain it?

And I couldn't find the stupid flash drive — where was it? Why hadn't I made sure it was safely in my pocket? How could I be so stupid? — and then, there it was!

My fingers closed on the drive. Panting, I rose to my feet, was about to spin around, to get out of there right away.

But I couldn't. My blood had turned to ice.

I didn't hear him. No, but I felt the energy emanating from him.

My head snapped around, and I saw him.

He was watching me. He was standing there, watching me.

How long had he been there? Had he seen me pick up the flash drive? Did he know it was in my hand?

Paul stood like a specter, tall, his face gaunt, his hair sticking up, watching. He was about eight meters away, between me and the clearing. The sun was behind him, tree branches above. Shadows sliced across him.

He looked at me. His gaze was blank, pitiless, and I wondered if he was carrying a weapon. If he would simply reach for his gun and shoot me.

What should I do? What should I do? *What should I do?*

He leaned against a birch tree, black on white. He folded his arms and crossed his legs.

"Do you know who I am?" he asked.

Fear drove bile into my mouth. I could not speak. I could not breathe.

"I am the watchman. The watchman," Paul told me, with a slow smile. His voice vibrated, but not with rage. "And who are you? What are you doing here?"

A strange force continued to radiate from him. I was its destination.

Would he recognize me? Would he realize I was Virginia's friend? I didn't think he'd seen me face to face in a long time, maybe not since I was ten or eleven, before I'd stopped coming over to hang out with Virginia. But I might look familiar to him just from living in the same neighborhood. If he did, everything would unravel. Bad things would happen to me. Virginia had warned me.

I was beyond fear. What I felt was different from fear. It was more like ... more like... I wasn't certain. I was amazed and overwhelmed. Was this terror?

I needed to get away. I needed to run. I couldn't speak. I couldn't move. I sank to my knees.

A great stillness had descended, and I was trapped inside it. Time had ground to a halt. I would be here forever. Paul was doing it. He was powerful and omnipotent. He was hypnotizing time. He was holding it hostage, and me.

"A babe in the wood," Paul said, considering me. "Are you afraid? Are you afraid of the watchman?"

I was trembling. I bent my head so he would not see whatever was in my eyes. What would he do? He had found me. He had found me here, spying on him, the flash drive in my hand.

He came a few steps closer. "Do not be afraid," he said, and he sounded like he was speaking a line from the Bible, something I'd heard before. Then, "Get up," he said, ominously.

I could feel him looking at me.

And I looked up. I had to. He made me.

Now Paul's blue eyes were locked onto mine, and something within me was continuing to shift. Despite what I knew and despite what I believed, despite my terror — was it terror? was it awe? — he was drawing me to him. I felt the stirrings of something inside me, something dark and deep and volatile. Something buried. Some potential that I did not even know was there. And it was recognizing itself, deep and dark, within him.

"Come here," he said. "Come to me. You look familiar. Who are you?" He held out a hand to me, and it was a command. "You must come."

He had stepped close to me. His voice was mesmerizing. He looked at me, and I was all he saw. There was no one else. Only me.

"Do you want to get to know God? God wants to know you. *You.* God is reaching out to you. Can you feel it?" He put out his hand to me, palm up. "God is reaching out to you. He wants you to be with him. He wants you to rise up to him when the time comes." He paused, and then he said the words slowly: "And the time is at hand."

I'd felt his pull as soon as we'd arrived here. But now it was ten times as powerful as that. One hundred times as powerful.

Infinitely more powerful.

Was it just Paul reaching out to me? Or was it God himself? I knew God would not be darkness. Even I knew that. But ...

I would put my face down and sink deep into the earth, melt away forever into nothingness, or I would go to him, reunite with the darkness, fall forward into his open arms, surrender, and give up the struggle, be embraced in whatever larger grand catastrophic experience he was dreaming of.

He stood there now, hand out, and I knew it would only take a tiny little leap — or less, even. I could slip out of the difficult struggle that was responsibility, integrity and will. I could slip; I could slide, and it would feel something like relief. There was nothing to stop me. Nothing. Like a feather let go into a swirling current, I would just float toward him, and he would be my fate.

I got up onto my feet, and I put out my arms, reaching out, or was I asking for mercy?

His eyes were hungry and blank. Like a snake about to strike, precise, thoughtless, patient.

Terror squeezed my heart and choked me, but I yearned, oh, I yearned toward Paul, and it was drawing me in, and I couldn't breathe properly, and yet still I was stepping forward. There was nothing to stop me, no one to help.

Paul stepped closer, close enough to touch me with his fingertips, close enough to grab me, embrace me. Tall and powerful, he loomed before me, and now I could even smell him, the tang of him.

Except … There was Virginia.

I saw her.

I saw Virginia.

She was there, right there. Virginia, still and complete. Her hair pulled back in a ponytail. Her T-shirt damp with sweat. Virginia, serene and mild.

How had she got here? How had she come here now, in this moment, when I needed her?

"Ivy," she said gently. She was there alongside Paul, as if she had been standing close by within reach, the whole time. Virginia.

Had she seen? Had she heard? Did she know?

She slipped between us, even though we were so close there was no room for her.

Paul was staring right through her. He did not see her.

He was repeating to me, "God is reaching out to you. Can you feel it?" But Virginia was there. She was in front of him, and he could not see her, and yet he hesitated. He drew back.

She was slight and as lithe as a willow tree. She was nothing to his great, overpowering form, but she changed everything. She was here. It was Virginia. And I could take a breath and recall myself. Become myself again. Take on the responsibility, the integrity, the will. Take it all back, the heavy weight of it, the joy of it.

And I did.

Time launched itself forward with a jolt that staggered me. I swayed. Maybe the earth resumed spinning.

It had changed, and when Paul said, beginning again, "Do you know who I am?" considering me, calculating, I looked at him directly. I swung the binoculars casually, so that his eyes shifted to them, and quickly I shoved the flash drive into the pocket of my running pants. I was still afraid, very afraid, but I could mask the fear. I had control of it. And my voice was steady and confident, and I was absolutely believable when I said dismissively, "No, sorry. I don't think we've met. Sorry I've bothered you. I'm bird-watching." I needed another breath to go on, and I took it and continued. "I dropped my binoculars, but I've found them. I've got to catch up with my friends."

As I was speaking, I was already moving away, and Virginia was gone now as if she had never been there, and maybe she hadn't. I was looking at Paul, and he was going to let me go. I was going to get away, and then I turned away from him. I put him behind me. And I was gone.

✝✝✝

*S*he watched them together, Ivy and Paul, and she stepped in to protect them so no one would get hurt. No one.

And she knew what Paul did not know, that she would

bear God's child and all his efforts would not be called for, would come to naught.

This is how it would come to pass.

She wanted to tell Paul now, so he could end it. All of it. She would bring him tidings.

But Gabriel had said it was not time.

So she simply stood and would not allow his sticky poison to seep toward Ivy. She knew that all the bad things would go away, and he would become like the brother she had once had, and he would be pleased with her and not so proud that he thought he had all the answers and could be the only one to help and had to be the watchman, the watchman who saw and did, set the fire and rang the alarm.

She had seen him look at Ivy and want her, and she would not allow it.

Chapter Twenty-six

There should have been three crows in our backyard that afternoon. *One is for bad news, Two is for mirth, Three is a wedding, Four is a birth ...*

My hair was still wet from my shower, but we were in a hurry. We had to get to the wedding ceremony soon. I lifted my arms and slipped my new dress over my head. It felt good.

I had told Dad I'd be home by 1:00, but it had been later than that. The drive out, sneaking through the forest, spying on the guys, searching the building and getting the data onto the flash drive had taken hours ... Confronting Paul ... that experience alone had seemed to last an eternity to me, but it must have taken only a few minutes because Joe told me that when he noticed I wasn't behind him and was about to turn back, he saw me coming toward him through the trees.

We reached the road and saw the car. Virginia's head was tilted against the window, and I had the fleeting thought, *How did she get back here before me?*, and I saw relief sweep across Joe's face. Then I put my hand on his arm, and we paused. I reminded him of the map, which I hoped I'd copied onto the flash drive. My voice shaking, I told him that the map might be the location of whatever violent act Paul was planning. I told him I'd look at whatever else I'd managed to put on the flash drive and then contact the police even if there was no evidence of any weapons because I just knew Paul was dangerous, and I could feel it coming — Paul had said to me "the time is at hand." I explained that I'd leave him out of all of it so Paul wouldn't know he was involved. Joe just listened and nodded, like he wasn't able to process anything I was saying.

We got in the car. "We're back," Joe said, trying to sound

energetic, cheerful, and Virginia reached out to him and put her hand gently on his shoulder, as if he were the one that needed comforting and not her.

"Are you okay? Did you stay in the car the whole time? Did you see anyone, Gin?" Joe asked, starting the car.

"I'm fine," she said, smiling at all the questions, her voice weary. "I was fine."

"I'm sorry for bringing you here, sis," Joe said apologetically. "Maybe it wasn't a very good idea ..."

"It's okay. Really," Virginia replied. She turned her head slightly, smiled at me. "But I think I'm going to sleep now, okay? I feel kind of exhausted." And she put her head against the headrest and closed her eyes.

We drove in silence the whole way, Joe and I each deep in our own thoughts.

It took us longer than we'd expected to get home. Dad looked worried and disappointed. "Ivy, it's Katie's special day," he began. "Couldn't you have tried to get here on time? Just for your sister ...?"

I muttered some excuse, and then he and I had a quick lunch and hurried over to the hall to help some of Katie's friends set up for her wedding reception. The afternoon sped by.

Thoughts of Katie and love mingled with thoughts of Paul and violence. Images of ribbons and lace became tangled with images of guns and explosions. It made me dizzy and slightly nauseous.

I desperately wanted to call the police, but there just didn't seem to be an opportunity. I knew time was running out. But it was Katie's wedding day, and the day was already half over. Standing on a chair dangling streamers from the door frame, I told myself I'd spend the next few hours helping her and thinking only about her, and then I'd call, right before the wedding itself. Paul's weekend leadership session was going right through until tomorrow, so it was unlikely anything was planned for this afternoon or tonight.

But now Dad and I were home again, and there wasn't time now, either, not really. I hadn't even had a moment to see if I'd copied the files onto the flash drive properly. I'd showered and done my hair, and my stomach was all aflutter. Katie was getting married! I moved to the bedroom window and began counting the crows as I struggled to do up the zipper on my dress.

One, two, three, four ...

There was a huge, noisy bunch of birds. Some had their shoulders all hunched up and their heads lowered. They were cawing like they were trying to argue a point. Others were hopping carefully on bent black legs from one branch to another.

Five, six ...

One came in for a landing, causing two others to take off and then hover nearby, disgruntled.

Seven, eight, nine ...

Another three suddenly dropped from a higher branch and looked for several breath-stopping seconds like they were going to fall forever, before stretching out their long, casual wings and curving away from death.

Ten is for sorrow, Eleven is for love, Twelve is for joy tomorrow ...

How could sorrow, love and joy be so intertwined, one lone crow separating them? How could sorrow and joy be so nearly one or the other — connected by and to love — and yet so incredibly opposite in fact?

And yet for me, today had held sorrow, and tonight would hold love. I hoped, for Katie, for all of us, that tomorrow would bring joy.

Zipper up, I turned to my bedroom mirror. Hurriedly, I smoothed down my dress and adjusted the shoulder straps.

For a moment, I stared into my own worried brown eyes. Then, I shot a quick glance at the clock and began scrunching my wet curls.

An angel had come to Virginia. That's what she believed. As I thought back to this morning, to her appearance in the clearing and her coming between Paul and me, I knew she hadn't really been there, couldn't have been, and yet at the same time I did believe that she was there. I had known it immediately, as soon as I saw her, as soon as I knew her presence and recognized that the snake that had been rising in me, a rough beast desiring to stretch out to its master, had been lulled back down into its coils.

Could you ask an angel for help? An angel could probably do anything. The only ones I had ever heard of usually came to give news, like telling the shepherds about baby Jesus being born, but maybe an angel could actually intervene.

Could you make a deal with an angel? Say you'd do anything in return for a sober mother? Say you needed help because there was a guy who was going to hurt people unless someone stopped him soon?

That's what I'd have done.

The crows outside my window called. There was a knock at my door.

"Ivy, are you ready?"

Dad came in and whistled when he saw me. "Hey, good lookin'!"

I grinned back at him.

"Oh, by the way," he told me, "your mother said to tell you that Virginia came by this afternoon looking for you, while you and I were out decorating the hall."

"Oh," I said with a casual nod. But my heart was racing. "So what did she want? What did Mom say Virginia wanted?"

"She only said she told Virginia you were out, and Virginia said it wasn't important and that it could wait." He hesitated. "Your mother said they had a nice chat — brief, but nice. She said you're lucky to have such a good friend."

I nodded. I couldn't speak. For some reason, absurdly, the image of Virginia and my mother speaking together, standing in our doorway, filled me with an overflowing sense of ... something. What? I wasn't sure. Grief? Hope? Sorrow? Love? I picked up my purse and stuffed a few things in it — a comb, some tissue — ducking my head, avoiding Dad's eyes.

I was ready to go, but first, Dad had to give me the Mom speech, which was basically the one I'd heard a million times in the past, every time we went out somewhere with her. It was useless to protest. He had to do it, like a ritual. It reassured him, made him feel like we were in control.

"Honey, I know you've heard all this before. But it's really important today. It's really important we both do our best. We'll take turns. You first, then me. Every half hour or so. One of us with her at all times. She told me she's going to go easy —"

"I *know*," I assured him. "I know, I know, I know."

"Okay, so come on then, Ivy," Dad said, with a smile. "Let's get this show on the road."

I almost got past the hall mirror without looking into it, but I couldn't quite. There I was. Long legs, small breasts, frizzy hair, even though I had just brushed it again, brown eyes, slim and still tanned from the summer. Until I was about seven, people had told me I looked like my mother. I would smile. I would catch sight of myself in a mirror and try to spot her there too. At the time, I couldn't imagine a higher compliment.

Mom was standing at the front door.

"You look nice, Mom," I said, slipping on my black shoes. She did look nice. Her hair was caught up in a bun with some loose curls dangling down in front of her ears.

She was wearing a blue dress with sequins across the bodice that I'd never seen before.

"Thanks, Ivy." Her smile trembled. "Listen, I want you to know —"

"Mom," I interrupted, "we don't want to be late." I moved past her, out to the car where Dad was waiting.

When we stepped out the door together, in the late afternoon sun, Mrs. Carlton was edging her grass where it met her front walk. She was down on her wide knees, her scissors in one hand, her ankle socks and her slippers poking out behind her.

"Joan, Ivy! Congratulations!" she cried, lifting up her hand in a huge wide wave, her voice big, loud and certain. "What a happy day! My best wishes to Katie!"

My mother nodded back and allowed the smile to spread across her face, as if indeed it was a happy day, and things were going to be all right and anything was possible.

✝✝✝

*J*oe *and her mother had gone to the wedding now.*

Earlier she had gone to talk to Ivy. She had already told her about the baby. Ivy was the witness. And she had had a sudden urge to tell her more, to make certain it was all set down, recorded. But Ivy wasn't there, and it was just as well, because she knew he would not have liked it. And in fact, he had not allowed it, because Ivy was not home.

She thought of Mrs. Morell coming to the door and opening it while she was standing there, and they had smiled at each other because she hadn't even knocked yet. They had spoken briefly about Katie's wedding, and she had said congratulations to Katie's mom, even though she wasn't sure that it was proper etiquette to congratulate the bride's

*mother. Mrs. Morell had smiled back at her, thanked her,
but the eyes of Ivy's mother were sad and weary and
carrying a heavy, deep pain. Remembering the woman's
struggles, Virginia had wanted to tell her that an angel
had come, and that she would be having a baby, and that
he was God's gift. He was a sign to them that they could
resist — all of them — what was life destroying, what was
drawing them into dark, dangerous places, and everything
would be all right. But she wasn't certain how to put all
this into words, because it was more about feelings and
faith, and so she had just stood there with her for a time,
on this wedding day.*

*Soon, she would go up to her bedroom where she would
wait for him to come. But now, in this brief time before
everything changed, she could sit for a while on the porch,
enjoying the evening air.*

*She thought about what she'd seen that morning, between
the time she'd left the car and the time she'd found Paul
and Ivy in the woods. She thought about seeing the boys
begin to start chanting, stretching, exercising, and how she
had walked on by and gone down the trail on the western
side of the field. Birds had been singing, warblers and
some chickadees, too. And when she got to the end of the
trail, to a small clearing, she had waited there for them.*

*There were targets at one end of the small clearing, and
when the young men arrived, jogging, they had lined up
in front of the large steel drum hidden beneath some rocks
that had maybe been pushed here by glaciers, across the
Shield, pushed and then abandoned, far from home,
standing out among the trees. Now Paul was handing
each boy a gun, and they were standing in a row and
shooting at the targets, and they didn't make a sound, but*

they were striking the targets because Paul would have them all stop and carefully put the guns down, and then they would move forward and check how they had done, and there was one boy who was the best. He was heavyset, with broad shoulders and a buzz-cut. And his face was one big smile. He was so happy and proud, and he said, "Will it be me?"

She had waited until they were done, and her heart had felt tired and worn, ancient, and it felt this way now. And they had gone. They had been singing a hymn as they ran back through the woods toward the clearing, and she had been sorrowful, full of sorrow.

Remembering, she thought, We all want to be picked. It's what we all want. Will it be me?

She sat on the porch. Evening fell, and she remembered, consoled herself. It will be me. I have been chosen.

But when a car pulled up, headlights sweeping across the lawn, she saw it was Janie's car. Paul got out, even though he was not expected until tomorrow night, and it wasn't him she had been waiting for. It wasn't him.

Paul came toward the house, hurrying, and she thought, His plans must have changed. *And seeing him, knowing what longings were deep in his heart and what darkness might drop, a great dread came over her — a great dread and a great sorrow. The time was at hand.*

Chapter Twenty-seven

The wedding was simple and just right.

Katie and Russ stood at the front of the room with the justice of the peace. The rest of us, a small crowd of about twenty-five, watched and listened.

Katie couldn't stop smiling. She was wearing a gray cocktail dress that she had made herself with a gray scarf in her hair, and she held a small bouquet in one hand. Her other hand never let go of Russ's.

Mom was tense during the whole ceremony, straining to hear every word, her eyes flicking back and forth from the face of the speaker to the responder. Every time Katie spoke, Mom's face softened. She exhaled slightly with Katie's words, as if they were being released with her breath, as well. When the couple were told they could kiss, Katie hugged Russ first, a long embrace with her head pressed against his shoulder, and I felt Mom finally relax.

I relaxed too. The first part was over and no matter what happened now, Katie had what she wanted. She had married Russ.

Now, chatting and laughing, everyone began congratulating Katie and Russ. Then they moved toward Mom, Dad, and me. An impromptu receiving line formed and we stood together, the bride and groom, the bride's mother, father and sister, shaking people's hands and being introduced to some of Katie's and Russ's friends. Russ's parents hadn't been able to come from Australia for the wedding. They were planning a visit in a few months so they could spend several weeks with their son and his new wife.

It seemed strange, the four of us and Russ, together and smiling, polite, pleasant, showing a rare common front. I felt good, content, and I wanted to just let it feel that way, but it was too new, too fragile. I knew we were too close to the possibility of danger, too close to the crumbling edge to relax into it.

After greeting us, the guests slowly began moving outside and down the City Hall steps, heading down the street on foot to the community hall where the reception was going to be held. Mrs. Donato and Joe were the last to squeeze Katie's and Russ's hands and wish them all the best.

Then Mrs. Donato turned to my father, my mother and me.

"Ian, Joan, Ivy. Congratulations! Thank you so much for letting me share in this happy day with you," said Virginia's mother, and without a second's hesitation, she gripped my mother's hands, then reached out and hugged her, pressing her pale face against my mother's flushed cheek. I couldn't help staring. This was the woman who had warned me that someone was going to get hurt. She had looked me in the eye and convinced me she knew what she was talking about. Then she had been hospitalized. And now she was here, weak but willing to celebrate love.

After a moment, my mother said, "Thank you for coming, Maria. It's been so long since ..."

"Yes, yes," Mrs. Donato agreed, waving it away. "But we all get so busy. So busy these days. Isn't that right?"

Mom nodded, accepting the kind excuse. "Ivy told us that you've been having some trouble ..."

For a moment, Mrs. Donato looked confused. Then, "Oh that," she said, waving this away too. She looked at me and put her hand on her chest, patting it. I wondered if she remembered her warning to me. "We all have our troubles. But not on a day like this. Not on a daughter's wedding day!" She smiled, including us all in her setting aside of everything but the joy of the day.

"Maria, Joan, let's walk together to the reception," my father offered. He took one of Mrs. Donato's arms and my mother took the other, as if they were old friends who had been apart for a long time and were reunited, and they headed down the steps.

Joe and I followed.

I was happy suddenly: happy about Katie's wedding; happy that Mom was with a friend; happy that the reception hadn't started yet and I wasn't yet anxious, worried, apprehensive; and happy to be moving beside Joe, his lean body handsome in pressed pants and a suit jacket. I was aware of my dress brushing my thighs, my hair blown back by the slight breeze, the heels of my black shoes hitting the pavement. Joe's stride was long, but it matched mine perfectly. I realized we were almost alone, and something in my chest tightened.

"They look good," Joe said, nodding his chin toward our parents. He had stuck his hands in his pant pockets. "They're enjoying it so far."

"Yeah," I agreed, reining in my thoughts, reminding myself of the reason Joe was here, reminding myself of his girlfriend. How strange and yet so perfect in my bizarre world that he and I were the ones chaperoning our parents and not the other way around.

We stopped at the edge of the curb and waited for a car to go by. Then we crossed, running a little to catch up to our parents. They weren't going quickly, minding Mrs. Donato's health, but my father was gesturing boldly, extravagantly, with his free arm, telling a funny story; my mother was swinging her head back as she laughed, and Joe's mother was smiling at one and then the other, the bridge connecting my parents.

"Joe," I said. "Virginia came to see me this afternoon, but I was out. Do you know what she wanted?"

He looked worried for a moment. "No. I haven't really seen her since we got home from ... our drive. I did some errands for my mom, and then I started to get ready for the wedding ..." He tugged demonstratively at his crisply ironed shirt collar, lifting his eyebrows to encourage a response.

"Very nice," I complimented him with a grin. Then I frowned a bit, considering. "It's just that ... Virginia hasn't been over to my house since ... well, since we were little. So I just wondered ... It may have been important."

Joe looked doubtful. "Well, I did see her right before we left. She came downstairs to say good-bye to us. She gave Mama a big kiss on the cheek and then a hug. She gave me one, too!" He grinned. "And she told us to have a good time. She seemed fine."

"Okay." I was somewhat reassured.

We stopped at another intersection and then crossed. I saw Dad take Mom's hand and swing it. They looked like kids. Unexpectedly, happiness caught at me again. It felt exciting to be outside and all dressed up, walking down the street on our way to Katie's reception. If only I could relax into the feeling, as comfortable as a warm blanket tucked around me or a warm embrace. If only I could give in and let it carry me through the evening. But I couldn't. My happiness was incomplete, edged as it was with nagging worries about Paul, and the phone call I had to make to the police.

I turned to Joe. "I meant to call all afternoon, meant to call the police, but I just didn't have time. I should do it now, Joe. I *want* to do it now," I insisted. "I just want to get it over with. Then I'll be able to truly focus on Katie and enjoy the rest of the evening. I keep thinking that if I don't, it might be too late. I could just give them a heads-up and tell them I'll explain all the details later, arrange to meet them at home in a few hours and hand over the flash drive. I haven't checked it yet but I'm pretty sure I copied the map onto it. And even if the flash drive is useless, I still want to tell them my suspicions, even if I don't have any solid proof, even if they're going to think I'm crazy."

"Ivy, I know you're really worried about this, but whatever Paul is going to do ... Well, they've been planning it for months, probably. It's not likely to happen tonight or even tomorrow. Another few hours won't make a difference." He pulled at his tie, loosening it. "Let's just wait another few hours, until the reception is winding up."

"But Joe," I protested. "What if it's too late?"

"Hey," he said, "relax." He threw his arm around my shoulders. "What if you call and the police want to rush in here and talk to you, and everything gets messy, and they need to speak to my mom ..." I couldn't tell if he was kidding, if he actually thought they'd take me seriously, if he really thought this was a possibility. "Let's just wait until after some food and the speeches okay? It would be nice to have some fun."

But I couldn't do it. I couldn't wait. What if something bad happened because I had delayed too long? What if Paul or one of the others noticed the open flaps on the boxes in the main building, or realized information had been downloaded from their computer and suspected someone knew about their plan? Maybe that would change everything. I was tired of waiting, tired of trying to second-guess the consequences of my actions.

"Joe, I'm going to call now. I have to," I told him, almost apologetically. "I'll be quick."

But when I did go and try to put the call through, using the phone in the corridor of the hall because I'd forgotten my cell phone at home, the operator who answered put me through to a detective, and then — "Answering machine," I mouthed to Joe.

He shrugged. "Leave a message."

But I was flustered, and it felt too weird. And there was

my dad popping his head into the hallway and frowning when he saw me on the phone. He was waving me toward the festivities. "Come on, Ivy!"

"Coming, Dad!" I called back. And then to Joe, "Okay, so I'll try again later, I guess."

All I could do now was put it on hold, put *all* my worries on hold — my worries about what Paul might do, and my worries about Mom and how she'd act in front of everyone on her daughter's wedding day — and immerse myself in Katie's happiness. I had to begin to enjoy myself or I would disappoint Katie.

We hurried down the corridor. It had been fun helping decorate the hall with streamers and flowers that afternoon. Now the tables were piled with food, mostly contributions from Katie's friends, and the bar was stocked. The disc jockey, also a friend of Katie's, had set up, and the music was playing.

As Joe and I stood in the doorway, Katie's friends had already started dancing and eating. One of them, Dave, came over, waving a chicken wing in one hand. Grabbing me with his other hand, he pulled me onto the dance floor. It was just what I felt like doing. Feeling the beat, rocking my hips and swinging my head, I danced. And then Katie was there, too, dancing right over to me, Russ twisting and shaking behind her, her friends whooping and hollering for her over the loud music. We gave each other a fierce hug and crazy grins, and danced together, two sisters and one setting herself free.

We danced and danced, one tune blending into the next. The songs were all fast and loud, and our bodies heated up the room. Sweat formed on my face, and I kicked off my shoes. Katie pulled the gray scarf out of her hair and swirled it in the air exotically as she danced.

Then finally the music slowed down. I stood panting, and as Russ put his arms around his wife and began to sway from side to side, I began to move off the dance floor.

But then Katie's hand reached out and tugged on my arm.

"Where do you think you're going?" she teased, lifting her voice. She pulled me to her and wrapped one arm around my shoulders, and Russ draped one of his around them, too. When I put my arms around their waists, hugging them close, we became an unbreakable ring, spiraling slowly together to the beat.

I leaned my head against Katie's and then, pressing my mouth to her ear, told her, "Congratulations." I saw her eyes go to Russ, and she smiled.

She looked at me. "Thanks," she mouthed back.

And then I saw Mom. She was at the bar, and she was pouring a drink.

I stiffened. *Where was Dad? Where was Mrs. Donato?*

My eyes flickered around the room. Mrs. Donato was sitting on a chair against the wall with a small plate in her lap. She was nodding to Katie's friend Sherry, who was squatting beside her, holding a plate of her own. Joe was there, too. And there was Dad, on the other side of the room, talking animatedly to a young man, another friend of Katie's or Russ's, no doubt.

Mom was all alone. *Why wasn't Dad watching her?*

Angry, disappointed, guilty, anxious, settling back to reality with a thump, I dropped my arms from my sister and her husband, began to pull away. The fun was over.

But Katie wouldn't let go of her grip on my arm.

"Where are you going?" she asked, raising her voice so I could hear her over the music.

I had seen her follow my gaze. I knew she had seen Mom.

"Where do you think?" I exclaimed sulkily, rudely. "The watchdog is needed."

I pulled my arm again, scowling, but still she held onto it.

"Wait, Ivy. Don't go," she insisted. She held my arm and leaned forward, looking into my eyes.

I laughed bitterly. She knew I had no choice. "Come on, Katie, let go!" I said. Yelling at her, yelling so she could hear me, seemed to fuel the resentment I was feeling.

"Ivy, don't," she repeated. She took hold of me with her other hand now, too. "You don't know what she's doing. Maybe she's having a soft drink."

Now I really laughed. "Katie, really." I rolled my eyes. "She's starting, and unless I get over there, it won't stop. You, of all people, know that."

Again I tried to pull away, but Katie's grip was strong.

"I *do* know." Her voice was urgent. Her look was intense. "You're right. I *do* know, Ivy. And what I know is that she doesn't need you."

I laughed again. What she said hurt me, distressed me. This was her wedding, and I didn't know why she was doing this now, here. "Katie, come on." I tried to stay calm. "I've got to go to her." I glanced over. Mom was sipping at the drink. As I watched she had a long sip, then another. "Katie, come on. I don't want her to wreck your party."

Katie was burning her eyes into mine. "Ivy, she *can't* wreck my party. Do you understand that? She can't wreck it." She shook me slightly. "She can't wreck my life. She's my mother, and she's your mother, but she can't wreck our lives. She can wreck her *own* life. It looks like that's what she's doing, and I'm sorry about that, but she can't wreck mine. She's not me."

Katie walked with me now, pulling me along with her closer to the wall where it was a little quieter. I kept my eyes on Mom. I saw her finish her drink and pause, her arms folded in front of her, a smile on her face.

"Ivy, you know all this. She's sick. It's like her body is controlling her mind. She won't accept our help. She has made that very clear. I couldn't stay home and watch her destroy herself, so I left." She shook me gently. "But it wouldn't have mattered if I'd stayed. She's right, in a bizarre kind of way. It was almost better for us to stop trying to change her, because nothing we were going to do could actually make her stop. Not pouring the alcohol down the sink, not yelling at her, not looking in all her hiding places for bottles, not smelling her water bottles — all those things that you and I were doing, Ivy, none of them stopped her then, and none of them would stop her now or tomorrow. She has to want to do it. She has to decide." Katie's words were softer now that she didn't have to yell, but more insistent. "You've heard it all before. But it's time for you to believe it."

Katie held my hand. I looked down and saw her wedding ring, newly placed on her finger. A smile flickered across my face.

"You can't save her, sis." Katie went on. "It's not your job. And *not* doing anything, controlling yourself so that you *don't* yell, so that you *don't* tell her to stop, so that you *don't* pour her drink into the garden, that isn't your job either. It's not up to you to make things right. And it's not good for you to keep trying." She shook my hand so that I looked back up into her eyes.

"Katie ..." Tears formed in my eyes. I'm not sure why. I looked at Katie, and now I realized it was Katie who looked more like Mom, and not me. I had the same hair as Mom, but she and Katie shared the same nose, the same mouth.

"Ivy, you have to let go. You can still love her, but you can't save her."

Mom was turning now. She was reaching out for another bottle. I saw her pause then. I saw her pause, her arm stretched out, her other arm back a bit, for balance. She looked as if she might just raise her arms once and lift off, as if she might grab the bottle, as if she might do anything. In that moment of hesitation, anything was possible.

"Ivy, you have to let her make her own choices."

And so I turned away. And I didn't watch, and I don't know what she did next.

Katie stroked my cheek gently with the back of her hand, and I reached out for my sister. I hugged her and she held me tightly, and she let me put my head on the shoulder of her wedding dress, and I don't know why, but I cried, and I think Katie did too. Anyone seeing us would think these were wedding tears, tears of joy, tears of letting go to enter a new life. And maybe they were.

✝✝✝

*P*aul *had hurried past, swept into the house. Shortly after, Teresa came out and stood on the porch, then sat. So Virginia knew she was not to go inside.*

When Anna Maria called them in for dinner, they ate, the five of them, silently.

Her siblings looked at her, waiting, when the meal was done, and so she went up to her bedroom.

The lights in the church, Paul's church, went on, and there was quiet in their house. And then maybe one or more people arrived, and there were again sounds of talking downstairs.

Teresa came upstairs and opened her bedroom door. "Stay in your room tonight, Gin," she told her. And it was like many other nights, but not quite.

And then some more time passed, and finally he came to her, as she knew he would. He was suddenly there, filling the room, as if he was all the molecules in it, as if he was in all the molecules and was expanding and the molecule walls, in turn, were pushing on one another, pressing, until the room was filled with this burgeoning pressure, as if something might be born, might burst into existence, or might simply explode, and there was no space here for anything else, no space for air even, no space for her.

Of course, he knew what had happened; he knew of her visit to the woods. But he did not speak of it, and she readied herself for his anger, but it did not come. Instead, he spoke and said, "It is too late."

Her heart stopped. Her lungs stopped. Her blood stopped. Her voice was thin. "But I told you right away. I told you right then, the first time you asked."

He smiled gently, sadly. "I know. That is not what I mean. I don't mean that your decision comes too late. I mean that the baby comes too late to stop your brother."

She was frozen. She was cold and still.

For a long time, neither of them spoke. He was waiting.

"When I tell him that I am having the baby, it will save them; it will save us, all of us." But she couldn't say it. She wanted it to be true, but now she knew it wasn't.

Gabriel said, "They have placed their hearts in his hands, and he must not disappoint."

She imagined the hearts of the Elite, throbbing, red, wet. She pictured her mother's heart, weakened, nestled on Gabriel's palm. She thought about the baby and when it would be inside her, and its tiny heart that would pump rapidly, racing to be born.

"Did you not hear?" He spoke sternly. "It will not be enough."

It was as if he could see inside her heart, inside her mind, see the picture there of her announcing her pregnancy to Paul, announcing the miracle, and he and his people believing that the baby would be born, and they wouldn't have to do anything now because God had chosen to send Him now. They could put aside their weapons. They were saved from committing a deed they should never have contemplated, saved from sin.

"You don't believe me?" he asked. His voice was icy. He turned his head away from her. He turned his back on her.

"I do believe you," she told him wearily. It was endless. It was exhausting to keep reassuring him, to keep this impossible faith buoyant and aloft.

"Good news will not stop Paul. He does not want good news." Slowly, his voice bitter, almost venomous, Gabriel explained. "He would not even hear the news as good." His back stiffened. "No, they have changed their plan. They have accelerated the Event. It is nigh. The time is at hand."

She waited, sick at his turning away, scarcely hearing his words.

And would he turn again? Would he look on her?

The waiting seemed almost a time to rest, for her heart to pause, for her to even wonder if she could bear it. Perhaps he knew, for his face was upon her. She bathed in his gaze, soothed, and rejuvenated.

"If you believe, if you believe me, even still there might be something else you could do, instead of the baby. Even still."

It was his voice. It was him, still him, the same. But

something had shifted, and it sounded to her like he was using his own imagination, coming up with his own ideas, and she didn't know if that was all right because she thought that he had come from God and that he was relaying God's word. If he was no longer a messenger but now an initiator, if he was speaking with the authority of God, with his voice, in his place, but was not him, was this all right? Was it still all right for her to follow blindly, with trust, with open arms, free-falling into faith?

"Rejoice." He leaned on the windowsill and smiled at her. "It could stop them," he suggested, as if it was a handout, this hope.

She trembled because there was a flicker of doubt in her heart for the first time, and she was ashamed.

She pressed her hand to her belly and felt hollow and empty, and she dragged her thoughts away from there to the clearing and what she had seen there, and she conjured it all up, what lay ahead, the immediateness of the threat, moonlight glinting on steel, blood spilling, perhaps the blood of people she might know, perhaps the blood of students in her classes at school, even, and how far it would splash, and how deep it would sink into the earth, and the stains that would never vanish.

And imagining it, seeing the future, she knew she had to continue to offer herself. She could not do nothing. It was not possible.

She had said she would do anything. And she would. And so she agreed before she even knew what it was he would ask of her.

Chapter Twenty-eight

Joe didn't exactly ask me to dance. He took me from Katie's arms and led me among the dancers, lifted my arms around his neck and put his arms around my waist.

We swayed and shuffled, and my tears dried.

Joe pulled me close when the next slow song started, and it felt ... wonderful. I knew he had a girlfriend. I knew he was here because he was helping out his mother. But I didn't care. I let myself enjoy being held by him. It didn't have to be anything more than that.

When the slow dance ended, Katie and Russ went to the microphone and talked a little bit. They thanked everyone for coming. They said they hoped everyone was having a good time. Katie read out a telegram that Russ's parents had sent.

Dad was standing with Mom, listening. I couldn't see the expressions on their faces. They were on the other side of the room. I took a deep breath. I didn't want to look too closely.

Then, just as Russ was finishing, I saw some heads turning. I looked, too, and there was Mom. She was pushing at Dad a little, and it might have been playfully. They were speaking, but I couldn't hear their voices from where I was.

Now Russ and Katie were looking toward them, too. Russ hesitated, his hand on the microphone stand.

My father was shaking his head toward Russ. Shaking it to say, "No, no. It's okay." But Mom had her hand up now and was moving it, waving it, as if she were a swimmer in trouble, signaling for help.

Russ looked at Katie.

So did I.

And now Dad had let Mom go, with everyone watching,

and she was heading to the microphone, weaving a little, her hand still up and waving, and then she got there and grabbed onto the stand as if it was going to hold her up.

The look on Katie's face was something to see. She leaned forward before Mom could speak, putting her arm around Mom's shoulder, and announced, "My mother." Her voice came out a little too loud, but it wasn't apologetic, and it wasn't apprehensive. It was a daughter's voice, respectful and calm.

She started to move back, and Mom put her hand up, catching her face. Mom kissed Katie on the cheek, and they smiled at each other.

Dad was standing there now, beside Russ. He was about to move in, but Katie put her hand on his arm and drew him back beside her.

We all stood there waiting. Joe was beside me. I could see his mother, still sitting against the wall, both feet planted on the ground.

First Mom laughed. It was like the middle of a laugh, as if she had been laughing all the way to the microphone and hadn't begun to get near to stopping. It was infectious. Some of the guests began laughing too, laughing along with her.

"You know, I'm having a very good time," Mom said. "A very good time." She held the microphone with two hands, and she looked out at the small crowd, here, there, including everyone in her gaze.

There were cries back to her of "Me too!" and "Hurray for Katie and Russ!"

"Katie is my daughter," Mom said. "And I am her mother. And she is getting married today. That is, she *is* married already." She was still smiling, and the guests quieted down a bit. "I didn't think it was a good idea ..."

I saw my father start to move forward, but Katie held him back.

I realized I was holding my breath for her. She might say anything. She might be angry, loving, hateful, kind.

"I know, I know ... I probably shouldn't say it out loud to everyone. But I don't know why young people would get married when they are so young, babies still really. What's the rush?"

Mom's eyes found Mrs. Donato's. Joe's mother tipped her head slightly, as if she could be agreeing.

"But, ah, well. It's done now. And Russ is a fine boy." This provoked whoops and a few cheers from some of his friends.

"He hasn't picked a very good mother-in-law though, I'm afraid," Mom went on. Her voice deepened.

I knew my face was pale. I was concentrating. I was trying to be me.

My mother was so exposed, so vulnerable. She might tell every secret we had. But now I knew they were her secrets, actually, not ours. They were hers to tell or not.

"I have a few troubles," she said. She brushed the loose hairs away from her face and sagged a little abruptly to the left, then caught herself. "But I'm going to try hard to do better. I love Katie and Russ. I love Ivy and Ian."

She put her hand up to her hair again. "We all have troubles, don't we?"

She looked toward Mrs. Donato. Then she dropped her hands from the microphone and turned to my father. She was finished.

Dad put his arm around Mom's waist and guided her away. Joe turned to me and smiled gently, without comment, and I was grateful.

Then Russ swooped in and spoke cheerfully into the silence. "We're going to cut the cake now, and then some more dancing!" he announced. Obediently, the guests responded with equally cheerful catcalls and hurrahs, and the party went on.

✝✝✝

"*Tell me,*" *she offered, reaching out, ready to grasp hold, and because he was everything to her, her guide, her love, her hope, because he was God's chosen angel, she listened, and she knew he must be right. She would give up the swelling of the belly, the months of anticipation, the delivery of promise and a second chance to the world, to the children, the men and women around the Earth who needed so much and especially this.*

But when he was finished explaining it to her, drops started falling on her hands. Reaching up, she touched one cheek, then the other. They were wet.

She was weeping.

Chapter Twenty-nine

I couldn't wait any longer. I had to talk to Joe, alone.

"Come here for a minute." Gesturing for him to follow, I headed to an empty corner of the room.

I leaned against the wall and sighed happily, weary from dancing. Joe stood near me. I thought back to when he had nearly knocked me down the steps of his porch, of how he had grabbed me, prevented me from falling, and then held me, just held me for a moment, and how I had responded so strongly to his touch. And not knowing him, and then speaking to him in the school hallway, going to Cameron's house, going to the clearing, and now we stood here together. It had seemed impossible that I would ever know him, and yet I did know him now, and he knew me, and that made me happy.

The music was soft, and I needed to talk to Joe, but he started to move toward me, and my pulse raced, and I could see the closeness of his eyes, the shape of his cheek, and I could feel the possibility of his lips against mine, his breath in my mouth. It was so real, and I longed for it. And in that instant, it was as if it was happening before the possibility had even been transformed.

He had only just started to move, only begun to lean toward me, so I don't know for certain whether he was going to simply whisper in my ear, or brush an eyelash from my cheek, or reach for me.

And suddenly, this seemed enough. It was enough for me. So, incredibly, I moved back slightly, and Joe leaned away at the same moment and maybe it had been nothing, maybe he'd just swayed forward. But even yet, it was as if it had happened.

I waited until my heart slowed again, until I could speak,

until the wave of emotion at giving up this moment was replaced by an equally powerful wave of emotion, the fear of not acting quickly enough to prevent whatever Paul was planning from happening.

"Joe, I'm going to try calling the police again. The reception is winding up."

He paused. Then he gave a quick nod. "Sure."

But I didn't move away just yet, and neither did he.

This was the last moment we would have together before the secret we shared, the secret that had briefly connected us, blossomed into view to the rest of the world. Nothing would be the same after that, I knew. I thought about it, gazed at him, felt it deeply.

Joe smiled at me. "I'm glad I came, Ivy. Thanks for inviting me."

"You're welcome," I replied.

Then I lightly took hold of his arm, gently shook it. "Joe, Joe Donato. Come on with me while I make the call."

We stepped into the hallway, and I dialed the pay phone. Joe had offered to talk to the police this time, and I knew he'd be really convincing, but I didn't want him to have to give his name. His brother would probably find out eventually that he was involved, but I didn't want to make it obvious. So I did it myself, and I tried to sound as credible and grown-up and reasonable as possible. This time, when the operator patched me through to a detective, he answered his line right away, and he didn't hang up on me when I told him my name and age, didn't hang up on me when I told him the story, even helped me sort it out and tell it properly by asking me all the right questions. I tried to keep it short, explained the urgency of getting to the leadership camp, of checking out the Donato house and the house behind theirs, giving him directions and addresses, and he seemed to agree. He said he'd take care of everything, and I shouldn't worry, that he'd be back in touch. And I didn't feel like he was just trying to humor me. It really seemed like he was taking me seriously and that he might do something about it.

As Joe and I came out of the shadows and walked across the room together, I felt like flying. A huge weight was gone. I couldn't begin to wonder what would happen now, or what this might mean for me, whether or not I was now in danger. I didn't care at the moment. Some guests were getting their coats on, saying good-bye to friends. I saw Joe's mother and mine, sitting side by side, arm in arm, watching us, their children, moving toward them, and I knew that we would all be going home now. The evening was over. My sister was married. My mother had behaved all right. My father had been pleased. It was a few hours of happiness in the life of the Morell family.

"Let's go, honey," my dad said to me. He turned to Mom and smiled at her. "Let's go home, love." And she smiled back.

And that's when we heard the sirens.

✝✝✝

*P*art *of her felt relief. Relief that it was finally time for something to happen. Relief that the waiting was over, that there would be no more waiting. At least one good thing was that there would not be nine months of waiting.*

Now she had instructions, clear steps to take. He was here with her, and he was telling her to do it tonight, not to wait anymore. She could finally act and end the horror before it happened, before they did anything, before Paul said "Now," and blood sprang from wounds and hearts exploded into grief.

It was also a sacrifice. Yes.

She was afraid, looking down, but this fear was acceptable and would soon end. What she couldn't continue living with was the dread of what was coming, of the guilt that would consume her if it happened and she had done nothing to stop it. It was stretching her mind, immobilizing her, pinning her to a place that felt like limbo.

The night was black. The stars were out. The letter was in her hand.

She didn't want to leave her room, but it was time.

"Now," Gabriel said. "It is time."

She would open her arms and save them.

Chapter Thirty

Was it possible?

Had an angel visited Virginia?

I think that it requires a leap of faith to be able to answer "yes," but what kind of faith?

Ask a thousand believers — Christians, Buddhists, Muslims, Jews, Hindus — whether it was possible that an angel had visited Virginia. Nine hundred and ninety-nine would probably say it was impossible, and one would say it could happen, it may have happened, even it certainly happened. Ask a thousand non-believers, and nine hundred and ninety-nine would probably say it was impossible, but one of them would likely say that sure, it could happen, it may have happened, even it certainly happened.

I'd say your answer depends less on whether or not you believe in God and more on how you think about life: Do you think that it's all up to us? Do you think that every single thing that happens is a result of what we each do, the weight of the world sitting squarely on our shoulders? Or do you leave room for the possibility that there is something more than the sum of our humanity, something that defies logic or molecules, something that can open a window and slip in to tip the balance, to offer hope or counsel disaster?

If you do leave room for that possibility, maybe that alone can make the difference. Maybe the empty space itself, that bit of room, becomes a fertile womb for a big bang of imagination, hope, longing, desire.

You can see it with kids. They're figuring out how the world works, and how things connect together, and most of them are wide open to suggestions of spaces in between that might be empty or, rather, full of possibility. I had seen it in the Hendricks's kids. At the lodge that summer, they had burned their marshmallows on the campfire. And the first time they did it, they cried out, and then they looked at me expectantly, as if maybe there was something I could do, as if there was some way I could step in and perform a miracle, transform those black burnt marshmallows back into white. And even though it was impossible, even though they had seen their marshmallows on fire, burning, they had seen the flames, and now the black charred shell was on the end of their sticks, simply in their hope, in their moment of looking at me so trustingly, with such desire and optimism, there seemed to be the chance of it happening, the possibility of possibility.

And when I reached down and grasped the black shell of each marshmallow and pulled, pouf! and the outer charred husks slipped off and the white gooey interiors remained intact, clinging to the sticks, their faces opened into grins and delight, their prayer for the impossible granted. A miracle had been performed: black transformed to white; the burning conquered, transformed into a fresh start. To them, reality itself was altered.

So had a miracle happened? And if so, had it occurred on the stick or in their minds, or both? And who had performed it? Me, or them, or both of us?

I still have so many questions, questions about miracles, love, and sacrifice, questions about Virginia and Paul, about what really happened to them, questions about what really happened the night of Katie's wedding.

Because we didn't see it all, of course. As we drove the short distance from the reception hall to our neighborhood, the sirens got louder and louder. I couldn't speak. I sat in the backseat, and my heart was pounding. I wasn't sure if this was something I had set in motion, if the police were screaming their way to the Donatos' because of my phone call, or if something bad had happened there already, and my call had been too late.

We reached our street and drove down it, and there were lights flashing as vehicles poured up the other end of it and stopped in front of the Donato house.

"What's going on?" Dad gasped.

He pulled into our driveway, and I leaped out of the car and ran down the street. Car doors were slamming, a fire truck was careening around the corner, neighbors were coming out onto their front porches and staring. I saw Joe and his mother. They looked like they'd just got out of their car, had arrived only just before us. And then I stopped at the front walk uncertainly, folding my arms over my chest in the cool night air, because I saw Donna and Paul, and Teresa, too, rushing out of the house.

Paul was there. How could Paul be there? Why wasn't he still up at the leadership camp?

He was pushing ahead of the others, was first down the steps. And for a moment, I thought he was coming for me. I thought he'd seen me standing there and knew everything, knew what I'd seen, where I'd been, what I'd done.

Then he was hurrying down the front walk, and suddenly I wondered, was he making a run for it? Had he pieced it all together? Did he know they were coming for him, and was he trying to get away?

Everything was happening so quickly, and suddenly the sirens shut off, and in the abrupt silence, something made me look up, a sound, maybe a cry. I saw it, high above us, a black figure with wide wings against the star-lit sky, poised for a moment, like sorrow itself.

I didn't know right away. Can you believe that for a split second I thought it was her angel, Virginia's, declaring himself and shouting faith be damned, here was proof, in the flesh, appearing before all of us, believers and non-believers, and now who would dare to doubt?

And then of course it struck me, like a fist in my gut, like

an impossible emptiness splitting open my heart. Standing
on the pavement, I shouted, "No! No, Virginia! Don't!" But
it was too late.

And everyone looked at me and then to where I was
looking, the top window of the Donato house, Teresa
hurrying down the front steps of their porch, Mrs. Donato
stumbling, and Joe clutching her waist, and I saw Paul's arm
rise, as if he might be pointing or beckoning or forbidding,
but now Virginia was no longer there on her tiptoes,
stretching, her face pointing up at the sky, her arms up high.
Now her arms were slowly descending, and like a swimmer
gliding through the water, like an angel slicing through thin
air, like a bird hunching its wings into a soaring, sweeping
escape, she leaned after them, tipping gracefully, graciously,
and although she should have soared, or wafted down like
a feather, or been cupped into the palm of God and placed
gently on the earth, she didn't, she wasn't. She simply fell.

✜✜✜

*I*t was just right. The police had come, as Gabriel had
planned, and her family was gathered, waiting and watch-
ing below.

She saw them pull up in their cars, and in her hand was
the message, the note to Paul describing what God really
wanted and how she knew, and the other note to the
police, sewn inside her shirt because that way, the medics
would find it and no one could remove it, sneak it away.

They would have to listen. Gabriel said they would, and
he knew. They would read the note, and they would
understand that an angel had come from on high to
intercede, and he had chosen her to bear the gift that
would save her brother, save his group and their targets,

save all the people, everyone. It would have been a baby — a baby! — but not now. Now it was this note, this sharing of the secret that her brother had plans, detailed plans, to gun down innocent people, and it listed the people involved and where the weapons were concealed. And Paul would know this also, know that there might have been a baby, but because of him it would not be so. The note would tell him that instead it had to be like this — this was the only way to stop him.

Standing there in the window, she turned to look back at Gabriel, hesitating, because she loved the sight of him, because he was there, and she wanted to be with him even now, knowing she would have eternity surrounding her momentarily. And because there was something still in her that would miss all the moments of living that would have been hers, that was grief-stricken at the loss of these possibilities.

"Don't be sad. Don't despair. Every moment, even this one, holds infinite possibilities." He smiled, and standing up, he spread his arms.

She turned, and she also spread her arms. And then she smiled, feeling his breath on the back of her neck, the whispering of air through his wings, and she fell, in love.

Chapter Thirty-one

The autumn sky is becoming bigger and bigger as fewer and fewer leaves remain on the trees. When the crows fly by, their black bodies look almost beautiful against the vivid blue.

It's Monday, late afternoon, and Mom is inside. She's actually making dinner tonight. I'm leaning against the porch rail, going over everything in my mind again, but calmly, slowly. So much seemed to happen that Saturday night, and yet it was really just one small motion, a leaning forward, that completed the story. That night, Virginia suffered massive injuries, including a broken arm, leg and ribs, but she didn't die. Amazingly, thankfully, when she fell, she did not die.

I watched as a medic flew out of the ambulance and across the lawn almost as if he thought he might catch her. And then, kneeling beside her, as she lay crumpled, as if he were her lover, he had kept her breathing while a second medic brought the stretcher. Once she was in the ambulance, they found a note sewn into her shirt, which they passed on to the senior police officer before racing away, siren wailing again.

Joe found another note on the lawn, near where Virginia had fallen. I saw him glance at it and then, glaring, weeping, thrust it at Paul, pushing it into his hand as if wanting to sear its message into his flesh. And then Paul turned and vanished in the commotion.

Two police officers came to talk to me a little later that night. Dad sat in the living room with me and listened. I gave the police the flash drive, showed them the few photos I'd taken and gave them the list I'd copied from Paul's desk. I repeated everything I'd already told them in the phone call, plus anything else I could think of. I couldn't look at

Dad's face as I told the officers that I'd broken into the Donatos' Turner Avenue house, that I'd been suspicious of Paul's activities, that I was worried about Virginia's state of mind, that I thought no one would listen to me if I told, that I'd eventually told Joe, because he was Virginia's favorite brother, and that he and I had visited Paul's camp in the Hardwood area. Again, I gave them the specific directions to the camp and repeated that they should search there and at Paul's church for weapons as soon as possible.

Finally, at the end of all this, the police told me that the emergency crews had raced to the Donato house not because of my phone call from the wedding reception but in response to a phone call from Virginia, who had alerted them to what she was about to do. The police said that the note they'd found sewn in Virginia's shirt had provided similar accusations and details about Paul's church and the weapons. So in the end, it was Virginia who saved the day, who exploded everything wide open, averted the violence Paul had planned and knocked down the castle walls.

Afterwards, when they had left, Dad came and sat beside me on the couch. As I wept, he bent to look into my face. "Ivy," he said, "I love you. I'm your father."

I nodded.

"You could have come to me. You could have," he told me.

I looked into his troubled eyes. I nodded. I think he meant it. I think I could have.

And then last night, Sunday night, Joe phoned. He told me that the police had searched Paul's church and the leadership camp. They confirmed that he had been training young men to handle and shoot several types of weapons. They had found some ammunition and a few guns in big boxes in the basement of Paul's church, and they had found many more weapons hidden in the Hardwood forest. Apparently, there was another small clearing at the end of the running trail that Paul's group had been using as a shooting range. Guns, silencers and bullets were temporarily being stashed there in a steel drum. The map on Paul's computer? They had matched it to a real location, a mall not far from our own neighborhood. The young men had been ordered by Paul to arrive at the shopping center at a particular time and commence shooting shoppers in the mall. It had been planned for yesterday, Sunday. The police were interviewing all kinds of people now, trying to understand the details of why anyone would do such a thing.

"You were right," Joe said for the millionth time. "You were right to want to call the police as soon as possible, Ivy. This was so close to being a bloodbath."

It was so bad and blurry and crazy and huge, and it's still almost impossible to understand. I'm certain Mrs. Donato didn't know any real details of what was going on. The police don't think so either. Joe says that after their first conversation with her, they pretty much left her out of their investigation. She must have known *something* was planned, because she tried to tell me something about it that day. She was clearly agitated and upset about it. But maybe what she knew was vague, and she couldn't figure out what to really make of it, or what to do about it. Maybe she *was* confused and not properly understanding things, like Anna Maria claimed. Maybe she'd even tried to confront Paul at some point or couldn't quite bring herself to believe that her own son could be involved in something so unimaginable. Maybe love for him had helped her find a way to transform it into something she could accept ...

I still can't believe that Paul planned it and thought it was the right thing to do, that Donna and Anna Maria thought so too, and Teresa, and Janie, and the man with her and the eight young men, including Cameron and Taylor, who showed up at the leadership camp, and the others whose names were on the list I'd found in Paul's church. How could they think injuring and killing people would result in some sort of good outcome? They'd have to somehow step back far enough that they could only see the bigger picture, say to themselves that the ends justified the means. They must have given themselves permission to avoid seeing the messy details, the dots that they were connecting, and imagine that God was only interested in the end result, the so-called greater good.

I've looked over at the Donatos' house to see if their car is there, but it's not. Joe must be out, maybe visiting Virginia in the hospital with his mother. Anna Maria, Donna and Teresa are all being held by the police, as well as the other two Elders, Janie Parke and Frank Camdon, who it turns out were the two people we saw at the leadership camp. Another man, whose name I can't remember, probably one of the other men I'd seen hanging out on their porch, was picked up, too. Cameron and Taylor were detained as well, and the other boys in the group — but Joe says some of them may be released soon on bail. Paul hasn't come forward yet, but Joe says he's certain his brother will turn himself in. "And then there'll be fireworks and pulpit-banging," Joe told me lightly. I know he's worried about Paul — angry, too, and scared — but he didn't want to talk more about him. Not yet, anyway.

Sitting out here on our porch, looking up and down my quiet tree-lined street on this beautiful afternoon, it's almost impossible to believe that these plans were being made here, that discussions about sacrificing the lives of others were taking place almost next door. It's as impossible to believe as Virginia seeing an angel, jumping out of the second-floor window of her house because he told her to and actually saving her family and probably the lives of many other innocent people.

And yet that's what she did. Last night, after Joe told me about the police search, I had so many questions about Virginia that Joe got quiet and thoughtful and then suggested that we meet and go for a walk, talk it over in person. So we did. We walked around the block a few times together. It was good. It turned out Joe had lots of questions, too. He asked me to tell him again about my conversations with his sister over the last little while, about the angel, about the pregnancy, and this time he really listened. Then he shared with me what he'd found out since Virginia had been in the hospital, things she'd told the psychologist there, things she wanted to share with everyone. "No more secrets," she'd said.

And I'd been right. Virginia's problems were connected to Paul's activities. She had known about his mission, known that he believed spreading more violence would please God because it would hasten the End Days. She'd known he was setting in motion something violent, and she was horrified by the consequences for any victims and how participating in this would affect Paul. She described the angel coming to her, telling her she was chosen to have God's baby, and how she'd agreed to take on that responsibility because it would take the responsibility for saving the world out of Paul's hands. She believed she'd be preventing the violence and saving him from causing it.

"She told me some of this — the angel, the baby — but not all of it," I told Joe. "Why wouldn't she tell me more? Why wouldn't she tell me everything?"

"Maybe she thought she had to take care of it herself, alone. Maybe she thought we wouldn't believe her, that we wouldn't help, even if we knew." Joe looked down at his feet. "Maybe we can ask her one day soon." He paused. "I've apologized to Virginia for letting her down. She didn't even turn to me for help, and when you finally did, I ... It took me a while to step up. I hope one day she'll forgive me. I hope she'll let me try to make it up to her."

Joe's voice trembled as he continued. He said Virginia had become terrified on Saturday afternoon, after we left for the wedding, when everything started happening so quickly, too quickly, when she realized the baby's birth would be too late to stop Paul. So when the angel told her what to do, she did it. She thought she was doing the right thing. She thought it was the only thing she could do."

It was painful to hear. I knew that helpless panicky feeling of having few options and no one to turn to. I felt horrible that Virginia had been feeling that way and yet hadn't chosen to confide in me. She'd told me about the angel and the baby, but she hadn't trusted me enough to tell me everything.

From the porch, I heard the calls of the crows. The birds had settled in the treetops.

One, two, three ...

All these things happened. They really happened. I guess maybe what they show is that a leap of faith can make a difference. Convictions can shape moments and actions. We have the ability to change our lives and the things that happen around us. If Virginia really thought that Gabriel was guiding her, then maybe he was, even if angels don't exist. Did God want Paul to take action? Paul believed he did, and the force of that belief almost ended real lives. I've seen that the world and what happens in it can be transformed by belief and faith, for better or worse.

Four, five, six ...

It's a habit for me to count the crows now, even though I don't really believe they can help us know what is to come. I do find it appealing, though, to imagine that what lies ahead is somewhat predictable, that we're pieces within a bigger picture, that we're moving toward something good and complete. But Paul used that to justify what he was doing. So I'd like to think that if there's someone or something greater than us, if there is some divine plan, some bigger picture that we're moving toward, then its final form is not really decided yet. And maybe it's what we do in the world — our individual choices, decisions, and beliefs, the responsibilities we decide to take on, and how we decide to fulfill those — that will shape the details of that picture, fill it in, give it color and substance, and even breathe life into it.

Seven, eight, nine ...

As soon as I can, I want to go and see Virginia. I hope she'll agree to see me. There are so many things I want to talk to her about. There are so many things I want to ask her. And most of all, I need to apologize to her — not for betraying her secret, because I know she'll understand why I did that — but for not being brave enough or generous enough to force myself into her world and stand beside her there, right beside her, shoulder to shoulder, so she'd know without any doubt that she could count on me.

Ten, eleven. There are eleven crows. Eleven crows against a blue, blue sky.

I turn to go inside, but something — maybe it was something out of the corner of my eye, or simply something in the wind, a faint whisper of air moving against feathers — makes me stop and look back. I don't turn quickly enough and so it's hard to tell them all apart now, the large group of them, one crow here, one crow there, overlapping against the others, hard to tell where one began and another one ended, but I think I saw one more, another crow, joining the flock. Yes, I really do believe I might have seen a twelfth crow, flying way up there, high in the blue sky with the others.

ACKNOWLEDGMENTS

I wish to express gratitude to my editor, Tara Walker, who, with her insightful comments and suggestions, guided this story toward its final destination. Thank you to early readers Monica Kulling and Sophie Coles. My thanks to the Ontario Arts Council for its support. Love and thanks to my parents, Raymond and Iris Hughes, and, of course, and always, to Ken Logue.